ISBN: 9798986311609

www.janekirrok.com
Instagram: @authorjanekirrok

BEST YEARS OF YOUR LIFE

A novel

To err is human; to forgive, divine.

Alexander Pope

FALL 2021

FALL 2021

Christine

I'm going to die this year. I'm going to die this year, and Joss can't even bother herself to remember my birthday dinner.

My foot taps the ground beneath the table, counting the seconds that she's not where she's supposed to be—here with us. It's closing in on thirty minutes. I check my phone again, then give my head a shake.

"Maybe Ma's just running late," Abbie says, and I know it's not because she believes it, but because she doesn't like to see us fighting. I'm not naïve enough to think an eighteen-year-old doesn't pick up on the coolness in her parents' marriage.

"Maybe," I mumble, trying not to let my frustration seep into whatever innocence Abbie has left.

I know Joss isn't coming. I can picture exactly where she is: hunched over the keyboard in our home office, zoned out from every and all obligation, typing away like her self-worth depends on it. Joss's research study hasn't just taken over the last year of our lives, it's wedged itself into our marriage like an unwanted third wheel.

When the waiter returns for the fourth time his eyes scream: *Eat or leave.* I let out an exaggerated sigh. "Well, Ab. Looks like it's just us tonight."

We order, and I shift my perspective away from how angry I am at my wife to appreciating a nice meal with the only person in this family who gives a shit.

At the two-top next to us, a couple holds hands across the table. They're leaned forward, as if pulled by a magnetic force. Young, thirties if I had to guess. Just wait, I want to tell them. That pull will loosen. Priorities will change. I didn't think it would happen to us, but here I am, at a dinner I didn't even want, only to take another back seat to my wife's work. We weren't always the versions we are now.

The Caesar salad brings little comfort, so I break off a piece of buttery roll—the one I purposely didn't ask for but was brought anyway—and eat it. Then another, and another until the whole thing is gone and on its way to my hips. Not a great choice for someone who's trying to stave off death.

"Steve said he's looking to hire someone full time," Abbie says. Her tone is light, hopeful, as though we haven't already paid fall tuition weeks ago.

"Abbie."

"What? Mom, I'm just saying. There's a job right there. You know how much I love the gallery." She extends an open palm to the table, like the job in question sits ready for taking somewhere between the salt and pepper shakers.

"We've gone over this," I say, to which Abbie sighs and slumps back against the booth. Her annoyance won't last long—she never stays mad at me. Before long, we're laughing about some ridiculous optical illusion the internet has exploded over.

"It's white and green!"

"Impossible! It's clearly pink and gray."

An hour and a full stomach later, I see it. The tell-tale glow of candlelight coming my way.

"Abbie, you didn't," I snap, shooting daggers across the table.

Her smile touches her ears. It's Joss's smile, though the way her eyebrows raise is all me—a contradiction I know isn't possible. Last time I checked, you can't create a baby with two eggs.

"It's a big birthday," she says, whipping out her phone and snapping a picture she'll undoubtedly enhance with an artsy spin and post to Instagram. I'll see it later. Unlike Joss, I caved to social media years ago as a way to safeguard our daughter. Who knew it would become my evening companion as of late?

"At least put a filter on that," I say, pulling at my crow's feet.

The waiter places the slice of cake in front of me, topped with a single glowing candle. They don't sing—thank God—but the fuss is still enough to attract the attention of the tables nearby, whose diners turn to look. My face burns. It probably matches my hair, making me look like a matchstick, all skinny and white with red on top.

"You know I don't like this," I say. Joss is the one who insists on birthday dinners. Makes sense for someone coming from a neglected childhood where each year only served as a marker toward independence. "But, seeing as it's my last one..."

Abbie rolls her eyes. "Mom, seriously. You're fifty. You're not dying." She leans in and blows out the candle for me.

"Yeah, well, I'm sure that's what my mother and grandmother thought, too."

She shakes her head. Abbie's heard this enough times to tell the story herself. How both my mother and her mother didn't live to see fifty-one, so I'm convinced I won't either. I've done everything in my power to stave off Father Time, but he carries on with little regard to my resistance. Who knows if I'll even make it to spring. Ha, the most important year of my teaching career, and I might not even see it come to fruition.

The cake is red velvet. We share it, Abbie starting at the back with the extra frosting. I used to share desserts like this with Joss. Back when we were a universe of two, who did more than just ramble formalities in passing. When we'd travel to and from campus together as a team—two unstoppable professors ready to change the world. When she didn't blow off important things like birthday dinners.

Those days are a distant memory.

"You good?" Abbie's voice rips me from my thoughts, and I realize I'm frowning at the cake. I straighten up and put on a plastic smile. It's not fair to drag her into it—she's just a kid.

"Fine." I take another bite. "Excited for tomorrow?" I say, changing the subject and infusing the question with extra optimism I hope will combat Abbie's reluctance.

She raises her eyebrows, stabs the cake. "Sure."

"C'mon, college is supposed to be exciting. You're going to meet so many new people."

"Oh yeah, 'cuz that's one of my strengths."

"Abbie."

"It's just going to be an extension of high school. I don't know why you guys are torturing me like this."

"You don't know that. And we're not torturing you. Art will be around forever. It's only four years. Give it a chance. For me. Okay?" I throw that last bit in there as a hook. If she's going to do it for anyone, it'll be me.

Her big, brown eyes lock on mine, and something softens. "For you. That's it."

Joss

It's pushing eight and Christine and Abbie still aren't home. Did Chris have a meeting? Did Abbie have practice? I can't remember.

I stretch, giving my lucky rabbit's foot a rub, then stand, using my toes to smooth the bottoms of the ankle pants Christine bought me. The Audrey Hepburn look doesn't work as well on a size twelve—the only thing I have in common with Audrey is the dark pixie cut.

I make my way downstairs, taking a detour through the kitchen, and grab a biscuit from the pantry. I eat it with my backside leaning against the counter, one arm crossed over the pooch above my waistband. Before I can finish the last bite—the center, the best part—the door slams. Abbie comes around the corner first.

"Where were you?" she hisses at me before adding, "Mom's pissed."

Christine's not three seconds behind, which gives me little time to form a defense to something I don't even know I'm supposed to be defending. I can tell by her face she's in a *mood*—jaw set, eyes dull.

"I was starting to wonder where you guys were," I say, and then immediately regret it, as Abbie's made it clear I forgot something important. I wrack my brain, but nothing.

Christine spares me no pity. She folds her arms across her chest. My defenses peak. "What?"

"Where *we* were? How about where *you* were? Or should I say where you weren't." Tears well in her eyes, and I realize she's more sad than mad. "How do you forget something we just talked about last night? It was your bloody idea in the first place."

She's slipped into my British vernacular, and that's never a good sign.

My wheels turn up empty. Something we talked about last night? My mouth opens, but no words escape. Frustration builds in Christine's face. Her eyes widen, waiting for me to get it, this thing I've apparently forgot. She finally blurts it out, like a dam unable to hold back the pulsing water.

"Dinner. For my birthday. Tonight," she says, leaning her head forward as she speaks.

Shit. Her birthday is today? I know I've been a bit detached, but I've never forgotten a birthday. My stomach is in my throat as I try to remember the conversation she's claiming we had. There's no way. I would have remembered. I stare at her with what I assume is the look of a fool.

"I tried calling you," she scoffs. "Abbie texted. You never responded." The hurt is splashed across her face and my hands go cold.

"I never got a call," I say, although it sounds lame even to me.

"I'd have liked to think you could spare one evening. I guess that was too much to ask." She doesn't have to spell it out—"research" has become a trigger word in our relationship.

"I swear I didn't get any calls or texts," I say at the same time I'm trying to picture my phone on my desk. Was it on silent all day? How would I have missed her call? Now that I think about it, I can't visualize my phone amongst my paperwork at all.

I go to the bench by the door where I keep my purse, but the bench is empty. My phone must be in my purse—if only I can find it. Why is nothing where it's supposed to be?

I spin around in place, sputtering. "I...I...where's my bloody purse?"

"What are you talking about?"

8

"My phone. It must be in my purse. But now I can't find my purse. It's not on the bench."

Christine's hands are on her hips. She thinks I'm making up excuses.

"Call it," I say in rebuttal. "Call my phone."

She doesn't react right away, doesn't want to play this game.

"Seriously, call it."

She pulls out her own phone and dials my number. We stand still. A faint ringing floats through the kitchen, muddled, like it's traveling through water. Our heads swivel, trying to locate the source. The ringing continues. I step to the right. It grows fainter. I step to the left, and the ringing gets louder. My eyes dart around the kitchen, wondering how on Earth my phone is somewhere here without my knowledge.

The ringing stops.

"Dial again," I say.

This time, I zone right in on the source: the microwave. Something is ringing inside the microwave. I fling open the door. My purse sits on the rotating plate, worn and floppy, like it's been cooked, even though it's just old.

My eyes struggle to focus through rapid blinking. This makes no sense. I look at Christine who's now beside me. She's dropped her hands, and her lips have lost their hard, angry edges.

"What's your purse doing in the microwave?" Abbie says, coming into the kitchen wearing a hoodie over red soccer shorts. Her confusion momentarily diffuses the tension between Christine and me.

"I have no idea." It's all I can manage. Nothing makes sense. I don't even reach for it, lest it jump out and bite me like a rattlesnake that sneakily slithered in there on its own. "I don't remember putting it there."

Abbie goes to the sink to fill up her water bottle. "You're losing it, Ma. Five hours of sleep ain't cutting it."

Christine and I stare at each other, the only two who seem to be grasping the strange weight of a purse in a microwave. Abbie twists the top onto her water bottle and leaves just as quickly as she came. We watch her go, and then Christine turns to me. I'm expecting her to comfort me somehow—a hand on my shoulder, perhaps. Anything to ground me in reality, because right now I feel very much out of it.

9

Instead, she deflates with a long exhale, like even though finding a purse in the microwave is concerning, she's just too tired to deal with it.

"I'm exhausted," she says. "Let's just forget about it and call it a night."

But I don't want to call it a night. I want to figure out how the hell my purse got in the microwave. At the same time, I'm knackered, too. This study is draining me more than any of my previous research. Chemical sensors, semiconductors, organic compounds—it's *deep*. Chemistry is how my brain works, but I'm having to re-read sections in order to fully grasp them.

My eyes crave darkness. Maybe a good night's sleep is what I need. I nod and reach for Christine's hand, but she moves before we make contact.

She's angry at me, angry at the study. But she just doesn't get it. What I've tried—and clearly failed—to explain is that it all comes so easy to her, teaching and parenting and eating healthy and basically everything else. Then there's me, the one who has things to prove. But that'll all change when this study is finished. Turns out mediocre students can actually reach big accomplishments, *thankyouverymuch* Mr. ninth-grade guidance counselor who said my C-average wouldn't get me anywhere.

I climb into bed while Christine does her nightly anti-aging skincare routine. When she joins me, it's without a word. We lay facing opposite directions, the space between us more miles than inches. But instead of reaching for her, I fall asleep to the thought of a research institute named in my honor.

Abbie

College fucking sucks. At least I know it's going to. I never wanted to go, to continue the line of *academic superiority*, but having two professors as parents sort of makes education non-negotiable. The gallery has displayed some of my pieces, and my Etsy shop was well on its way, but *apparently* selling art—my art—isn't good enough. The only reason I gave in was because Coach showed interest. And the only reason I would have tried soccer in the first place was because Uncle Fisher suggested it, and I'd do anything for Uncle Fisher. At least I would have. Now, I'm one of only two freshmen who made varsity.

Art and soccer: the two things I care about, the two things I'm any good at. Too bad drawing landscapes and still-life for a living doesn't bring in the big bucks my moms want me to make. You try living up to one mom as Research Extraordinaire and the other as Teacher of the Year.

Jesus.

I hear footsteps coming up the stairs and I know it's Mom because she's lighter on her feet than Ma's purpose-driven stride. Their bedroom door shuts. I wonder if Ma will soon follow. Probably not. If I had to put money on it, I'd say she's back in her office. I get the research is important—I've seen Ma present to a room full of people—but come *on*. There's more to life.

I open the camera app on my phone and tap the screen to switch into selfie mode. I hold it out, soften my eyes, and look into the distance—like those famous sisters always do. *Click.* I check the picture, then decide to take one more from the other side so the monster zit on my chin isn't visible. *Click.* Yeah, that's better. Do I look cool? Wait, scratch that. Selfies are not cool anymore. It's all about the candid shot and the surrounding scene—the ones that are planned to look un-planned.

I slide down to the floor and lean my back against the bed, knees tented, feet turned inward. I aim the camera at the full-length mirror on the opposite wall, and raise the phone to cover my face. The coolest posts now are the artsy ones—the ones that make it look like you're in some urban hot spot instead of small-town Virginia. Like you're not even trying when really it's your sole mission.

Click.

Ugh. Maybe it would be cool if I weren't in soccer shorts. Or if my walls weren't plastered with half-finished sketches. Jesus, why the fuck am I so awkward? At least with Trina, we were equally *un*cool. But then she had to go and apply to school a million states away—really? Nebraska?!—and I became friend-less.

I add a grainy filter and post the pic to my feed. Within two minutes there are thirty-seven likes. Maybe I have more "friends" than I thought—at least behind their phones.

A comment pops up. Fierce, it says, followed by three flame emojis. I blink at the name. Stacia King, captain of the soccer team. I didn't realize she followed me. A butterfly dances in my belly at this newfound knowledge. Stacia King! I smile and "heart" her reply.

The picture is actually kind of pretty, now that I stare at it more. The angle hides my round, tortilla face. Mom says she loves my face, but I think that's just because it reminds her of Ma. They've never told me who my official bio mother is, but I'm convinced it's Ma. We both have dark hair, olive skin, and lips that come to crisp little points at the center. Mom's all Irish and freckly and has eyes so blue they're almost transparent. But then there's the fact that neither she or I can curl our tongues, and Ma can. So...who the hell knows.

It didn't even become a thing until middle school when people started to ask. Before then, the thought never occurred to me. I have two moms and have never known otherwise. But then I became curious. Whose body did I come out of?

"It doesn't matter which of us actually gave birth to you," they'd say every time I'd try to bring it up. "We're both your moms, and we love you equally. That's all that matters."

I call bullshit.

I came from rando donor sperm mixed with one of their eggs. That, they've confirmed. But just which one of their eggs, and which one of their bodies, they refuse to say. When I press, they dismiss. There's not a single pregnancy photo that exists. Plenty of each of them holding me as a newborn, but none with either Ma or Mom swollen in a hospital bed.

They're not fooling me. I'm totally Ma's kid. And this ploy to get me to love them equally regardless of DNA just makes me laugh. Ma is clearly my bio mom, which is why I'm confused we're not closer. Aside from our resemblance, we have about zero in common.

Mom ran the carpool. Mom cut the crust off my pb&j because she knew I wouldn't eat it otherwise. She's my Target shopping partner, the one who asks me about something that happened weeks ago at school. Ma, on the other hand, doesn't listen enough to retain anything meaningful.

Sometimes I wish I had a dad instead.

I click on Stacia's profile and thumb through her perfectly-curated, friend-filled posts. In one, a group cascades down the front steps of what I assume is someone's off-campus apartment. They're all in various states of laughing—open-mouthed, a head tossed back. I stare harder. There's a vacant step near the top, and I picture myself on it. Not front and center—I'd be fine with being the tail end—just included.

It's getting late. I go to my closet and lay out leggings and a tee for tomorrow, then fall asleep watching a YouTube video of a dry brush technique I want to try.

Christine

You'd think faculty would get prime parking on campus, but that's just another misconception about the "luxury" of being a college professor.

I wedge into the only open spot next to a beater that's over the line, and have to all but sexually violate the door just to shimmy out the inches it gives me.

"Damn students," I mutter, though the inconsiderate parking job could be another faculty member for all I know.

It's the first day of class and it's raining. Not just rain, but humid, mid-Atlantic rain. Lovely. There goes my hair. Still, MacAmes is stunning—a tranquil, leafy campus, even under the gloom of rainclouds. I still get a little tingle every time I pull through the wrought-iron gates.

I reach back through the tight opening for my purse and computer bag, all while juggling to keep the umbrella above my head. I'm a contortionist in a pencil skirt—neck twisted, back arched, one leg lifted off the ground.

A box of donuts is perched on the console between the seats, and I reach for that too, unsure how I'm going to carry it all. I extract the donut box and set it on the hood of the car—temporarily risking the cardboard turning soggy—while I rearrange the bags over my shoulders.

It's eight in the morning and I've already sweated through my bra.

"Need a hand?"

I jump a little in my frazzled state, the deep voice catching me off guard. I look over my shoulder to see a student in a hooded jacket, his arm outstretched toward me. *Where's your umbrella*, my parental instinct thinks, but he just stands there, unbothered. "I can carry those for you if you want." He points to the donuts whose box is close to being soaked through.

"Oh," I say, flustered. My heavy tote bag slips off my shoulder, taking the strap of my sleeveless blouse with it, and I yank it back up.

He doesn't wait for me to respond before crossing the few feet toward my car and grabbing the donuts. How kind. But while his clothes are protected by his jacket, my donuts—the anthropology department donuts, I should say—are still getting wet. It takes me a second to put it all together.

"Here," I say, stepping next to him and raising the umbrella to cover us both. He's taller than me by several inches, even with my heels. "Thank you, I appreciate the help. It just had to downpour on the first day, right?"

"Not a problem." His white teeth contrast his light brown skin, and his smile is warm enough to blast away the chill from the rain.

We walk toward the stately stone building ahead, my shoulder bumping into his bicep. If it were Joss, she'd put her arm around my waist to keep me close. At least, that's what she used to do. My outside arm is getting a little wet, but it feels awkward to move any closer. I'm not sure, in all my twenty-five years of teaching, I've ever been in such physical proximity to a student.

Beds of tulips and dahlias in an ombre of pinks line either side of the sidewalk. I'm always impressed with MacAmes' landscaping efforts at the start of the year. Nothing says "welcome" better than a rainbow of flowers.

"Pretty," my walking mate says. "Even in the rain."

I assume he's referring to the flowers—because quite frankly, everything else looks a bit waterlogged—so I nod. "I'm not much of a tulip fan."

"Is that what they are?"

"The taller ones, yes. I'm more of a sunflower girl. Something about their vibrancy. They just seem so happy." What a dumb comment. Still, it's true. Joss used to surprise me with sunflowers. I loved them so much it's what I carried on our wedding day.

A foggy memory pokes my mind: running through a field of sunflowers with Fisher, two ginger-haired kids, laughing, open-mouthed, front teeth missing. Not a care in the world. My brother, my best friend.

We reach the door and he opens it, motioning for me to go first. A gentleman, I think, and I silently praise his parents for instilling good manners. But I can't go through because I'm the one holding the umbrella.

"You go ahead," I say.

"No, here. I'll take it." He grabs the umbrella, shifting the donuts to one hand, and I reluctantly let go.

I step through the doorway while he lowers the umbrella and gives it a shake before following me into the dry foyer of Avery Hall, the palatial building that houses my office.

"Thanks again," I say, rain dripping down my left arm and catching on my wedding band.

"Want me to carry these for you? Where are you headed?"

"Oh, no. That's all right. I think I can manage now that I'm not worried about ruining my colleagues' breakfast. I appreciate your help." We exchange smiles. I take the donuts and let the umbrella strap dangle from my wrist.

"No problem."

"Have a good day. Happy first day of classes."

"My *last* first day of classes."

"Senior year? Ah, well, enjoy it. Senior year's the best."

"That's my goal."

He gives me a slight nod, pulls his hood up and turns back out into the rain. I watch him go for a split second, wondering how many other students would have gone out of their way like that. Thank God there's still humanity in the world.

Abbie

"I'd like you all to break up into groups of four. We're going to play a little ice breaker game."

The sociology professor is young, but he's wearing a suit and tie like he's trying to appear older. He doesn't fit in here, I can tell—and I should know. It's easy for one outcast to recognize another.

Mom has told me stories from her first years of teaching. How she'd wear outfits much too matronly and how she'd toss in words her mother used just to trick the students into thinking she was older. "Fake it til you make it" was her motto before her true confidence in the classroom kicked in. I get the same vibes from this guy.

A muffled grumble circles the room at the words "ice breaker." Guess I'm not the only one who hates this first-day ritual. I mean, we mostly all follow each other on social media anyways, so what's the point of talking in real life? I'm pretty sure I can pinpoint who won't like me without hearing their valley girl voices.

I give the girl at my two-person table a sidelong glance while keeping my head straight, but she's already flagging down a group in the back. She only sat next to me by default—the last open seat left when she came sashaying in ten seconds before the start of class, plopped her heavily-stickered MacBook on the table and didn't so much as peek in my direction.

I pick at my nails under the table, wishing Baby Professor would count off by fours and dictate our groups. Most students don't like this micro-managed approach, but at least it would put me in a group, spare me the humiliation of being the only one no one wants.

No such luck. Baby Prof busies himself with papers at the front table. I catch him tugging at his collar like it's choking him.

I look to the left and right, cursing under my breath at this particular form of torture. My classmates happily pair into chatty foursomes. I overhear Cody Marshall, the star quarterback, at the next table say something about Thirsty Thursday. God, he's gorgeous. I wonder what his hair smells like. Fucking stop, Abbie—like you'd ever get close enough to Cody Marshall to smell his hair.

Everyone moves chairs into tight circles like it's no big deal. My throat tightens. Why is it so hard for me when it's so easy for everyone else? I bite the inside of my lip and stare at the desk, wishing my breath didn't suddenly feel so restricted.

"Everyone ready?" the professor says, looking up.

I slump down in my chair. Maybe he'll be like the rest of the world and not even notice me. Maybe he'll conduct the entire first day of class, listening to everyone talk about their siblings and their hometowns and their hidden talents, and he'll skim right over the girl in the middle row with a walk-in salon haircut and knockoff athleisure.

"Are you in a group?" Damn. He's looking right at me. Guess I can't get out of this one.

"No," I say, keeping my eyes forward. Seeing pity from thirty people my own age would be like salt in an already open wound. No thanks, humiliation from one is plenty.

Baby Prof bops his finger in the air, counting the students who've formed groups. *Onetwothreefour, onetwothreefour...*

"Well, I guess we have an odd number today. Anyone want to welcome—" He trails off, with a hand in my direction, like it's a tray he wants me to place my name on.

"Abbie."

"—Abbie. Anyone want to welcome Abbie to their group?"

The room's quiet. No one makes eye contact.

Not again. The corners of my eyes prickle. I knew this is how it would be. I tried to tell my moms, but they just wouldn't listen. Now here we go—another four years of torture.

Finally, a greasy-haired guy in the front raises his hand. "You can come with us."

"Thank you," Baby Prof says.

I hesitate, feeling my outcast status creep even higher, but then reluctantly scooch my chair over to join the land of misfit toys: a boy in black who looks even more pissed than me to be here, a girl with a bad case of sunless tanner streaks, and two other guys, including grease head.

For the next thirty minutes, we go around the room, telling the class "something interesting" about another member of our group. It encourages communication and collaboration, our annoyingly enthusiastic teacher tells us. There's nothing interesting about me—literally nothing at all. I'm an art freak who lives at home. The last thing I feel like sharing is that my moms—lesbian moms!—teach here, which would only put more of a sign on my back: *Hi, I'm different!*

"Lukas has a winter home in Aspen."

"Janelle just topped fifty thousand followers on Instagram."

"Brooks made all-team for basketball."

A girl in glasses, but not the trendy oversized kind, stands when it's our turn. "This is Abbie Graham-Maston," she says in her mouse-like voice, and I cringe on the inside—even my double last name makes me different. "She can name every Impressionist painter from the late 19th century."

A few students snicker under their breath. I don't think I'm getting any new friends today.

Christine

Here's the funny thing about teaching: every year I get older but the students stay the same.

A group of three girls shuffle in, wearing what Abbie calls "mom jeans" and rib knit crop tops. Their hair is thrown up on their heads to look haphazard, but I know they probably pulled and tucked those locks into the perfect place before stepping foot outside their dorms—I've seen Abbie do it.

Mine hangs limp from the rain, a red curtain, despite blowing it out this morning. I was them once. Heck, when I started teaching, I wasn't much older than them. My mind drifts back to those early years—the bountiful energy, the tighter skin. Getting old is so depressing.

My phone lights up, snapping me back to the classroom, but it's just a news alert. I frown. Still no text. She always texts me on the first day of class.

I smooth my blouse and check the time on my watch. Its double G logo is backwards since it's a knockoff from some overseas supplier, but it's close enough to Gucci to make me feel relatable. The last thing I want is to be lumped with the other over-fifty female faculty at MacAmes.

Five minutes after the hour. I clear my throat and step out from behind the podium, my heels clicking on the linoleum.

"Good morning," I say. "Welcome to Foundations of Anthropology." Their attentive faces return with polite smiles. God, I love freshmen—not yet jaded like the upperclassmen. "Let's see who all is here, shall we?"

I call roll, my eyes bouncing up and down to place names with faces. Three Emilys and I'm not even halfway through. Reminds me of the couple years when I was inundated with Ashleys in every spelling under the sun. I have to admit, there's not much diversity here—Admissions does its best to make campus a melting pot, but every year we stay just as white, just as upper-middle class as ever.

Christine is a classic name, and while it doesn't bother me as an adult, there were times when I wished I'd been given something as unique as Fisher.

I continue down the roster. When I get two-thirds down the list, my finger stops.

Johnson, Micah. Senior.

My face pinches. What's a senior doing in my freshman-level course?

I look up and scan the class, and that's when his face jumps out at me. The same friendly smile I met this morning. Donut boy—er, donut man. Man-boy. College is a weird age. They're adults in the eyes of the law, but still seem like kids to me. It's not like I'd consider Abbie a *woman*.

But something about this pupil is different.

Either way, the student who helped me two hours ago is sitting in my class. Only now, without his jacket, I get a full look at him. Bleached tips on his high fade, eyes as dark as two ink blots, fringed by thick lashes. He's reclined, with a quiet confidence foreign to first-year students. A small smile pulls at the corner of his full lips.

I tap my finger on his name. "Micah Johnson?"

"Here," he replies so smoothly it sounds like syrup.

"It's you," I say with a hint of familiarity. Our gazes catch and recognition passes between us. For a brief, bizarre moment, the room disappears. It's just him and I, the two of us, yards apart but somehow close enough to hear each other breathe.

21

Someone in the class coughs, zapping me from this weird trance. I clear my throat and put my professional voice back on, as though the class might discover I'd shared an umbrella with this student before. As though I'd done something immoral. "Mr. Johnson, would you mind coming up here for a quick second?"

He stands and shimmies out of the row. His jeans are slim, hugging his backside. My chest constricts. Did I just consciously check out a student's butt? Something about him pulls me back to that post-grad fling I had with a tall, dark and handsome junior accountant.

I return my gaze to the roster as he approaches. When he's a few steps away, I slide back behind the podium, thankful there's something between us, though I don't quite know why.

"Hi," I say with a sunny smile. "You didn't tell me this morning you were taking my class."

He cocks his head, grinning. "I didn't know who you were."

I consider the irony only for a second. "Ok, well you do know this is a 100-level freshman course. Sometimes people get mixed up, especially with classrooms getting moved around at the last minute. Don't want you to sit through something if it's not where you're supposed to be."

"I'm right where I'm supposed to be." He taps the podium.

An instant warmth rushes over my body. How can you feel like you know a perfect stranger? His eyes burn into me, like they can see all the way to my soul. My smile falters for a split second, but before I can say another word, he's halfway back to his seat.

Okay then.

I push my hair back off my shoulder, hoping my face doesn't match its strawberry color. I've had hundreds of male students over the years, but never a reaction like this to one.

You haven't done anything wrong. The words feel phony, but they're enough to bolster any would-be accusation.

Accusation? Why am I even toying with these scenarios? A student helped carry my things when my arms were full. We shared an umbrella. What, was I supposed to say, "No, you must stay out in the rain"?

I step out from behind the podium again and begin my typical stroll around the front of the class. Teaching is my comfort zone, where I feel most alive. I guess you could say it's in my blood, coming from a long line of educators.

"We'll be covering the pillars of anthropology," I say, "the basis of a humanistic experience." I hand a stack of syllabi to a perky girl in the first seat. She takes one and passes the stack to the left. "Who can tell me the essence of anthropology as a study?"

A boy in a concert tee a few rows back raises his hand. "Understanding the past?"

"That's a part, for sure. But what else?" I twirl my hands, figuratively pulling the answer from him.

"How the past connects to the present?"

"Bingo. A hundred imaginary bonus points to you." I pretend to roll up something in my hand and lob it in his direction. The boy plays along, reaching to catch the invisible toss. The class hums with interest. "Anthropology is all about studying human behavior, which of course, includes patterns. We can't understand and accept who we are as a species today unless we know where we came from."

I'm in a groove. This—this interaction—is my favorite part of being a college instructor. It's like a high, and I can't grasp how Joss doesn't feel the same. The research component of my contract is an obligation, but the teaching is a thrill.

We go over the syllabus I'd meticulously prepared—the semester-long project, the research paper, the exams. At that section, I catch a couple students eyeing each other. I know, I know. My tests are on the hard side—something I've garnered a bit of a reputation for. They must not be *that* hard; my rosters are always full.

We're cruising along nicely until my eyes scan the sea of students and land on Micah Johnson. The rest of the class is taking notes, as good freshmen do, but he's locked on me. My stomach does a weird flip that I'd love to chalk up to skipping breakfast this morning. *Stop staring*, I want to say, but I don't because there's another voice in my head, too, and it's saying the opposite.

I check the time and consider calling it a day, dismissing the class early and getting away from Micah's burning eyes—but I can't. Not this year. Not when I'm up for tenure in the spring. Not when every move I make in this place is noted by the Rank & Tenure Committee. I've got to be on my best behavior, and things like letting students go early is highly frowned upon, though professors do it all the time.

Thirty more minutes creep by. Thirty minutes of me rambling while my mind is elsewhere. Finally, I slap my binder closed.

"See you all Wednesday."

The first day is supposed to be mindless, but this boy has got me on edge and I don't like it.

The students filter out, a few giving me polite "thank yous" on their way past the front table. I keep my head down despite the urge to watch Micah leave. *Please just go.*

I stuff my materials into my leather tote, ready to get back to my little hole of an office and unpack the unsettling feeling in the pit of my stomach.

When I lift my head again, the classroom is empty. I release a long breath.

***

My office is at the end of a long hall lined with identical gray doors and overflowing bulletin boards. A name plate announces my credentials.

CHRISTINE GRAHAM, PH.D
ASSISTANT PROFESSOR OF ANTHROPOLOGY

Even after two decades, my heart still sings when I see it. I've come so far in my career, from junior level instructor all the way to assistant professor. Tenure is the next—the last—big thing. Tenure and a promotion, then I've made it as far as I can go. What a relief. Fulfilling, but still a relief. Too bad I won't live long enough to enjoy it, not with the Graham family curse coming for me at any moment. I don't know what it'll be—the sneaky attack of heart disease like my mother? Or a freak accident like my grandmother? The poor woman never saw the fall coming.

I drop the tote on the floor behind my desk and check my phone. Three hours into day one and still no text. My body sinks an inch. I know things have been distant, but I didn't think she'd forget the same text she

24

sends me on this day every year. Then again, I didn't think she'd forget my birthday, so...

About halfway through a stream of emails that have flooded my once-empty inbox, there's a quiet knock on the door. I look up and a jolt of electricity zips through my chest. Micah leans against the frame, his hands shoved into the pockets of his jeans. He wears an expression of relaxed ease like he belongs here, like we're casual enough for him to press his body against something that's mine.

I sit up straight. "Oh, hi, Mr. Johnson. What can I do for you?" I rustle papers on my desk, as though I'm incredibly busy.

He enters and pulls out a chair opposite me, removes his backpack and takes a seat. "I just wanted to say how much I enjoyed your class today," he says. His head's at a slight tilt, giving even more definition to his jawline. His Adam's apple bobs as he talks, and I've never once been so fascinated by a body part.

I blink twice. What did he say? Oh, class. He enjoyed it. But it was only the first day, and we did nothing.

"Well...great," I say, which is true, but mostly because I don't know how else to respond. "I'm glad."

"I'm super interested in culture and stuff. You know, like why people behave the way they do. It's captivating stuff."

What student uses the word *captivating*?

"Yes, I agree...obviously." My eyes dart around.

I don't know where this conversation is going, but I try to act like I would with any other student. An awkward silence hangs between us for a beat. I don't know what to say, what he wants me to say. His chocolate eyes will not let me go. I give a half laugh. He saves me.

"Maybe I could swing by again? To talk about class stuff?" His eyebrows raise and his mouth parts a little, tips into the slightest smile.

I shift in my chair. Something about this feels dangerous. Somewhere in my head a flag waves in panic, a red-hot signal of danger, but all I can think about are those glowing student evals I'll need come tenure decision. I can't turn a pupil away. *Availability to students*, one of the benchmarks states. Yes, I think, but what *kind* of availability?

"I have an open-door policy," I say chirpily. "My office hours are posted."

"Great. Looking forward to it."

I swear he winks when he says it. I can't be sure, though, because I might be having a stroke. Great, this is how it ends. My fate is a stroke, right here, right now. How did my air-conditioned office suddenly become a sauna?

Micah takes two long strides to the door, then turns back over his shoulder. "See ya Wednesday, Dr. Graham."

"Bye, Mr. Johnson," is all I manage to get past a thick tongue.

He chuckles, and even that is velvety. "You can call me Micah, you know."

And then he's gone.

I stare at the empty doorway for a minute before returning ten tingling fingers to the keyboard. I keep hitting the wrong keys, as I realize my fingers aren't the only part of me that's tingling. I push back from my desk and shake my hands.

What on earth is happening?

My gaze pans to the bookcase at my right. Mixed among textbooks and binders sits a photograph in a chunky gold frame. Three grinning faces. My family.

Me, my wife, and our daughter.

A throb pumps in my chest. I am gay, right?

Joss

Thirty-six. That's how many pages I've written this morning, and it's not yet noon. If I keep up this pace, the paper will be done well before deadline.

I run a thumb over the rabbit's foot resting on my lap. An unsought image of my father materializes in my mind, his permanently downturned mouth, voice like sandpaper. The ever-present glass of Scotch. "Luck," he'd said, as I wrote the "ss" in my name backwards. "You're gonna need a lot of it."

Maybe it was his complete doubt in me, the distaste that seemed to flow from him as early as I can remember, but when eight-year-old me finally saved up enough money from walking Mrs. Hammond's mini dachshund, the rabbit's foot—luck—was the first thing I bought.

The second thing was escaping to another continent the minute I graduated high school.

I give the rabbit's foot a squeeze. It's lost a bit of smoothness over the years, and its keychain top is now more rust than gold, but this little good luck charm has served me well. I've dedicated the last eight months of my life to this research study in the hopes that it'll land in medical journals. It's all I can think about, which is why I've locked myself in our home office every day to focus. Only four more months of sabbatical and then I'll be back in the classroom.

I know so many tenured faculty who use their sabbaticals to nap liberally and faff about on holiday, then submit some dinky paper to a mediocre journal as something to show for it. Not me. This study has the potential to go big time. Like CDC big. Richard, my research partner, and I are presenting at the American Chemical Society's annual conference next month. My name could very well land in the national spotlight.

Take that, I want to say to the Ivies that didn't accept me out of high school.

The old pendulum clock on the wall chimes, making me look up from the computer screen. Noon. I jerk up straight, as a little ping of panic hits my chest. I forgot to text Christine.

Damnit.

I grab my phone, knowing it's too late—she's already had a class or two—but hoping a late text is better than no text.

My finger extends and moves, but then stops, hovering over the collage of colorful icons. I stare at the phone in my hand, and all of a sudden the strangest sensation grabs hold: I don't know how to use it.

This is a phone, that I know. It's used to call people, that I also know. But as I study it further, it becomes even more unfamiliar. What button do I press? It's like someone just handed me a rubik's cube and asked me to solve it.

I let out a laugh and shake my head, squeeze my eyes shut. Too much screen time is starting to mess with my head. But when I look back at the phone, I'm no clearer on what to do with it. Alarm seizes my gut, and I drop the phone to the desk like it scalded me. I stare at it, horrified.

This is the most bizarre experience I've ever had.

I close my laptop with a swift hand. I clearly need a break from work. My legs are stiff from sitting so long. It doesn't help my backside, which is already flat enough to begin with. Twelve-hour days in front of the computer haven't been kind to my waistline—my fingers are often the only things getting a regular workout—and it's not like I've ever been naturally thin like Christine. I really thought by the time I'd turned fifty, I'd have lost all self-consciousness about my body, but turns out even middle-aged women still care.

Well, to a degree.

In the kitchen, I reach behind my wife's healthy snacks for the carton of Goldfish and pour myself a bowl. I eat them four at a time—always four, never three or five—and crush them against the roof of my mouth until they're a smooshy glob of cheddar goodness. The salt wakes up my taste buds.

After a few minutes in the kitchen, I feel refreshed. Blood sugar leveled. My mind trickles back to research and the deadline I've given myself. I head back to the office, Goldfish in tow. My phone leers at me from where it lays, a foreign object. At least it's here and not in the microwave. I should try to text her again, but even as I stare at it there on the desk, the buttons all blur.

Instead of simply flipping it over, I shove it in the top drawer. Out of sight, out of mind. Christine will forgive me. Now, it's time to focus on what's more important.

***

A door slams and footsteps come up the stairs. I check the clock. Four-thirty already? Where has the afternoon gone?

Abbie passes the office door in a blur.

"Hi, Ab," I call. Her response is more of a grunt, as she heads to the cave she calls a bedroom, but I still yell out after her because that's what good moms do. "How was your first day?" She's already gone. I close my eyes and give my head a shake. Daughters. Teenage daughters.

I return to the screen, trying to regain focus. Where was I?

A minute later I sense a presence behind me. Christine. I hate when she just stands there—it's hard enough for me to concentrate let alone when someone is watching over my shoulder.

"Hi," I say, not taking my eyes from the computer. The *click click click* of the keys is the only sound in the room.

"How's writing going?"

"What? Oh, good. I've really been on a roll today."

29

"Mmmm."

I can hear it in her voice. The way she's lingering means there's something else she's not saying. I continue to type. Not because I don't want to talk to my wife, but because I'm so close to finishing this section of the paper, I don't want to lose momentum. Can't she just give me thirty more minutes?

"You forgot to text me this morning," she says.

There it is. I was hoping she wouldn't have remembered.

My fingers stop moving. Their pads sit lightly on the keys. I look to her. Her arms are crossed like she's heated, but her face looks sad, and that does something more to me than her anger ever could.

I consider my options. I'm mortified at the thought of telling her the truth. That I actually *had* remembered to text her, but that my phone was some sort of alien object my brain couldn't process. And after the microwave incident, it sounds even worse. I mean, Christ. I'm fifty-four, not eighty.

"Sorry, Chris. I've been glued to the computer all day." I resume typing.

Her hands slowly drop to her sides like weights sliding off a cliff. "I guess I'll let you finish."

"I just really need to get this chunk done." I glance over my shoulder. She's already at the door, her back to me. It's the first time I've seen her all day.

"It's fine."

"I'll wrap up before dinner. Promise."

Then she's gone. Guilt churns, but only for a moment. I swear, sometimes she doesn't get how important this research is to me. I need it like oxygen. If I can't prove myself through work, then what am I? A nothing, just like Dad said I'd be.

I stare at the screen again, trying to regain focus. Abbie's music thumps next door. I moan through gritted teeth. It's so much harder to concentrate when they're home.

***

30

The next time I check the clock, it's pushing eight. I've been writing for thirteen hours and it feels like no more than a blip—time's funny like that.

"Shit," I say, before hitting save on my file and closing my laptop. Downstairs the dishes have already been cleaned. Christine and Abbie are on the couch watching *The Voice*. They're nestled together, Abbie's feet tucked under her mom's legs. A whole living room of seating, yet they *choose* to be close. My heart immediately flares.

"Hi," I say awkwardly. "Care if I join you?"

Abbie's response is wordless, but the slightest nod tells me I'm welcome. I plop down on the other side of the couch and peek at Christine from the corner of my eye.

"Sorry about missing dinner."

She doesn't look at me. "There's a plate in the fridge if you're hungry."

Great. The text and now dinner? I'm officially in the dog house.

"Okay. I'll do the dishes, then."

"Already done."

I'm not surprised. The one time I tried loading the dishwasher, Christine hovered over me like some sort of Type A maniac before insisting on doing it herself. Apparently, there's a precise method to top drawer/bottom drawer. ("*Never* put plates in opposite directions.")

"So," I try, "How was your first day?" I say it to both of them, hoping at least one will respond. Either the daughter I don't understand, or the wife that's mad at me.

"Dumb," Abbie says.

"First days are always a little silly," I say, attempting to relate.

"No, not just because it was the first day."

I sigh. I thought we were past this. "Come on, Abbie. It's been one day. This is your future we're talking about. You know, it's not too late to get campus housing. You're going to miss out on so much. You could join the art club."

"I'm not interested, I've told you both that a hundred times."

I clench my jaw, wanting to push the issue, but not wanting to suffer her wrath.

"Let her be," Christine says, running a hand through Abbie's short brown hair. It frizzes at her temples, despite her every effort to tame it with a flat iron. "You'll find your way, won't you, Ab?"

Abbie lays her head on Christine's shoulder. I hate that I'm jealous.

We finish the episode and then Abbie starts to yawn. She grabs her phone and stands. "Night, guys."

"Goodnight," we say in unison, though Christine adds "sweetheart" to the end.

With the buffer of Abbie's presence gone, Christine rubs her neck. "I think I'll turn in early tonight too." She gets up without waiting for my response. I contemplate whether to follow her. I can't remember the last time we went to bed at the same time.

My phone illuminates the dark living room. A text from Richard.

Methodology section almost done.

My brain flips back to work mode. Christine can wait—she's not going anywhere—but my paper can't. I head back to my office.

Abbie

I'm in the car waiting for Mom when she comes flying out of the house, her hair streaking behind her like the tail of a comet. It's thinner than it once was, and has lost a bit of its luster, but Mom is still insanely beautiful. I just wish she thought so herself. Hell, she looks way better than most moms her age, but her ridiculous aging complex prevents her from seeing it. I'm pretty sure Mom's healthy eating and weekly spin classes will take her all the way to one hundred.

"Ugh, sorry, sorry. Running a little behind this morning," she says, as she tosses her bag into the backseat. She's wearing a shift dress with a button down underneath in mis-matched patterns that still somehow works. Very J.Crew-like. Very un-me-like. I wish her sense of style would rub off on me a bit.

"It's fine. I don't have class until ten," I say, trying for tenderness, as I try to buff out a paint stain from my jeans. It's Uncle Fisher's anniversary, a sore reminder to Mom that half of herself is no longer here. We talk about Uncle Fisher a lot, but not today. Today's too hard.

"Yeah, but mine's at nine." It's eight-fifteen and we normally leave at eight. Mom backs out of the driveway. "I hate being late for class."

"Mom, chill. We're not even late. It takes ten minutes to get to campus." Five, if Ma were driving.

"I know, but I need time to get settled."

She's frazzled in a way I'm not used to seeing. I take a bite of the cinnamon Pop-Tart I found in Ma's hidden stash. A trail of crumbs drops to the seat. "Oversleep?"

"Seriously, Abbie?" She reaches over and brushes the crumbs to the floor, and I know she'll have the Shop-Vac out later. "Yes, I overslept. Tossed and turned all night. Woke up at three something from a really bizarre dream and couldn't get back to sleep."

"What was it?"

Mom doesn't respond. She looks lost in thought, and her brows knit a little, like she's perplexed about something she isn't saying.

"Mom?"

"Hmm?"

"What was the dream?" I say through one side of my mouth, the other crammed with breakfast that Mom loves to remind me has basically zero nutritional value and will leave me starving again in an hour.

"Nothing. It was nothing. Just weird. You know how dreams are."

I nod. "Did it wake Ma up?"

"She fell asleep in the office last night."

"Again?"

"Yes, Abbie, again. Ma is working on a really big study right now, you know that. Let's not patronize."

Her tone is snippy, but I see through it. I know they've been disconnected lately. I'm not blind. The fact that Ma slept in her office doesn't shock me, but it does sit in my gut like a little cloud of darkness. Parents aren't supposed to sleep apart.

Mom changes the subject, softens her expression. "So, first game next weekend, right? Are you excited? I can't believe you're starting varsity." She reaches over and squeezes my thigh.

"I guess," I say with a shrug.

"You guess?"

I roll my eyes, not wanting her to misconstrue my excitement for the game as acceptance of enjoying college life.

"Oh, that's right," she says. "You hate everything about college. Wouldn't want to be enthused for a small piece of it or anything. That's not in line with this angsty persona you've got going on."

I can almost taste the sarcasm coming out of her mouth, and I give her a look. She punches my shoulder and I dramatically fling myself into the door.

"Ow! Now you're abusing me too?" But I'm smiling and then we're both smiling. I can never stay mad at Mom for long. Even though we've never said it out loud, we both know there's something different about our relationship, something special. Mom gets me—even if she's not letting up on the whole college thing.

I crumble up the Pop-Tart wrapper, careful not to drop any more crumbs on Mom's beloved seat—like we're not in a Toyota Camry, but whatever. "Coach called an extra practice tonight to run drills. It'll be late. I'll see if someone can drive me home afterward." *Who would want to drive me home?*

"We can come get you, we don't mind." By *we* I know she's referring to herself.

"It's fine. Someone can drive me." I say it without believing it, but feel bad making her leave the house after nine. "Maybe you and Ma can have a nice dinner or something."

Mom mumbles something under her breath, something I can't quite decipher. Then, more clear, "Alright, well, I'll see you when you get home. Text me when practice is over, okay?"

We pull into campus and find a spot in the overcrowded lot. I have to admit, MacAmes is a really pretty school. When I was a kid, it reminded me of Hogwarts, with its Gothic architecture, pale stone buildings, and tall, pointy steeple.

Mom tosses her bag over her shoulder. Few students mingle outside at this hour—only the underclassmen get stuck with eight-A.M.s, but I was lucky to use my moms' pull and avoid that time slot altogether.

The sidewalk splits, Mom heads left and I go right.

"Have a good day, sweetie."

"You too."

I do a double take. I didn't notice it in the car, but now in the sunlight it's more obvious. Mom's wearing...lipstick?

Christine

I spend the entire walk to my office trying to convince myself the dream had no meaning. Dreams are dreams, and the dreamer has no control over them. What was it I learned back in school? There's no reliable evidence that dreams can be connected to real life. See? No connection. But wasn't it Freud who argued the manifest content of a dream? I don't know what to believe.

I fall deeper into thought. The details were so vivid, I feel my face flush just remembering it.

I woke to a hand sliding up my calf, under my night shirt and around to my stomach. Not yet turning over, I smiled. *She's finally come to bed.* The hand traveled up to my breasts, cupping the soft flesh. Flashbacks of our younger days danced in my mind. We'd always been so good together, our connection electric. I've missed it. "Thank you for coming to bed," I whispered, and my body quivered at her touch. She knows my body well. I rolled to face her, the face I've known and loved and missed.

But it wasn't Joss.

It was Micah Johnson.

Then I woke up for real. My skin sparkled with sweat, and a steady throb pulsed between my legs. No, no, no. I bolted upright in bed, utterly disoriented. Joss's side was empty. Placing a palm on my chest, I tried to steady my breathing.

After that, it was hard to fall back asleep. Every time I closed my eyes, I saw him—us—doing things I hadn't done with a man in nearly three decades, things I hadn't found any pleasure in for a long time. A sex dream about a student? You might as well profile me on *Dateline*.

***

My knee-high boots clap on the hallway tile as I navigate toward my office. I've had these Michael Kors boots for ages, and every time the sole wears out, I drive an hour to a cobbler to have them fixed. If they're good enough for Kate Middleton, they're good enough for me.

The clacking zones me into a trance. That dream. I can't shake it. Did I like it? And if I did, what does that say about me as an educator? What a cliché—the teacher and the student. It happens more than people think, including to a girl I was friends with in school who was lured by a religious studies professor. Religious studies, of all things. But she was seduced, baited. Am I baiting? Good Lord, Christine, no. I've only exchanged a few sentences with the kid.

I shake my head as though I can erase the thought like an Etch-A-Sketch, then glance ahead to where I'm going. My heart jumps into my throat when I see a figure on the bench outside my door. Micah. I know it's him even at a distance—his dark hair stands out against the white walls. He's leaned forward, elbows on knees, studying his phone.

A gush of heat surges through my body, and I'm surprised how quickly underarms can feel damp. It's eight-thirty in the morning. What is he doing here? I want to turn the other way, dart into another office and wait him out. He can't sit there forever. But what if he already saw me? What if he heard my boots and looked up before I did? My mind's whirring even as my feet keep moving, one in front of the other.

Relax, I tell myself with a deep belly breath like my yoga teacher taught me. *This is nothing more than a student coming to office hours.*

I'm getting closer. I'm going to have to say something, but my mouth is like the Sahara. Finally, when I'm a few steps from the bench, the words form.

"Hi Micah. You're here early. Everything okay?"

He lowers his phone and stands. "Hey Dr. Graham. Do you have a minute?"

I look around, as though letting him in my office were some sort of frowned upon behavior. Is there anybody watching? I'm not sure if I want someone to be or not. Maybe I need a witness, someone to stop this before it starts. Please, someone pull me away. Where's Kerry when I need her?

"Of course," I say. "Come on in. Just let me put my stuff down real quick." I drop my bag and take a seat behind my desk, establishing my dominance. The heat has traveled from my underarms to my chest, and I feel an actual drop of sweat make its way down my cleavage. Is this what a hot flash is like?

I fold my hands on the desktop. "What's up?"

He pulls out a chair and sits. "I was looking ahead on the syllabus and wanted to run some ideas past you for the term paper." He leans forward when he talks, and in turn I lean away, moving my hands to my lap.

"The paper? You do realize that's not due until after midterm—like eight weeks from now."

Micah grins, and I notice his smile is ever so slightly lopsided, higher on the right than the left. A small dimple makes a divot in his cheek.

"Right," he says. "Just trying to be proactive."

"Well, I give two thumbs up to that." The second it comes out of my mouth I cringe. Two thumbs up? Who am I? A corny, aging Gen Xer, that's who. Why am I trying to act cool in front of him? I feel like a first-year faculty again, all nervous and clumsy.

He doesn't take my cue to wait on the term paper, and since I technically don't have class for another twenty-five minutes, I feel obligated to appease him.

We go over topic ideas, but it's mostly me doing the talking. At one point, I grab our textbook and open it on the desk facing him, flipping to the chapter on regional dialects. I point to some of the areas we're going to be studying this semester.

"There's tons of English-speaking dialects in Europe. Even within a single country, there could be a dozen or more." I'm babbling, both because I'm flustered by him and also because I'm genuinely excited to have a student so eager. Maybe I can help guide him to grad programs in this field. There's nothing better than students discovering their passions.

My finger is firmly planted on the United Kingdom and I'm mid-sentence when Micah reaches out and covers his hand over mine. He drags my finger across the map.

"What about here?" he says, slowly, drawing out the words. He stops my finger in the Atlantic, off the coast of North America. My eyes fix on the page, but in our close proximity, I can tell he's not even looking at the book.

Not sure there's dialects in the middle of the ocean, I want to say. But something tells me he's not really interested in the paper after all. When I look up, his eyes bore into me. Our hands are still clasped, his over mine, and it's then that I notice the differences. My skin is loose where his is firm. An age spot has formed near my center knuckle, while his hand is unblemished. He's new and shiny next to me. I used to have young hands, a body people wanted—one my wife wanted.

Fifty. My mother died at fifty. My grandmother died at fifty. Surely that means I'm next. He has his whole life ahead of him, while mine's about to wrap up.

"I...I...," I stumble.

But then there's a knock on the door. I yank my hand away and straighten up in my chair. Micah sits back, leaving the textbook between us like a ticking bomb.

Kerry Viotto, my department chair, pops her head around the corner. "Hey, Chris, just a reminder we're meeting at ten." Oh, Kerry, couldn't you have been fifteen minutes earlier?

"Right. Yes. Thanks for reminding me." I answer short and fast, adding the meeting I forgot into my mental schedule.

Kerry stands there for a moment, and I wonder if my cheeks are as red as they feel. She smiles and leaves, so we must be in the clear.

I look back to Micah. "I have class soon. Is there, uh, anything else you needed today?"

"Nah, I think I'm good. Thanks. Maybe I'll stop back again tomorrow?" His face is hopeful without giving it all away. We're speaking in code and we both know it.

It ambushes me, this sudden feeling—not only as a married woman, but also as an educator. Cardinal rule of teaching: don't cross the professionalism line. I feel like I'm teetering awfully close, but not by my own doing. Something, someone, is pulling me.

This is the moment I'd look back on and question my sanity. The undertones are as loud as a marching band, though we say nothing aloud. He doesn't need to explain. I know the connotation. And with five little words, I set forth on a new, dangerous trajectory.

"Sure, that would be great."

Micah smiles, knowingly. He tosses his backpack over his shoulder. "See ya then, Christine."

When he calls me by my first name, I know I'm screwed.

Abbie

Coach runs us hard tonight. I'm pretty fit—definitely one of the cleanest on the team—but even I am huffing good once he finally blows the whistle to end practice.

All of us collapse on the pitch, starfished on our backs, staring up at the sky, all shades of black and blue like a three-day bruise. After a few minutes, some of the girls roll over, climb to their feet and disperse. It's nine and I still have a couple hours of homework, but what I wouldn't give to just lay here for another hour.

"Hey, Jules, can I bum a ride home?" I say to a girl sitting near the edge of the group. Out of everyone, Jules is the most like me, an outsider, what with the glasses held on her face by a thick head strap. Like Trina all through high school, Jules feels "on my level." Plus, she's a sophomore and I know she has a car. If I'm going to ask anyone, it's going to be her.

"Sorry, Abbie. I'm actually staying to meet up for a group project. Euro History." She twists her face into a gag, and I can't argue. Euro History—oof.

I'm mentally calculating how long it will take me to walk home when another voice chimes in. "I can take you."

It's Stacia, and she's addressing me with a friendly smile. I nearly look over my shoulder to make sure she's not talking to someone else. Now *that* would be embarrassing.

Her perfect blonde hair is pulled into a ponytail, and a few wisps frame her face. Even after a brutal, sweaty practice, she still somehow manages to look Instagram-ready. Me, I probably look like the last remaining contestant on *Survivor*.

"Thanks. You sure?" My body tingles. I still can't really believe she's talking to me let alone offering me a ride home. It's one thing to comment on people's Instagram posts, but it's another to socialize *in public*.

"It's no problem!" She says it like we've been besties for ages.

We walk to her car in the lot below the soccer field. I stay one step behind, as though there were some seniority rule like anyone who walks with the Queen of England. Even though we've played together for weeks now, I'm rendered mute as we cross the parking lot. Aside from hollering soccer plays at each other, we've never had a real conversation. Plus, she's just so popular, the alpha. Even with three thousand students, everyone on campus knows Stacia. The girls want to be her and the boys want to sleep with her.

"So, are you pumped to be playing varsity this year?" she says after taking a long pull from her stainless-steel water bottle.

"I'm a little surprised, to be honest. I thought maybe Coach made a mistake and was going to change his mind."

"Stop it. You're really good, Abbie."

My skin prickles. I roll my head side to side, like it's hard to accept her compliment because it is.

"No really, you are." Stacia gives me a playful shove.

I want her to do it again.

I slide into the passenger side, embarrassed that my sweat-drenched clothes are going to leave a mark on her seat. I sit rigid, trying not to rest all my dripping weight on the cushion. Stacia rolls down the windows as we pull out of campus. The September breeze is a relief and helps to dry my forehead. I need a shower STAT before this sweat invades my pores and gives me another giant pimple.

"So, what's it like going to the same school where your parents teach?" Stacia says.

I chuckle. This has become a frequent question since school started. Once people find out I'm Dr. Matson's and Dr. Graham's daughter, it's usually the first thing they ask. That, or the lesbian thing. Oh, if I had a dollar for every time I got *that*.

"It's not that big a deal, I guess. MacAmes is big enough that I don't run into them every day."

"Yeah, but don't you ever worry about them hearing about things you do?"

I stifle a laugh, not wanting to offend her. "I don't really do much." Then, after a second, "But even if I did, my mom's pretty cool."

"Which one?"

"Oh, they both are," I say, feeling the need to be a good daughter and not favor one parent over the other, "but I was referring to my Mom."

Stacia's forehead scrunches, and I realize I've made no sense. To me, they're Mom and Ma, and can never be confused or interchanged. But to others, the term "mom" is used a bit more loosely.

"Sorry," I say, "I mean Dr. Graham."

"Yeah, she is cool. I'm in her class this semester. Theory of Gender Studies."

"I've heard that's a tough one."

Stacia's eyes grow wide. "That's an understatement."

"Oh yeah?"

"I mean, your mom's really nice and she's a great teacher, but yeah, the class is *hard*."

I laugh awkwardly, not sure how I should respond, then finally settle on, "I can't take my own parents' classes even if I wanted to...which I don't." I'm downplaying it, but I've seen the reviews on Rate My Professor—Mom's tests are a bit notorious.

"Our first exam is coming up next week," Stacia continues. "My roommate took the class last year and said the tests are brutal. I'd *kill* for a copy of that exam." She gives me a side glance before returning her eyes to the road. Her words linger in the air between us, caught in the mini dream catcher that hangs from her rear-view mirror.

A chill crawls down my back, and I'm not sure if it's my body temperature regulating or a reaction to what Stacia said. I switch the conversation back to soccer, asking about our upcoming match. We run down stats, and my body relaxes with the change in topic.

When we pull into my driveway, I reach for the drawstring pack at my feet. "Thanks again for the ride, I really appreciate it."

"Absolutely, no prob. See ya tomorrow."

I'm a few paces from the car when she rolls the window down and hollers to me. "Oh, and Abbie? Don't repeat what I said about the test."

I roll my eyes. "Duh."

* * *

Mom has chicken and broccoli for me in the fridge. I could really go for some carbs to replenish what I just burned at practice, but Mom is a little scared of carbs. Ma's my pasta partner. Together we can demolish a box of penne faster than you can say cellulite.

The kitchen is dim with only the pendant lights above the island giving off a soft glow. Mom's reading student papers at the counter. She lowers the one in her hand when I enter, removes her cheater glasses. "How was practice?"

"Killer."

She kisses my forehead, despite the fact it probably tastes like salt. I join her at the island and eat while she continues grading.

"You like all your students this semester?" I say.

Her head whips up, but she's still chin down in order to see me above her frames. "What's that supposed to mean?"

I stop chewing. "Nothing...geez Mom," I laugh, "don't bite my head off. Just making conversation."

"You've never cared about my students in the past."

"Mom. Relax. It was just a question."

Her face softens, the set of vertical wrinkles between her eyes smoothing flat. "Sorry. Long day, I guess." She takes my empty plate to the sink, rinses it and puts it in the dishwasher.

"I can do that, you know."

She shrugs. "Habit. Guess moms never stop mom-ing, even when their kids leave the house."

"But I still live here."

"You know what I mean," she says with a wink.

My legs are screaming to be elevated. As I swivel off the stool, my quads throb. I'd so much rather soak in the tub than do school work.

Mom finishes wiping up the counter. "You heading up?"

"Yeah. Got a couple more chapters to read for English Lit tomorrow."

"You and me both," she says, tapping the stack of papers with her red pen.

I climb the stairs and trudge past the study where I know Ma is knee-deep in research, but then stop a step later and reverse. I crack the office door enough for a single eye to see through. Her dark pixie cut is haloed by the computer screen's glare.

"Night, Ma," I say.

Ma glances back over her shoulder. "Oh, hey. Didn't realize you were home."

She smiles in that way I know she's trying to be an interested parent but she really just wants to get back to her work. We're in a stare-off. I wonder what it would be like not to have an awkward parent.

"Anyway, just wanted to say goodnight," I say through the crack.

I walk the rest of the way to my room, too exhausted to fight the internal struggle I feel toward my bio mom. The questions will still be there tomorrow and the next day: How can two people who are linked by blood feel so distant, while two people who share no DNA seem connected by a higher power?

My bed is a welcomed oasis. I grab the thick textbook from my nightstand and open to where I left off. By the second page, my eyes travel the lines, but my brain is gone. I'm thinking of Stacia and our drive home. Her friendliness. Her complimenting my skills on the pitch. Butterflies swirl in my belly. Could we actually be friends?

Christine

Micah comes to my office every day for three weeks. At first he left the door open, but by the following week, we are regularly shut inside the solid gray barrier. The first time he closed it behind him, I opened my mouth to protest, only to clamp it shut without uttering a word, the opportunity passing like a ship under a bridge.

If the day's nearing its end and he hasn't come, my pulse begins to throb and my skin grows itchy. Maybe this will be the day he doesn't show. The day he wakes up more interested in the girls with tight little bodies and no bags under their eyes. But then, just as I'm on the verge of despair, he appears, glides into my office and shuts the door. And just like that, my pulse regulates, my heart settles back into its proper place in my chest, we fall back into the conversational rhythm I've come to enjoy, and everything is okay.

Micah is leaned back in the chair across the desk from me, arms crossed, one ankle resting on the other knee. He wears sneakers from that rapper's new fashion line—something I know only because Abbie showed me and we'd both guffawed at the insane price point.

"But when does it go from appreciation to appropriation, hmm?" Micah says with a shrug. We've been discussing the latest celebrity receiving backlash for wearing cornrows in her hair.

"A hairstyle? Braids have been around for thousands of years. This was a Bo Derek nod." He gives me a look and it hits me: he's too young to know who Bo Derek is.

"Nah, this was clearly Black style. Plus, she's pushed boundaries before. Remember the bindi incident?" He taps between his eyebrows. "I'm pretty sure she's not Hindu."

"Point taken."

I'm impressed with his stance on the topic—and that he knows what a bindi is. I've heard my fair share of racial slurs when students don't think I'm listening. Even in this woke culture—another term I've picked up from my students—kids can be mean. But not Micah. This depth, this level of respect, is refreshing.

"Young people do dumb things," I say. "But I agree, sometimes you just scratch your head and wonder how they thought they could get away with something so obvious. And especially today, everyone has to watch out for—"

"—cancel culture." We say it at the same time and laugh.

This isn't the first time we've finished each other's sentences. It's so strange. Over these last few weeks, it's like our brains are melding. I haven't had a student so engaged in years.

Micah props an elbow on my desk and rests his chin on his fist. "You know," he says, "I'm thinking about applying to grad school."

I feel my face brighten. "That's great. What programs?"

"San Diego State has a Master's of Applied Anthropology program."

"San Diego, as in California?" I try not to let my smile falter even though a sudden heaviness wants to pull it into a frown.

"Yeah. I mean, maybe. Who knows. It's just an idea. I'd have to get in first."

"Why wouldn't you get in?" It's the encouraging, supportive teacher response, but in truth, I have no idea what Micah's grades are like. He's not my advisee, I can't see his transcript. He could have a 4.0 GPA or be flunking for all I know.

"Nothing's a sure thing."

"I'm happy to help with your research or application materials if you want," I say. "I remember that process, it can be stressful."

"Where'd you go?"

"University of Kentucky. Best years of my life."

"Did you always want to teach?"

I look to the ceiling, considering his question. Did I ever have another path in mind?

"I think teaching and anthropology go hand-in-hand. They're both a study of people. I guess it felt like a natural choice. Ultimately, I just want to make a difference." *Before I die*, I almost add. "The school gives a teaching excellence award every year. Sometimes I envision myself getting it. It's a pretty big deal, recognition from my peers. But then again, there's a lot of great teachers here."

I flush, embarrassed to have gone so deep, so vulnerable. I highly doubt he cares about my dreams for the future. But to my surprise, he's nodding along.

"I can see it," he says, raising a hand to paint an imaginary scene in the air. "Dr. Graham, Professor of the Year. No really, I can. You love it, don't you, teaching?"

"I do."

"It's obvious. You're really good at it."

My face warms.

"I hope I find a career I love someday," he says.

"You will."

Our gazes fix and for a long minute we do nothing but drink in each other's eyes, smiles, every freckle, every blemish. I look away first.

"Well, why wait?" I say, slapping my hands on the desktop. "Let's pull up some programs and start looking."

* * *

The next day, a small woman in jeans and a polo shirt knocks on my office door.

"Delivery," she announces in a cheery voice. "Someone really loves you."

She steps in, leading with a small bouquet of sunflowers.

"Oh my." My ears prickle, as I stand and meet her at the front of my desk. I take the vase with two hands. The aroma delights my nose, its subtly sweet scent a pleasant mood lifter. Sunflowers. Joss must be feeling guilty about her distance. Olive branches aren't her typical M.O., but this comes as a pleasant surprise. It's a small arrangement, but I don't mind. Flowers are flowers.

"Thank you," I say.

"Enjoy!"

When the woman's gone and I return to my chair, I pull the vase close to take another long inhale. My eyes land on the tiny white card, hidden under a petal. I pluck it off the plastic stem.

For the sunflower girl, from an aspiring anthropologist.
Thank you for all your help.

The card is light in my hand, and I hold it in front of my face, re-reading, as though somehow I've imagined the words. These flowers aren't from my wife at all. But the place where disappointment should be is suddenly filled with something else, something new.

I tuck the card under a notebook in my desk drawer. The flowers are like a blooming sun. I take another deep whiff.

Looking back, it's so obvious what was happening. I knew it. We both knew it. But like a runaway train, the steam was already pumping too hard. I couldn't stop it.

Couldn't, or didn't want to.

April 1998

*P*edal!" *It's a joke-command, and I can see her smile even though I'm on the back seat of this tandem bike.*

"I am pedaling!" I say. It's amazing how we can banter even at the tail end of a ten-mile ride. It was her idea, renting an old-fashioned bike and taking it for a spin around the lake for our anniversary. But this slight incline is no joke, and my legs are screaming.

We crest the hill. There's a park bench ahead and I suggest stopping for a short break. She hops off the bike first, removes her helmet. The hair around her temples is flat and damp, but she still looks gorgeous to me. Sometimes I pinch myself—this cannot really be my girlfriend.

"Whew! I'm beat," she says, flopping onto the bench.

I slide in next to her, wrap my arm around her shoulders. Not even the musk of sweat can drown out the minty shampoo she uses. It's become my favorite scent.

"One whole year," I say.

She nuzzles her head into mine. "The best year."

My stomach flutters. There's something I want to say, something I've been thinking about for weeks now. I've known it in my gut since the beginning: this woman is it for me.

"We make a good team, you and me," I say, and our faces turn toward each other. She leans in and kisses me, and our lips hold tight while we breathe each other in. No need for a full-blown make out session in public—we have plenty of those at home.

"And I don't see that changing," she says, interlacing her fingers with mine.

My heartbeat had just regulated from the climb, but now it races again. I know she feels the same way about me as I do about her. We've said it to each other enough times. I need to just do it—say what's been burning inside me.

"You know," I start, "I've never been happier."

"Me too."

"I love you. I love you so much."

"I love you too." Her eyes light up, like she's sensing something big is about to happen. She's right.

"Let's do this thing together—life, all of it. What do you say? Will you marry me?"

I didn't think it was possible for her smile to get any bigger, but it does. She flings her arms around me, and when her mouth is next to my ear, I hear the sweetest word: "Yes."

"Yeah?"

"Yeah," she says, nodding. We're both laughing, like two giddy little girls in a toy store.

A blast of dopamine surges through my body. I feel like I could take on a hill twice the size of the one we just climbed. Her cheeks are flushed, but the smile hasn't left her face.

"But wait, there's one thing," she says.

"Anything. Whatever you say, it's a yes." As long as it's not a honeymoon in England—I swore I'd never go back there.

"Fisher has to be my man of honor."

I laugh. "Of course."

"And one more thing. I want to be a mom someday."

I'm weightless. If I thought I'd reached bliss with her as my future wife, I've now just hit the ultimate jackpot. Motherhood? It's a no-brainer for me, something I'd always envisioned, but was never quite certain would happen.

"Is that a deal breaker for you?" she says.

"Couldn't be more opposite." I reach for her again, pull her close to me. "You'll be an amazing mother. We...we'll be amazing mothers."

Christine

It's the fourth week of classes and I'm in a department meeting with three other anthro faculty, plus Kerry, our fearless leader. She takes a swig from her Yeti thermos, then spins the top closed.

"Course updates, everyone? Make sure you're checking your rosters for no-shows who forgot to drop, or people coming to class who never officially registered. We're a month in, retention is important. Admissions is riding deans, who are riding chairs, which means, unfortunately—"

"—you have to ride us," I say.

"Exactly."

"My course is full, no drops," Will says. He's young and cocky and thinks he's God's gift to our campus. I've also heard his father's a big donor and helped get him his job, so...

"Christine?"

"No drops." I'm humbler than Will, but add in, "a few still on the waitlist," so he knows he's not the only popular professor around here.

Everett, a forty-something stoner who happens to also be an excellent baker (his burgeoning belly proves it), tips his chin in my direction. "Heard you've got an exam coming up. I can pretty much pinpoint what week of the semester it is based on before and after class chatter. 'Dr. Graham's exams are the worst. Gender Studies exam next week—fuckmylife.'"

His impression of students makes us all laugh, both because it's hysterically accurate but also so wrong coming from an overweight man with thinning hair.

"I've heard it too," Trish chides.

"Hey, hey," I say. "Listen, I'm not about to ease up on my standards after twenty-five years."

"Yeah, but those semester evals," Will says.

"—have always been just fine. Kerry, back me up here? Do you think my exams are a problem?"

Kerry folds her forearms on the table. "You're a tough grader, Chris, the students know it, we all know it."

"I expect a lot. I'm not doing them any favors by hand-holding them for four years."

"I didn't say it was a problem. But, you know, it's tenure year. Just something to think about. Student evaluations are one of the heaviest factors in the committee's decision, like it or not. Let's face it, keeping students happy is part of our role. No students, no job."

I nod and pinch my hand under the table to keep from arguing. I swear this place is so backwards sometimes.

Unlike Will, who regularly bribes students, or Everett who's too high to write his own exams, or Trish who's too scared to take off points, I value firmness and fairness. So my tests are hard? It'll be fine. Integrity is one of the few things you have control over in life, and I'd never let something rock that.

***

Four hours and two classes later, the morning meeting is a distant memory. Micah's sitting across the desk from me saying something about alliances and antagonisms in relation to ethnic identity. I can't hear what he's saying, though, because I'm too focused on his fleshy lips and how they stretch and curl with each word. I haven't studied a man's lips so hard since high school when I tried to force myself into finding Michael J. Fox attractive just because all my friends did. College was my age of experimentation, when I was finally comfortable enough to admit my attraction to both sexes. But ever since Joss entered my life, it's been her and no one else.

Micah stretches to point to something in the textbook, but can't exactly reach.

"Here, let me get closer," he stands, moving his chair from the front of my desk around the side so that it's directly next to mine. He hasn't crossed the threshold of my desk up until this point. Somehow, having three hundred pounds of metal between us was enough for me to justify our little meetings. But now...now our shoulders nearly touch. I smell his cologne. Or maybe it's deodorant. Do guys today wear cologne? Whatever it is, it makes me shiver.

"Ethnocentrism and patriotism are two very different things," I'm saying, though I sound a hundred miles away. I don't even know if that's what he's asking about. We sit there, side by side, looking at a textbook neither of us cares about in this moment.

I keep talking. I keep talking so I don't do something else, something I know is very, very wrong. From the corner of my eye, I see his hand lift. It meets my face, and I freeze. He trails my cheekbone with a finger. When he makes it all the way to my chin, I turn to face him, meet his piercing stare with a version of my own. An energy of charged particles bounces between our bodies. My insides are on fire. I'm waiting for my conscience to interject, but it doesn't, so I do nothing to stop him.

There's no "wait, this isn't appropriate."

No "Micah, you're my student."

No "you're twenty-one and I'm fifty."

Nothing.

When I meet his eyes, it only takes a second for our lips to touch. His mouth is just as soft as it looks. I close my eyes. Is this really happening? I can barely breathe. He brings his other hand up to cup my face, and I grab his wrists. Whether to tear his hands away or desperate for them to stay put, I don't know. Even his wrists feel strong under my fingers.

It's so quiet, only breath against breath. My heart pounds in my chest. His mouth tastes like mint, and I can't help but wish I would have had a splash of mouthwash myself. The almond breakfast bar I had this morning left a bitterness on my tongue, but it must not be bothering Micah because his strokes against mine without recourse.

My insides fire alive. I haven't been kissed like this—so tactile—in what feels like ages. So different from a close-mouthed peck. This is whole body awakening, a feeling I've forgotten, but now remember how much I used to love—even though it was with someone else.

Joss.

No, don't go there. Here. Stay right here.

We kiss for another long minute, until I pull back. Adrenaline courses through my body, and I think I might throw up right there in my little plastic trash can. Semester evaluations are now the last thing I need to worry about.

"Oh my God," I say, bringing a shaky hand up to cover my mouth. It's two-twenty-six on a Thursday afternoon and I just kissed my student.

"I've been wanting to do that for so long," he says.

"Oh my God," I say again. It seems to be the only phrase I can form. "What just happened?"

He strokes my arm. "We kissed."

"What? Yes, I know we kissed. But, how, I mean...oh, God." I put a palm on my forehead.

Micah grins and when he does I want to pull him to me again. He's so calm, it appears I have enough nerves for the two of us.

"It's okay, Christine," he says, putting a tender hand on my shoulder. "You better go."

He drags the chair back to its right position on the other side of my desk. "See you tomorrow?" And again, there's hope where there shouldn't be.

I can't speak, so I just stare dumbly. My body is numb, my head spinning. Micah doesn't wait for a response, not even a nod. Just casually opens the door and disappears, taking with him every ounce of sanity I have.

Abbie

I barrel into Mom's office a little after three.

"Hey," I say. She startles when I come around the corner, as though it weren't something I do every day at this time. "Whoa, sorry. Why so jumpy?"

Mom's body relaxes. "Hey Ab. Sorry, I—" She shakes her head. "I was just so focused I didn't hear you come in."

She's on her computer. Her desk is cluttered with file folders and stacks of paper. A coffee mug that reads "girl boss" sits near the far edge. It's Ma's mug, a gift from us when she got department chair a few years back. We started calling her Joss the Boss, and let me tell you, nothing has ever been more accurate.

I plop onto one of Mom's chairs. She looks dazed, like she's seeing someone else in my place.

"What?" I ask.

"Nothing."

"Are you okay? You've been acting super weird lately."

"What do you mean? Of course I'm okay." She returns to typing. "I'm just trying to focus. Need to get this exam written before we leave. I'm almost done. I don't want to have to worry about it tomorrow." Mom raises an eyebrow and smiles. "Big game, and I suspect we'll be going out somewhere to celebrate your win afterward."

"Don't jinx me."

"Honey, you're going to do great. Ma and I can't wait to watch you soar."

"Okay, Mom. Seriously, you don't have to be so cheesy."

I pull out my phone and scroll Instagram. There's a post from Trina in front of the anime posters that line her walls. We went to a convention together last year, but now that doesn't feel like something I want people to know—liking anime is basically putting a "weirdo" sticker across your forehead.

I keep scrolling. Stacia posted a pic of herself and another blond mid-laugh, with the simple caption: IYKYK ♡. No, I don't know, but I want to.

"Spill the tea," someone commented.

"You live rent-free in my mind," another said.

Most everyone on the team liked the post, so I do too.

A woman's voice filters into the office before she's even made an appearance. "Chris? Can I steal you for a— Oh, hey Abbie."

"Hi, Dr. Viotto." Mom's friend—Kerry, as she calls her at home—is a skinny little woman with frizzy blonde hair cut at a length that's not quite a bob, but too short to be considered shoulder length. It just sort of juts from her head like a yellow triangle. She wears little makeup, and even though she's the same age as Mom, she seems older. I think she has that stereotypical "enlightened professor" mentality—the one where looks don't matter, even though of course they do.

"I hear you've got a big game tomorrow?" she says, leaning against the doorframe.

"First varsity match."

"Good luck. Kick 'em hard, er...or whatever you say about soccer."

I chuckle, and Dr. Viotto returns her attention to Mom. "Chris, do you have a sec? I was hoping we could chat quickly about schedules for next week."

Mom pushes back from her desk. "Sure." She checks her watch. "We don't need to leave for a bit. Abbie, that okay?"

"Yeah, I'm fine." I wave my phone. She hates that I'm always on it, especially after watching a documentary on the addictive qualities of social media. Ever since, she's on me about too much screen time. All I hear is blah, blah, blah.

Mom rolls her eyes and turns to follow Dr. Viotto. "I won't be long."

I rotate through Instagram, Snapchat and TikTok, mindlessly scrolling, until my eyes start to cross. When that becomes boring, I toss my phone into my bag. I look to the bookcase behind Mom's desk. A framed photo sits on the second shelf. Ma, Mom and me. It's old—I think I was in eighth grade. I get up and walk over to look at it closer. My eyebrows are bushy and I'm wearing a Hannah Montana t-shirt. No wonder I wasn't in the cool crowd.

Behind me, Mom's computer dings, and I look over. A popup notification for a new email. It flashes once, then disappears, leaving my gaze squarely on rows of questions, each followed with four responses: A, B, C, D.

The exam.

A zap pings my gut. Could it be?

I reach down and scroll to the top of the page. There in the header, the title of the course: Theory of Gender Studies.

Stacia's class.

I recoil like I'd touched a flame. My body knows something's dangerous before my brain's even put two and two together.

I've seen my mom write dozens of exams over the years. I've heard her read questions out loud to Ma and ask, "Does that wording make sense?" I've picked up exams from the printer for her on more than one occasion.

In short, I've been privy to test questions—and answers—soon to be in students' hands.

But this is the first time I've been a student here, too. And this is the first time the thought has ever crossed my mind to be unethical.

Stacia's words ring in my ears: *I'd kill for a copy of her exam.*

Before I even know what I'm doing, I'm in Mom's chair and hitting Print. My hand trembles, but it's not fear, it's thirst.

The copier is at the end of the hallway, thankfully in the opposite direction from Dr. Viotto's office. I peek my head out the door. The hallway is empty. How much time do I have? Minutes? Seconds? All I know is I'm wasting them standing here. If I don't go, someone else could grab the exam from the printer, bring it to Mom and then I'll really be screwed.

The thought thrusts me forward. I speed walk with urgency in my limbs, six doors down to where the big printer lives. The pages are there waiting for me. I snatch them from the tray. They're still warm in my hand.

I pause. Holding the test makes it all real. What am I doing? I could get in massive trouble. Not only from Mom, but from the school. There's a paper shredder on the table. Every ounce of me says to slide the pages in and watch them come out in little strips on the other side. No one would have to know what I did...what I planned to do.

The clunky black box taunts me. *FEED ME.*

But I don't shred them. Instead, I hurry back to Mom's office and tuck the exam into my bag with a giddy-sick feeling in my bones. I'm high—high on so much adrenaline, I feel like I could run a hundred laps around the field. My body feels the pricks of a thousand needles.

I take the same seat across from her desk. It's still warm from moments ago—that's how quick it all happened. My bag is next to me, and I can almost feel the exam through the heavy nylon, its power to elevate my standing at MacAmes. This single set of paper could be the key to all my problems—the ticket to the "in" crowd. My fingers tingle as I grip the straps tighter. I pull the bag next to my hip, as though keeping it close will prevent what I know I'm going to do next.

"Sorry, sorry." Mom flies back into her office, flapping her hands. Her voice jolts me back to the present. I peek at the time on my phone and realize I've been daydreaming for nearly twenty minutes. Mom rounds her desk and leans down to type a few strokes of the keyboard without sitting down. "Let me finish these last two questions, and then we're out of here, okay?"

Wait, will the screen show that the document had recently been printed? Fuck, this might be bad. I hold my breath. The distinct smell of coffee has followed her in here. It's strong and bitter, and my senses are so heightened, it makes me gag. I look to my backpack as a distraction. I can't believe what's inside.

Mom types without a word. I must be in the clear.

"Alright." She snaps her laptop closed. "Abbie?" I whip my head up; I've been daydreaming again, the one where I'm the first choice in gym class, instead of last one picked. It's only symbolic, of course—thank *God* there's no more gym class in college—but those middle school traumas stick with you.

Mom eyes me. "You're quiet today. Thinking about the game?"

"Yeah," I falter. "Just thinking about the game."

Christine

After that first kiss, I told myself never again. It was beyond wrong. A colossal mistake. I could lose my job. But even more than that, I'm *married*. I've always taken pride in being faithful, unlike so many spouses Joss and I know. I never understood those couples, the ones who cheat. I swore it'd never be me. I'd speak up, I'd say something if my relationship was in trouble. Cheating is never the answer. But I *have* spoken up. Joss knows things have been strained.

Yet here I am sliding down the center of a volcano, staring at the approaching lava and trying not to get burned. Joss and I had a good marriage before priorities slipped. Maybe it could have been salvaged. Now I've gone and ruined it.

What was I thinking?

A complete moment of lunacy. It could never happen again.

But then Micah shows up the next day, and I let him in without hesitation. What happened yesterday electrified me—my senses are sharper, my mind focused and awake. I want more.

He closes the door and doesn't even bother with pulling the chair close. He's on me in seconds. Our hands fly wildly around each other's bodies, pulling at clothes and squeezing flesh to the point it hurts.

Micah hikes my dress up to my waist, and for a second I wonder if I'd subconsciously chosen it knowing this might happen. Pants would have taken longer to remove, but a dress...a dress in September offers easy access.

I push the stack of papers back and he lifts me to sit on the desk. We don't speak, our lips are too busy. The act is fast and furious. I bite my bottom lip to keep from making any noise.

Whoa. This is crazy. Crazy good, and just plain old crazy.

The urgency is intense, and I don't even have a chance to think about what's happening. No time to take in the sounds, smells, or even second-guess what I'm doing.

Micah's head flings back at the end, and then he collapses forward, his forehead resting on my shoulder. Our breathing is ragged. My hair has come undone.

It's then, as I feel the wetness between my legs, that I suffer a momentary stab of panic. Did he use a condom? Of course he didn't, there was no time. My insides tighten. I haven't thought of birth control since college, and even then, was pretty sure I'd never need it.

But I'm fifty years old. Fifty-year-olds don't get pregnant. I let my head fall back and I count the rows of panels in the drop ceiling. It's what an old therapist once described as a method of grounding myself when I felt like I was slipping out of reality: find one thing you can hear, one thing you can smell, one thing you can touch, and one thing you can see.

I see fluorescent tube lights on my ceiling. The ceiling of my office. My office, where I'm half naked with a student.

Maybe I should slip out of reality again.

When I straighten and glance back, Micah has righted himself and is buttoning his fly. He gives a small smile, then leans in and kisses me, softer this time.

"That was just as amazing as I imagined," he says against my lips, and I wonder how long he's been envisioning this. Me. Out of everyone he could have, he wanted me.

I run a hand over his cropped hair. The texture is polar opposite to Joss's fine, smooth strands. I'm caught in a moment of fantasy when muffled voices outside the door snap me back to reality.

"This is crazy," I whisper. "No one can know."

I push him back and stand to straighten my dress. One of my pumps came off, so I'm lopsided with one foot flat on the floor. I grab the shoe with my toe and slide my foot in. Now I'm eye level with his neck—that Adam's apple—and I tilt my head up so he can see the gravity on my face.

"I'm serious, Micah."

"Tomorrow's Saturday. I can't wait all weekend to see you again." His voice is urgent. "Where can we meet?" He grabs my face and kisses me again, hard.

"No, I can't. I have my daughter's soccer game. I'll be home with my family. I can't." The oxytocin vanishes like a dream upon waking. Was I really euphoric only moments ago? Now, panic sits in my gut.

"We can find a way."

"No, really." More voices pass by on the other side of the door. My pulse races, thinking about someone knocking and wondering why I'm locked inside with a student. Oh, God, what did I just do? I'm seized by guilt. It never felt like this with Joss, the basking afterglow of lovemaking. Maybe that's because it was never as wrong as this.

A small whimper escapes my lips. I physically turn Micah and push him toward the door. "Go."

He unlocks it at the same time I'm smoothing my hair behind my ears. As he leaves, I clear my throat and call behind him, a little more forced than necessary, "Thanks for stopping, Mr. Johnson. I'm always happy to give study tips."

It's not until he turns around and winks that I realize how misconstrued it could sound—especially behind a closed door.

Joss

Christine insists on getting to Abbie's games unnecessarily early. It's not like we're at a D1 school with a packed stadium. I really could have used the extra half hour to write.

Parents and friends sprinkle the two sets of metal bleachers. Half of the students are on their phones the whole time anyway, which always puzzles me. Why even bother coming if you're not going to watch the match?

"Did you bring a hat?" Christine asks me. "I didn't realize it would be this sunny." You'd think September would be fall, but in Virginia, it still feels very much like summer, especially at one o'clock on a Saturday afternoon. I toss her the ball cap I was planning to wear to cover the greasy hair I haven't washed for a couple days. She burns easy, and then she's cranky and I'm not in the mood for cranky.

"Thanks." She slips on the faded khaki hat embroidered with a large ACK monogram, pulls her ponytail through the hole in the back and tucks flyaways behind her ears.

I love this hat on her. It makes her look like she's twenty-five again, like when we met. Reminds me of the travel we did before we had Abbie. That trip to Nantucket was after we'd been dating for a few years, when lust was still a constant in our relationship. We'd booked a B&B, with intentions of sightseeing around the island, but ended up spending the entire weekend in our room. Maybe we'll go again—after my study is complete.

The players are stretching on the field. I look for Abbie. She's standing near the center, one leg bent back, heel touching her butt. Her hair is in a high, braided ponytail like all the other girls. A vague memory surfaces of a young Abbie standing in front of Christine, whose hands twist and weave our daughter's long brown locks. Hair duty—thank God it was Christine's thing and not mine.

"Hi, Dr. Matson," a young blonde says. I recognize her from one of my classes last year, but can't place her name.

I give a polite smile. "Hi there."

Christine unfolds a chair. "Hi Morgan," she says, saving me. "How's your semester going?"

"Pretty good, Dr. Graham. Although my classes aren't quite as interesting as yours."

I see Christine's cheeks pink. She's humble, but I know comments like these make her soar. The students love Christine. She's got that natural way in the classroom that lets her courses be both fun and educational. In truth, she's a much better teacher than me. I've never been able to connect with the students like she can. Maybe that's why I've always been drawn to the scholarship side of my job. Chemistry—the sciences, in general—are research-heavy compared to many of the humanities.

We pop open our folding chairs and the ref blows his whistle to start the game. Abbie's playing midfielder. I watch her sprint up and down the field, amazed by her endurance. It looks effortless. She's barely out of breath. Me, I couldn't run to the mailbox without panting.

The back-and-forth motion of the players lulls me like a rocking boat. If I'm being honest, soccer isn't the most action-packed sport to watch. Okay, it's painful—and that's coming from a Brit who was bred to love it. I'll never forget Dad making fun of me for cuddling up with a book instead of joining the rest of the extended family in front of the telly for the World

Cup. When I left England, I wanted to sever all ties, but then Fisher gave Abbie a soccer ball for her fourth birthday, and the rest is history. Sometimes I wish she'd have picked basketball or even hockey. Better yet, no sports at all. After a half hour, my eyes glaze over, until I hear Christine shout.

"Yes!"

I blink and realize everyone's clapping.

"She scored! You saw it, right?"

"Of course I saw it." I clap enthusiastically along with the rest of the crowd. Christine eyes me, but then turns back to the field, beaming. "Nice one, Ab!" she yells, as Abbie jogs back to position.

I'm careful not to nod off for the rest of the half. When the whistle blows, we rise to stretch. Christine makes small talk with a few more students, while I stand awkwardly by her side with my hands in my pockets. It's always a bit humorous to see student's reactions to faculty outside of the classroom, as though they can only picture us in front of a lecture hall, wearing tailored office clothes. Christine and I are both in MacAmes t-shirts and jeans today, although she looks better, of course. Her white adidas sneakers are the same the kids wear. From a distance, she could probably pass for one of them.

When the second half starts, my Apple watch beeps. An email from Richard. Probably sending his pages for review. God, I want to read it, but I resist the urge, mostly because Christine will berate me for not being present.

Forty more minutes and then I can get back to my research.

MacAmes is up three goals to one. Our coach calls Abbie off the field, replacing her with a short, muscular girl who looks more like a compact gymnast than a soccer player.

"Good hustle, Ab," Christine calls.

"Yeah, good hustle," I echo because that's what feels appropriate.

Play resumes. A girl heads the ball and everyone cheers. Another goal for MacAmes.

Next to me, Christine fidgets in her seat. She looks over her shoulder into the bleachers. Not once, not twice, but repeatedly. What's so interesting? I follow her glance, but all I see are students.

A few minutes later, Abbie's back in. She charges the ball, stealing it from her opponent like it was nothing. The players on the sideline holler their approval.

Christine touches my arm. "I have to use the restroom. I'll be right back."

Now? But Abbie just got back in the game. *Why didn't you go five minutes ago?* I want to ask, but she's gone before I can say anything. I watch her walk briskly toward a small cinder brick structure that serves as a concession stand. A uni-sex bathroom is attached at the side. I shudder— I'd rather hold it than use that.

I bring my attention back to the game, knowing I better concentrate in case something happens that Christine will ask me about when she returns. I'm so fixated on the game I don't realize how long she's been gone, only that when she finally does return, her hat is cockeyed and several pieces of hair fall around her ears where they were once neatly tucked.

Christine

It's not until after halftime that I spot Micah in the stands. He lifts an arm and waves so casually, like a friendly neighbor passing by. I quickly snap my head around, shocked to see him outside class—or my office. What is he doing here? My brain spins for a moment before stilling. It's nothing. Maybe he's a soccer fan. Maybe he's friends with girls on the team. Then it strikes me: Wait, could he be friends with Abbie? Did I sleep with my daughter's friend?

I peer over my shoulder again—nonchalant, at least I hope so—and sure enough, Micah's eyes are nowhere near the field. His lips stretch into a grin, and in that second, my insides come to life. I know exactly why he's here.

Next to me, Joss is in a daze. She finds soccer about as stimulating as watching grass grow, but it still unnerves me that she doesn't put in a little more effort. This is our daughter's passion, after all—one thing she actually cares about.

I vividly remember reading parenting books when Abbie was little, highlighting and dog-earing pages I'd return to time and time again, desperate to be the best mother possible. So much of the research talks about being present. All kids want from their parents is time and attention.

Now look at her, eyes glazed over. She's probably counting down the minutes until the game is over. It makes my decision easy. I'm tired of not being seen—of Abbie not being seen—and even though the game and Joss's apparent boredom has nothing to do with me, I want to punish her. Punish her for not caring about me, about us, about anything but herself.

I turn once more and give Micah the smallest nod. It's not much, but I suspect he'll know what I mean.

Joss's skin is clammy when I reach out and touch her arm, the sun taking effect even after less than an hour. I tell her I need to use the restroom, then stand before she has a chance to respond. I went before we left the house—a habit I'd formed after those early years of teaching Abbie—but I'm hoping she doesn't notice.

There's a little snack stand that sells overpriced bottled water and bags of candy. It sits a hundred yards or so away from the field, its back butting up against a small grove. I head in that direction, eyes focused straight ahead, as though any sort of distraction might stop me from doing what I know I'm about to.

Within a few feet, I smell the public restroom—sharp and ammoniacal—and know I have to alter the plan. No way am I going in there. I stop at the bathroom door and look back to see if Joss is watching me. She looks more alert now, back straight, head swiveling to follow the play of the game. No one's paying attention to the woman taking a bathroom break.

That is, except for the person walking directly toward me, hands in his pockets, shoulders relaxed, as though he could be going anywhere, though I know he's not.

I dash around the back of the building, simultaneously brushing my arm against the brick's rough corner. The contact leaves an instant mark, the finest layer of skin peeled away, a tail of white like a jet line in the sky.

"Damnit," I whisper, and twist my arm to see.

"Eager to see me?" Micah's here quicker than I expect.

"I scraped my ar—" But I don't have the chance to finish because his lips are on mine and before I know it, my back is pressed against the cold, gray blocks.

We're hungry for each other. The risk of it all fuels a new level of forbidden excitement. Someone could walk around this corner at any moment. I'd be finished. Fired and left with nothing more than a scarlet A on my chest and a white scratch on my arm. That danger—real and impending—sits heavy in my stomach, but I brush it away because not even the threat outweighs how glorious this is.

"What are you doing here?" I breathe as his mouth explores my neck.

"What do you think?"

"But, all the people."

"You want me to stop?"

I grab his face and we lock eyes. "No." I test the word out and decide I like how it tastes. If death is coming for me, this is a pretty good way to go out.

Micah turns me around. My jeans are at my ankles. He has my hands clenched in his, extended up and pressing against the wall for leverage. For a second, I almost swivel back to face him—something about the thought of him watching my ass jiggle takes away a bit of excitement. At least I went to spin class this morning. But still, fifty-year-old skin doesn't look the same at twenty-year-old skin. Sure, I'm slim and generally in shape, but there's a difference between dressed skinny and naked skinny.

I push modesty to the side. Enjoy it, Christine. Don't think about wrinkles and body parts that aren't where they used to be.

It's fast and clumsy. Then I'm panting and laughing, rebuttoning my jeans and stealing a few more kisses before emerging back into the sun on the front side of the snack stand.

"Don't come right out after me," I say before leaving.

His head lolls. "Christine, I'm not stupid."

As I walk back toward the game, his words ring in my ear—*Christine, I'm not stupid*—and the only thing I can think is maybe he isn't. But am I?

Abbie

We win by a single goal, and even though it could have been any of the six scored by my team, I like to think it was mine that clinches the win. My first varsity game, a goal, and a W. Exhilaration! Seriously, what could be better?

The girls gather in the center of the field after shaking hands with the opposing team. We huddle and do a little dance, then Stacia pumps us up even more with some final words.

"We kicked ass today, ladies!" She's across from me in the huddle, and I notice how perfect her braid looks even though she just played ninety minutes of intense soccer. My sweaty arms slide against the girls on either side of me. But my body feels light, the high of winning threatening to lift me off the ground altogether.

"Abbie, you killed it," Stacia says. A few other girls echo, making me fly even higher. I'm the youngest one on the team, but I feel so much a part of it now. Acceptance is addictive, and I can already tell I'd do anything not to let it go.

We all put a hand out to the middle, layering sweaty palm on top of sweaty palm. "Major slaps to Abbie today, girls," Stacia says. "On three." Our hands pulse, *one, two three*, and we shout: "Lady Foxes!"

I jog off the field. The bleachers are mostly cleared of students now. Only a handful of parents remain. Ma and Mom are standing with their folding chairs slung over their shoulders. Their full-faced smiles make my heart swell as I approach. I'm lucky to have them here, unlike some of my teammates who live out of state. Even Ma, who saw it in her heart to put me above her work.

"Oh, hey, superstar," Mom says, extending a hand for a high five. I grin and roll my eyes, even though her comment sends joy through my body.

Ma claps my back. "Well done, love. You looked brilliant out there."

"Thanks," I say. My breath is still regulating. I take a long swig of water.

"Uncle Fisher would have been so proud of you," Mom says, pulling me into a whole body hug even though I'm drenched and smell terrible. She holds me a beat longer than normal, like she does whenever Fisher's name comes up. When she finally releases me, she's blinking away watery eyes. "How about a little Tar-jay run on our way home?"

"Oh, I was actually going to get a ride with Stacia, if that's okay."

Mom looks dejected, but shrugs and says, "Sure."

I jump in to soften things. "Some of the girls were going to go grab a bite to eat to celebrate and they asked me to join."

"How nice," Ma says. She eyes Mom, whose expression lifts. They're probably just happy to know I'm not sitting in my bedroom alone.

Mom gives a light smile. "Of course, hon. I'm glad you're doing more things with friends. Go. Have fun. See you at home later."

I head back to the bench where a few girls sprawl on the ground, unlacing their cleats. Before I'm too far, I wheel around and holler to my parents. "Thanks for coming, guys."

They smile at the same time. "We wouldn't have missed it," Mom calls back. She waves, then they both continue to the car.

Stacia is sitting on the bench when I get there. She peels off her jersey, replacing it with a dry tee. I do the same. "Your moms are so cute together," she says. "Sort of like Ellen and Portia, only...brainier."

How many times have I heard this comparison? Oh, only several hundred. Still, I grin at Stacia. "Something like that." It's not worth it to point out stereotypes.

She continues. "They seem so cool. Really laid back and hip. I mean, wasn't that a Goyard bag Dr. Graham was carrying?"

"Maybe?" I lie. Of course I know it was a Goyard bag. Ma freaked out when she found out how much Mom had spent on it. But Mom claimed she deserved it. After all, she'd said, it's not every day you finish your PhD.

"Well, I'm pretty sure it was. Must be fun to have someone to share clothes and stuff with. My mom is still stuck in the early nineties—not cool-again-nineties, original nineties. It's bad."

We laugh. The rest of the girls finish packing up, cinching their drawstring bags and tossing them onto their backs.

"I'm starving," someone says by way of transition. My own tummy rumbles. Amazing how many calories are burned during a soccer game. I could eat a footlong sub right now and still be hungry for more.

"Henry's?" Stacia asks, although the diner as a post-win tradition is a given. The girls call dibs on rides.

"I'll ride with you?" I propose to Stacia, with a newfound confidence I didn't have even a week ago. I wait, hoping no one else will jump in, and am relieved when no one does.

We hop in her car. I clamp hold of my bag and the precious cargo inside. It's a short drive to Henry's so I need to be quick with what I'm about to say. I twist the braided straps. My fingers are tingly, like before a class presentation. I don't want to screw this up.

"Hey, so, remember how you said you'd kill for a copy of my mom's exam?" I blurt it out awkwardly and without any lead up. I've never claimed to be the smooth and suave type, so why start now. Besides, we'll be to Henry's in five minutes.

Stacia looks over at me. "Yeah?"

I open my bag and with a single, triumphant yank, pull out several pieces of paper, folded in the middle. I hand them over to her. "Here you go."

"You're kidding."

"Nope."

"For real?"

"Yes," I laugh.

Stacia glances from the road to the papers several times, blinking wide eyed. "No. Freaking. Way. Oh my God, Abbie. How did you get this?"

"Printed it from her computer. I'm in her office by myself often enough."

"Oh my God," she says again. "You're a lifesaver. This is so huge. I honestly have been studying, but I've been so worried I won't pass the class. I can't afford an F senior year, it would kill my GPA."

I don't know what to say, so I just sit there, beaming and basking in Stacia's praise.

She hugs the test to her chest with one hand, the other on the wheel. "Thank you *sooooo* much."

"You're welcome. But, hey, don't tell anyone, okay? I mean, I could obviously get in major trouble. Can we just keep this between us?"

"Oh my God, absolutely, Abbie. Of course. I won't tell a soul."

She stuffs the exam in her own bag at her hip. My body is flooded with relief. It's over. The deed is done. I'm satisfied. And even if I wasn't, it's not like I can ask for it back now anyways.

We pull into Henry's at the same time my phone rings. Trina. I send it to voicemail without another thought, then return my attention back to the one who determines whether I'm going to sink or swim at this school. Several of our teammates get out of their cars. Stacia parks. As we walk toward the group, she links her arm in mine. I feel weightless.

"Sup, Foxes?" she calls to the girls ahead. A few howl back. It's then that the irony strikes: I may be a fox—in more ways than one—but doesn't the fox always get caught in the trap?

Joss

This year's conference is in Atlanta, which means my go-to oversized sweaters aren't going to cut it. I asked Christine to pick me up a couple new short sleeve tops at Target, and she ended up coming home with an entire new wardrobe. Her judgment is better than mine when it comes to what's on trend—if it were up to me, I'd probably be shopping at some old lady store or something. The last time I bought a new top for myself, Abbie and Christine vetoed it with an "absolutely not," before it was even all the way out of the bag.

My flight leaves at one-thirty. I know this because I had to go back into my itinerary four times to double check the departure time. There it was, in bold blue numbers that even a blind man couldn't miss, but it just wouldn't stick. Must be nerves. Even though I've presented at countless conferences over the last twenty years, I still get those pre-speech jitters.

One-thirty.

Or is it two-thirty? Bloody hell. I open my Outlook calendar again. Yes, one-thirty. I repeat it three times. *One-thirty, one-thirty, one-thirty.* I nab my rabbit's foot from my desk and toss it in my bag, hoping to take the good juju with me. It's never failed me before.

When Christine and Abbie left for campus earlier, I gave them each a hug. Christine was rigid in my arms. She pulled away quicker than I wanted, especially given that I wouldn't see her for a couple days. There once was a time we'd even get teary when the other was leaving. This morning, she barely looked at me.

"No kiss?" I'd said.

She retraced her steps and gave me a quick peck on the lips. "Sorry, in a hurry. Have fun on your trip."

Have fun? This is a business trip, not some jaunt to Tahiti with friends. Sure, I love presenting, but it's not like it comes without pressure.

I waited for more. *I'm going to miss you. Best of luck. This is huge. You'll do great.* But she says none of these.

* * *

I leave my car in short-term parking and make my way toward the terminal. Security is packed and it takes close to fifty minutes to get through the queue. People pack against each other, and I hear my father's voice in my head: *What's the point? You're just hurrying up to wait some more.*

Dad. I try hard not to think of him often, the man who called me chubby and didn't think I'd amount to anything. The one who disowned me when I came out.

Look at me now, Dad. A top researcher in my field...and still gay as ever.

As a first-generation college student, the weight of the world was on me to succeed. I could never—*never*—live the same simple life as my parents. Academic success was my ticket out. And once I got a taste of it, there was no turning back. Which was why attending university in America made the most sense—tons of great schools back home, but they were too close. Too much a reminder of what I wanted to escape.

On the other side of security, I grab a sandwich and find a seat at the gate. It's nearly full—a lot of people must be going to Atlanta.

I pull my laptop from my carry-on tote, open to the conference website and click on past presentations. Preparing for speeches isn't just about practicing in front of a mirror—which I do—but also commanding the stage. My fellow academics are pros, and I'm always trying to hone my skills. I pop my ear buds in, as a smartly-dressed man fills the screen and begins talking about enhanced halogen formations. Goosebumps prickle my arms. This is where I belong.

***

My phone vibrates. It's a reminder I'd set—just in case.

Flight to conference, 1:30

Yeah, yeah, I say to myself, dismissing the reminder. I know what I'm doing. Those odd forgetful moments—the phone, the purse—seem like ages ago. Complete one-offs. It must have been lack of sleep.

I check my watch. One-fifteen already. Fantastic! The video has made the time fly by. I look up, but no one else is moving. I'm surprised they're not boarding yet. I wait another five minutes. They better get this lot boarded or we won't take off on time.

Finally, people around me begin to stand and form a queue near the jetway entrance. I power down my laptop and put everything back in my bag, eager to get going. I fall in line behind a couple holding the hands of a little girl with brown curls. She skips in place, her princess backpack bouncing off her bottom. Her unbridled joy reminds me of when Abbie was young, and I can't help but smile to myself.

The queue inches forward. The desk attendant lets the little girl scan her own boarding pass, much to the child's delight. Then, it's my turn. I run my boarding pass under the scanner, but instead of admitting me with a green light, it flashes red, and makes a noise different from everyone who went before me.

"Let me try that again," the attendant says.

The scanner gives the same sharp beep. The woman frowns. She takes the slip of paper and brings it to her face. I watch her eyes narrow as she scans the ticket. With an emphatic look, she extends the boarding pass back to me. "Ma'am, you're at the wrong gate. This isn't your flight."

Not my—what?

I stare at her, hearing the words but not sure how they can possibly be true. I want to laugh at her like she's some incompetent newbie. Of course I'm not at the wrong gate. It's not like I've never flown before.

She points to the bold, black words. "You're going to Atlanta. This flight's to Minneapolis." She's flapping the boarding pass at me, and I reluctantly take it, but my feet won't move.

"I'm sorry, ma'am," she says, empathy gone and replaced with irritation, "but I'm going to have to ask you to step out of line. I need to get these passengers boarded. I'll be happy to help you when I'm done."

She's annoyed now, like I've interrupted her very serious job. She must think I'm delusional, a first-time traveler who can't follow simple procedures.

I fumble backwards toward the wall, still confused. I look back and forth like a tennis match between the boarding pass and the digital sign next to the gate number. Sure enough, it's there in big, bright letters: MINNEAPOLIS, DEPARTING AT 2:05, ON TIME.

A tremor trails down my spine. If this flight is on time to leave at 2:05, what does that mean for my flight that was scheduled for one-thirty?

At once, I'm off. I grab my rolling carry-on and run through the terminal like those absolute nutter parents in *Home Alone*. People lunge out of my way as I come barreling through. I can just picture what they'll say later: "Yes, some slightly overweight woman with boobs bouncing out of her V-neck blouse nearly toppled us over."

As I pass an airport shop selling slippers, I curse the stacked heel booties Christine said were "cute." I feel a blister forming at my pinky toe, so I take the moving sidewalk, but that doesn't help.

When I get to my gate—the correct gate—the area is empty. A balding man in thick rimmed glasses is behind the desk, and I practically trip over myself to get there.

"Did it leave already? Did I miss it?" I'm out of breath, and I can already feel sweat trickling down my back.

He startles at my explosion into his calm area. "Flight 1215 to Atlanta?"

"Yes."

"I'm sorry, you missed it. Pushed back about ten minutes ago."

I groan. "What? No. I was here. I was in the airport. Just at the wrong gate. Why didn't someone page me?" My voice has an edge to it. This whole thing is ridiculous. Now I'm going to be late getting in and will miss the opening dinner.

"Let me see your boarding pass," the man says. I hand it to him. "Oh, Mrs. Matson. We paged you several times."

"You did? That's not possible." Then I remember. My ear buds. If my name came across the intercom, I never would have heard it.

"I'm sorry, ma'am. Would you like me to look up the next available flight to Atlanta?"

I'm in a daze. I replay the last hour. Arriving at the airport, security, my sandwich. I checked the departures board. I know I did. Gate B7. I saw it, I went there. Why would I have sat down at any other gate besides my own?

"Ma'am?"

A lump grows in my throat. I've been looking forward to this conference for months, I'm not about to let a silly slip-up ruin in.

"Please," I say, straightening up. Professional Joss kicks back in. Competent Joss, the brain behind this whole study. I mentally brush off the annoyance of missing my flight. There's still time to get there.

The desk attendant presses a couple keys, speaks to the computer. "Looks like there's still a couple seats left on the 5:25 flight."

"I'll take it."

"One second," he says, type type typing, then giving the final key a dramatic strike. "Ok, all set." A flimsy boarding pass materializes from under the counter, and he extends it to me. "A7," he taps the bold gate number. "That's in a different wing. Follow the signs to—"

"Yes, I've got it. Thank you." I'm quite capable of navigating an airport.

"A7," he repeats, and though his tone feels like a discount of my intelligence, I repeat it in my head, too. A7, A7, A7.

Three hours and two Manhattans later, I'm wedged into a middle seat at the back of the plane, ear buds in and eyes closed, running through my speech and trying with all my might to dismiss a pesky tug in my gut.

November 2000

O kay, on the count of three, pick a straw," I say.

We're in the dining hall at a small, two-person table near the salad bar. We try to meet here for lunch when our schedules allow, which isn't that often, if I'm being honest. Not with the pressure MacAmes puts on junior faculty to wear a gazillion hats: teacher, mentor, advisor, researcher, committee member...the list goes on.

"That's not fair. You know which one's which."

"I don't."

She gives me the look, the one where she wants to be mad but can't help but smile. I've loved this look for the past three and a half years.

"Okay, fine."

"One, two—"

"Wait! What is it again? Short one or long one?"

I sigh. We've gone over this five times now. She's stalling, but I know it's not because she doesn't want a baby. It's because she wants to be the one to carry it. Most couples don't have this luxury—if that's what you'd *call it—this ability to choose. But with two women, there isn't a default to who becomes pregnant. And since we've both been given the clear from our doctors, it's up to us to decide.*

"Whoever draws the short one is whose egg we'll use," I say.

She nods, presses her hands flat to the table, and takes a deep breath. We're surrounded by students eating pizza and burgers off of red trays. They're unsuspecting of the two young faculty members whose knees bump under the table. And why wouldn't they be? We look like two friends, laughing over bowls of watery tomato bisque. Our rings clearly indicate we're married—but most students don't realize it's to each other. With demographics like theirs, I wouldn't be surprised if they knew a single gay person.

I hold out my hand, which is clasped firmly around the bottom of the straws. I try to feel the ends against my palm, try to decide which is the shorter one. Do I want to choose it?

She reaches, her thumb and pointer finger pinching the tip of a straw. She pulls. We have our answer.

Christine

"What are you thinking about?" I run my thumb over Micah's bottom lip. It's full and pouty, and all I can think about is the fact that this lip has traveled my body. We're in my car, tucked into the back of a deserted parking lot, a safe distance from campus. The backseat is cramped. The windows fog every time, and all I can think about is Jack and Rose in that stowed-away Coupé de Ville on the Titanic.

My car has become our go-to. Less risky than my office, or any hidden place on campus, though we've tried those, too. The soccer field was dangerous. When I think back to it, I can't believe I was so impulsive. I'm not generally a rash person. Then again, I never would have thought I'd be sleeping with a student, let alone a male student. If this is a sexual identity crisis, I have no way of explaining it.

"You're far away," I say, dismissing the conflicted thoughts and gently turning Micah's face toward mine. "Tell me something."

"Like what?" He kisses my mouth.

"Anything."

"I never thought I'd fuck a professor."

It's exactly what I'd just been thinking, though the coarse word choice makes me cringe inside. I ignore the sourness of it. This isn't just fucking.

"Assistant professor," I correct him. "Won't be a full until I'm tenured."

"Same difference."

Maybe to students, I think. He doesn't get the politics of higher ed, how I was disregarded in many ways by administration all those years on the non-tenure track, like I was a mere peasant in their kingdom. Tenure's coming to me so much later than most professors my age, but that was my choice—everything's about timing.

"Here's a question," he says. "What would you do if you weren't teaching?"

"Outside of education completely?"

"Yeah. Like what'd be your career in another life."

I think for a minute. "Maybe medicine. A nurse, perhaps. Taking care of people." I picture Fisher, shriveled and bald, the disease eating him from the inside. "Or a researcher looking for life-saving cures."

"Nurse Graham...I could see it."

"But that other life isn't real—this is."

"Yes, this."

He moves so he's back on top of me. Our legs have to bend awkwardly, and I try to imagine we're sprawled on Egyptian cotton sheets instead of faux leather upholstery that's seen better days. One of Abbie's stretchy soccer headbands peeks out from where it's fallen between the passenger seat and the center console. Its neon orange screams out from the dark crevice that's been its home for who knows how long, and instantly grounds me as a reminder of home.

It doesn't belong here, not in this sacred space. I can't have any piece of Abbie or Joss witnessing me like this. I shift so the headband is out of sight, and try to focus on Micah. If the headband doesn't exist, then neither does my wife and daughter.

He's kissing my neck now. I'm struck by how attracted I am to his body. It's tight and well-muscled, with a youthfulness that hasn't yet experienced the hardships of life. I haven't seen a man naked since college, when I finally stopped forcing myself to pretend I was straight.

Maybe I'm straighter than I thought.

"Why'd you choose me?" I ask.

He straightens his arms so he's hovering over me. "Look at you. You're a *snack*. You look like you're twenty-five, not—"

"Watch it, buddy. Don't even go there." I don't want to hear my age come out of his mouth. Instead, I let the compliment soak in. I'm hot. I'm still desirable.

His phone blinks awake. A string of texts line the screen.

"I told my roommate I'd be home an hour ago," he says, and I realize I don't even know if he lives on campus. I assume not—most seniors don't.

"Where's home?

"Apartment. Just down from Jolly's Ice Cream. Me and a couple guys."

The phone lights up again, and I catch the time. I have class in thirty minutes, but that doesn't stop me. I know exactly how much longer we can stay. After a little trial and error—twice late to class, a little more disheveled than normal—I've perfected the duration of our little getaways. Three minutes back to campus. Two minutes to fix my hair and makeup in the car. Five to walk across the quad to my class.

That means we have twenty more glorious minutes here. I want every one of them. He lowers onto me again and our bodies move in rhythm.

Joss

The conference is set up in a hotel ballroom lined with windows along one side, overlooking Centennial Park and the grand SkyView Ferris Wheel. It doesn't look nearly as spectacular in the daytime as it does when the sky goes dark. Last night, I'd crept into the ballroom and stood at the window. The room was empty. I ambled the perimeter, grounding myself in the space, as I like to do before any big presentation.

Now, the ballroom is full, packed with conference attendees whose name tags swing from lanyards around their necks. They mingle, sipping coffee, while Richard and I prepare at the side of the stage.

"Here, let me," I say, clipping his mic to the lapel of his suit jacket.

"The steadiest hands," he says with a chuckle.

"Why wouldn't they be?"

"Oh, I don't know. Maybe because we're about to have several hundred eyes on us? You don't get nervous at all?"

"No need to. We've got this." I give his chest a pat. Richard's brilliant, a leading scholar in our field, and together we're about to knock it out of the park.

"Yes. We've got this."

The room hums for another ten minutes before people make their way to linen-covered tables, each place setting arranged with notepad, pen and water goblet. The emcee takes the stage, her heels clacking all the way to the podium. She tucks the ends of her short bob behind her ears.

"Good morning!" she trills, and the crowd hushes. "Welcome to the American Chemical Society's Annual Symposium. We're so pleased to have you here on this beautiful Atlanta morning. It was wonderful to see so many new faces at last night's dinner, and I'm sure you're all eager for this afternoon's breakout sessions. But first, I'm honored to introduce our keynote speakers to kick off this two-day celebration of minds. Joss Matson is a professor of chemistry at MacAmes University, where, along with a full teaching load, she oversees the school's Institute of Applied Sciences. With expertise in molecular composition and cellular changes, her current research focuses on the impact of functional organic materials. Richard Hughes is a professor of chemistry at Florida State University..."

I tune out the rest of the introduction, as my brain prepares the sequence of events at hand: Go on stage, warm welcome, explain study, dive into findings. I've done this dozens of times—hundreds more in my head.

A round of applause snaps me from my thoughts, and Richard's hand presses gently on my lower back, guiding me to the small set of stairs at stage right. I climb them, then give my blazer a straightening tug and roll my shoulders back. We make our way to center stage, the huge projector screen displaying our study's title like a movie marquee. I smile into the audience and a familiar ease comes over my body. Here we go, this is my *moment.*

"Good morning," I say. "Thank you, Gina, for that kind introduction. We're thrilled to be here to present our—"

Richard leans in close to me, reaches toward my waist, and my instinct is to step back. What is he doing?

There's a tiny click. "Might help to turn your mic on," he says, his voice booming where mine had been quiet. The crowd laughs at his joke, but my cheeks burn. Our eyes meet, and he gives me an encouraging nod.

"Jetlag," I quip, though my flight was barely two hours and in the same time zone. Richard steps to the podium, and clicks our presentation to the next slide. I take a cleansing breath. Words fill the screen. Words I should know—I'm the one who wrote them—but now look like gibberish. Words I can't seem to pronounce in my own head let alone from my lips.

My breath becomes suddenly short, my feet cinder blocks glued in place. I'm stuttering, and when I make eye contact with Richard again, he must read the panic on my face. His brow scrunches, though he tries not to show it.

"Would you like to explain our methodology?" he prompts in effort to jog my memory. But it's no use. I don't remember why I'm here or what I'm supposed to be talking about. The room narrows, the walls squeezing in, and the swirl of the carpet only makes me feel even more unsteady. Hundreds of faces stare back at me, heads cocked, expressions confused. A couple people turn to their neighbors and whisper.

"Richard?" I say, and it comes out louder—and shakier—than I intend. I hear his footsteps approach, as my vision blurs. Two clicks—he turns off our mics.

"Joss, are you okay? What's going on?" He's in my ear, and I'm clutching his arm.

"Where are we? Why am I on a stage?"

I can barely finish the sentence before he leads me behind a heavy gold curtain.

"Someone get her some water," I hear him say. "Joss, Joss can you hear me? Are you feeling alright?"

But I can't speak because I'm shaking and scared and want to go home. Christine. Where's Christine?

"Is she okay?" It's a woman's voice this time. A gentle hand on my shoulder. "Go ahead, Richard. I'll sit with her."

"Thanks, Gina."

He walks back on stage and I hear him offer an apology before resuming his speech. For the next thirty minutes, he's confident, strolling the width of the stage, speaking with passion that awakens something inside of me.

As I sit, the room widens again—slowly, inch by inch, until the entire ballroom comes back into focus. Ballroom. Stage. Windows. Ferris Wheel. Flight.

I'm at a conference. I'm a presenter.

I look to the screen and the words—my words—make sense. I stand, thankful there's a back exit so I don't have to face these people again. Gina tries to protest, but there's only one thing on my mind: getting out of here as fast as possible.

I make it back to my room before the tears come. They run down my cheeks like hot rivers, dripping from my chin and leaving two wet rings on my breasts. What is happening to me? I grip the bathroom counter until my fingers go white, and even after ten minutes, I can barely get them to dial the number I know I need to call.

Christine

It's Wednesday—the longest day of the week—and I'm struggling to get through the slog. When I get back to my office after class, I'm shocked by an unexpected visitor.

Joss is here.

My heart thunders in my chest—she hasn't been on campus for months. Even though we've both worked at MacAmes for two decades, spending countless hours in each other's offices, she looks out of place sitting in the chair by my desk.

I want to tell her that's Micah's chair, but instead I say, "Whoa, hey. What are you doing here?" It comes out accusatory, and her face scrunches.

"Gee, thanks for the warm welcome. Am I not allowed to visit my wife at work?"

I toss my bag on my desk. I've had sex on this desk. "You know what I mean." But I keep staring at her, waiting for a real answer as to why she's here.

"My appointment?" Joss says. "I'm picking you up? You said you wanted to come with me? Abbie's taking the car? Jeez, Chris, I'm supposed to be the one forgetting things, not you."

She's making light of it because that's what she does, but I can see through that tough exterior. It's what happens when you spend so many years with someone—years where you once thought your souls had meshed into one.

When Joss returned from Atlanta, she was a different person. That night, she'd opened a bottle of California red and drank most of it herself. I listened in horror as she told me what happened at the conference. Her face was pure white—not even the wine able to flush away her terror. Her voice trembled when she spoke.

Joss's voice never trembles—she's the strongest person I know.

In that moment, the little pestering gut reaction from the microwave incident solidified. There was definitely something bad going on. I could see it in her face and hear it in her words.

"Of course I didn't forget your appointment," I say now, and immediately feel guilty. Not three hours ago, I was having sex with someone other than my wife. I wasn't thinking about her or the frighteningly confusing things she's been experiencing. What kind of partner am I?

I push away the shame with a firm hand. This isn't all my fault. If Joss hadn't been so absorbed with work, none of this would have happened. She's been physically present, yet mentally absent, a combination that's simply not sustainable.

"I didn't think we were leaving for another hour," I say, checking my watch. "I have a meeting with Kerry in a couple minutes."

"That's fine. I can wait."

"I'm surprised you can tear yourself away from your computer for this long." The comment is harsh and unhelpful, but I can't help the resentment I feel, even when it sneaks out in a snarky tone.

"Ouch, Chris."

"Sorry," I mumble. Even I'm jolted by it. *Jesus, Christine.*

"Campus is one of the few places I feel like myself, okay? You of all people should understand."

Her eyes turn down, and I sense the vulnerability she's trying so hard to protect. The brave façade has cracks, after all. I get it—campus does feel like home, as much as we joke about practically living here.

Joss stands and leans in to give me a peck on the lips, only it feels obligatory, not genuine. I meet her for the briefest second, before quickly pulling away. I can still smell Micah on me—his crisp, woodsy scent. I've all but memorized it the last month, even going so far as to buy a car air freshener that's as close as I could get to mimic. A little pine tree that hangs from my rearview mirror. Micah, dangling and swaying wherever I go.

I grab my notepad. "Why don't you come with me to say hi to Kerry? She's always asking me how your research is going."

"And what do you say?"

"That I don't really know since you don't really talk about it."

Joss huffs. "That's not true. You don't ask. I'd tell you all about it if I thought you actually cared."

I give her a little smirk to diffuse this conversation from turning into an unnecessary argument. "I'm kidding."

But I'm not really kidding. I could be interested in hearing about her study. Every time I try, she's either so zoned in she doesn't realize I'm in the room, or she's too exhausted to get into it. She spends more time in her office than anywhere else, so what does that tell you? There've been three of us in this marriage for a while, and Joss has made it clear which one takes priority.

I catch her staring off into the distance. The thought of Joss being sick, of her not being able to continue her work, tosses uneasily in my core. Of course I don't want my wife to be sick. But the study? Give it the disease. Let the study come down with some incurable illness so that it crumples into nothing and goes away.

An image pops into my head. What if this is the exact thing that brings Joss back to me? A moment of reckoning. The catalyst that finally makes her realize that she's been neglecting—us. Something bubbles inside me. I think it's hope.

She fiddles with her phone. "This doctor's appointment better be quick. I have a conference call with Richard at five."

I deflate like a popped balloon. Joss might be scared on the inside, but she'll never let debility—or the threat of it—steal her glory. She will continue to work even on her deathbed.

Instead of arguing, I give a lifeless nod. She'll miss dinner with us again. It's becoming a new routine—plating dinner for two, and putting Joss's straight into Tupperware for later.

"Knock, knock." I hear the voice before I see the person, and my mouth goes dry. No, not now. Micah comes around the corner, stepping into this space like he owns it. He stops when he sees Joss. "Oh, sorry, Dr. Graham. I didn't realize you were in a meeting."

My face flushes, and I know there's probably bright red hives splotching my neck. I wish I was wearing a turtleneck. Hell, I wish I was wearing a full mask.

"Micah. No worries." My tongue feels fat in my mouth, like I just came from the dentist after receiving Novocaine. "You know Dr. Matson?" I gesture to where Joss sits. She has on her default teacher smile, gummy and wide.

"Hi, there," she says.

"Nice to meet you." Polite Micah. Gentleman Micah. The one who helped me through the rain. Not the one who whispers vulgarities in my ear.

He looks back to me. Joss is still facing him, but I know her head will swivel to me at any second. I quickly shoot Micah a look. *Not now. Get out of here.*

"I was just going to, uh, run this assignment past you before next class," he says. "But that's okay, I'll try to catch you tomorrow."

We were just together mere hours ago. The fact he clearly wants—needs—me again sends a pulse throughout my body. He's addicted. So am I.

"Okay, sounds good." My voice is high pitched and chipper. Joss looks quizzically at me. I'd normally never brush off a student with unanswered questions or concerns. Micah lingers, and I silently beg him to leave. I busy myself with papers on my desk for a beat, until another voice fills the room.

"Ma! Didn't expect to see you here." My head whips up to see Abbie coming through the door. She excuses herself as she brushes past Micah.

My already racing heart picks up even faster to the point I'm sure it will beat right out of my chest. Time stops. The room freezes. My knees go weak. In the space of a few feet are my wife, my daughter and my lover.

Abbie

Ma gets up from the chair and reaches out to where Mom sways unsteadily. "Chris, are you okay?" Mom's white as a ghost—I didn't know her skin could get more pale. Her hands grip the edge of the desk.

"Mom?" I help lower her onto the thick office chair. She's blinking like there's something in her eye, but her gaze is glossed over.

A long minute later, she's present again. "I'm fine, I'm fine." She looks to the door, and I follow, too. No one's there.

Okay, that was strange. Maybe Mom's paranoia about dying isn't all in her head. Was that a stroke or something? No thanks. Don't really feel like driving to the ER right now.

"That student left," Ma says. "You didn't have to send him away just because I'm here."

"No, no. I'm sure it's fine." She flaps a hand like it's no big deal. "I'll catch up with him before class tomorrow."

"Your students always so casual?"

"What?"

"'Knock, knock?' Just seemed overly comfortable. Like you two are on a first-name basis or something."

I listen to them go back and forth and feel like I'm clearly missing a piece of the puzzle. What did I walk into? This banter feels edgy—like one mom wants to be playful, and the other's not in the mood. Like that one week of each month when all three of our cycles align and it's just a moody bitchfest.

Mom laughs. "I don't know what you're talking about."

Ma turns to me, points a thumb to the door. "D'you know that guy?"

I plop into an empty chair and pull my phone out of my pocket. "I think his name's Micah. I know *of* him."

"What's that supposed to mean?" Mom snaps. "*Of* him."

My hands go up in surrender. "Whoa, nothing, just that he's well known on campus. His name gets tossed around a lot. Pretty sure he's a player. Someone said he bangs a new girl every weekend."

"You don't know that. College campuses are complete rumor mills," Mom snips.

Jeez, *someone's* defensive. I give Ma a sideways glance and she shrugs. It's not like they never talk about students at home. I've heard it all. The girls who dress slutty to class, the guys who reek of alcohol at nine in the morning. The ones they catch cheating.

Mom is so out of it lately—testy as a landmine—and I don't even know how to deal with her. I mean, it's gotta be the stress of being up for tenure. I've heard them talk about coworkers going through the process. A woman who was denied tenure and then didn't get a contract renewal. So yeah, I get it. But I've got my own weirdness to deal with, I don't need hers. Maybe Ma's not the only one who needs a sabbatical.

"I've definitely heard his name floating around before," I continue, opening Instagram. "Here, let me find his profile."

"Abbie, enough. Just drop it, okay?" Her nostrils flare. She looks like a bull ready to charge. Then she takes a breath and her jaw softens. "We've taught you better than to talk behind people's backs."

I stifle a laugh. Seriously? Gossip is what college life is built on. They're just as guilty. Still, her jab stings, and I drop my eyes back to my phone. I'm not used to Mom snapping at me. She's supposed to be good cop.

"What are you doing here so early anyways? I thought you had class til three," Mom says.

"Canceled."

"Who is it?"

"Williams."

Mom grumbles. "Figures. All these tenured faculty do whatever they damn well please. It's us untenured folks busting our butts in the classroom. *We're* the ones the students like because *we* actually care." She sits and types heavy-handed on the keyboard.

I've heard this rant from Mom before. Ma gets defensive because she's been tenured for years, but I see Mom's point. I have a math professor this semester who's literally the worst teacher ever—everyone agrees—but he'll never get fired because he's protected by some ancient, backwards system. Being a freshman sucks. We always get the worst professors.

Mom flips open a binder on her desk. The hives have disappeared from her neck, and she seems normal again. "Why don't you stick around on campus? Meet up with some friends or something—now that you have extra time."

Poor Mom, she's trying so hard to make me social.

"Stacia said I could kill time at her place. We're meeting when she gets out of class."

"Want to keep me company while you wait?" Ma asks. "Your mom has a meeting with Dr. Viotto."

The last thing I feel like doing is sitting in a cramped office with Ma, making awkward small talk and pretending we know anything about each other. Pretty sure the last thing Ma could pin point about me was my Justin Bieber phase about ten years ago.

I make up something on the spot.

"I'm actually gonna make a pitstop at the bookstore for a bagel...sorry."

Ma's hopeful smile falters. "Oh, all right."

"I won't be long with Kerry, and then we can get going," Mom says, breaking the tension.

"Where are you guys going again?" I ask, not that I really care, but more so because I can't remember the last time they went anywhere together.

They blurt different things at the same time.

"Dinner."

"Shopping."

"Shopping, then dinner," Mom clarifies with a nervous laugh. Her shoulders are high and tensed. A pinched smile crosses her face.

I eye them. It's not even close to dinnertime. And Ma hates shopping.

"Okay. I'll make myself something to eat later."

Mom gives me a hug, tucks in the bra strap poking out from my shirt.

As I'm leaving the office, I hear Ma's voice call out. "Save us some food for when we get home!"

I pause mid-step, scrunch my face, then continue, wondering what in the hell is going on with them.

Christine

"Chris, come on in."
      Kerry's office is no bigger than mine, which is to say it's about the size of a sardine can. It's walled with overflowing bookshelves and bulletin boards. A worn leather loveseat takes up a third of the space and serves as the only seating for visitors. There's no window, no natural light. It's completely unglamorous—far from the shiny department chair offices of large state universities. I always get a kick out of movies that depict college life as this world of grand mahogany desks and Persian rugs. I can tell you one thing, my desk is metal, and it's rusting at the corners. If schools had extra money, trust me when I say it wouldn't be spent on sprawling offices for faculty.

      I take a seat opposite Kerry, unsure how to feel about this unprompted meeting. We're friends, as well as coworkers, but for the duration she holds the chair position, she's also my boss, and will be one of the people deciding whether I'm awarded tenure in the spring. I'm confident I have her vote, but that doesn't mean I'm still not on my toes.

"How's your semester going?" she says, removing her tortoise frame glasses. They remind me of Abbie's, though Abbie's are only blue-light glasses—more ornamental than anything, one of her attempts to stay on top of trends. Glasses make me feel old, so I've stuck to contacts. Oh, to have perfect vision again.

"Good. Great." I cross my arms, before quickly uncrossing to seem less defensive. I fold my hands in my lap. I have nothing to be defensive of. Well, that's not true exactly, but as far as Kerry knows, I'm still doing my job as usual. "It's always a little crazy at the start, but things have fallen into a groove, as they always do."

"And you like your classes?"

"Yes...?" I draw it out a little, my voice creeping up at the end like it's a question. Why is she asking me this? I've taught these classes for years and have never once complained.

"Okay good. I just like to check in. You know, make sure everyone's managing." She's studying me hard. There's something in her tone that's making me uneasy. I don't like it. And I especially don't like it when I have something as big as tenure staring me in the face. What's she getting at?

"Is there something I should know?" I ask.

Kerry shuffles a stack of papers, puts her glasses on and takes them back off again. "I'm sure it's nothing." She flicks her hand like she's shooing away a fly.

"What's nothing?" Now my pulse is thumping. Her comment can only mean one thing: she knows about Micah.

"Just something someone said," she says with a shrug.

Shit. I thought we'd been so careful. My mind races. How am I going to get out of this?

"Who said? What did they say? Kerry, you're making me nervous." I laugh, trying and failing to lighten the tension that feels lethal.

She lets out a deep exhale and folds her arms on her desk, leaning slightly forward. "I got a note. It was on my floor yesterday morning. Like someone had slipped it under the door through the night."

My vision swims. I feel faint. "What did it say?"

She opens her top drawer and pulls out a single sheet of white printer paper, folded in half. She passes it to me across the desk. I open it with shaky hands.

KEEP AN EYE ON CHRISTINE GRAHAM.

"I don't know what it's supposed to mean," she says, "but I figured you ought to be aware."

"Who would write this?" I say, trying to keep my composure. Rattled equals guilt. Calm equals innocence. This is the moment I seal my fate.

I look at the words on the page again, as though trying to identify the slanted, all-caps handwriting. Who saw us? I replay the times Micah and I have been together, but there's far too many at this point, they all start to blur.

"Got any bitter students this semester? Anyone who recently flunked an exam and is feeling resentful?" Her voice has a tinge of hope to it, like she's giving me an out.

A lightbulb goes on. Yes, that's perfect.

I toss the note onto her desk like I can't be bothered with such silliness. "Yeah, actually. There's one girl. Tried to argue a few points out of me but I wouldn't give in. She was damn persistent though, I'll give her that."

Kerry nods. "You know how girls can be. Spiteful."

"You're telling me. I live with two of them."

We both chuckle. The conversation is turning a corner into lighter territory, which makes my pulse steady. Still, I'm not a great actor, and my foot taps rhythmically on the ground. Breakfast rolls in my stomach. This meeting has to end. I need to get out of this office.

"Well," Kerry says, taking the note, "I'm sure it's nothing then."

She puts the note back in her drawer. I want to stop her and tell her to rip it up. Why is she saving it? But I need to act like nothing's wrong, so I just force a smile.

When I stand to leave, she stands too. "Thanks for meeting with me, Chris. It's a big year for you. Just don't want anything to derail it."

I leave before the surge of nausea makes it all the way to my throat.

Abbie

Stacia's bedroom looks like it stepped out of an Anthropologie catalog. In fact, the entire apartment does, including her roommates' rooms, the small living room and kitchen.

A furry, white chair with slim metal legs sits in front of her computer desk, which is cluttered with candles, floral teacups and dozens of beaded jewelry but somehow manages to look neat. Clutter chic, I'd call it—the quintessential bohemian aesthetic. If I tried to achieve it, I guarantee my room would just look straight up messy. It's just another thing Stacia's able to do without trying.

"Try this one," she says, flinging a green top in my direction. She rifles through her closet, him-hawing over each piece with such nonchalance, while I practically salivate at the thought of sharing her clothes. I slip the shirt over my head.

She gives me the lookover. "Yaaaaas, girl. You've gotta wear that one tonight. In fact, keep it. It looks way better on you than me."

"Really?"

"Abbie, it's just a shirt."

I plop onto her bed, covered in a sunburst quilt. The pattern reminds me of a sketch I did last week, then digitized and uploaded to Etsy. I trail my finger around the thick stitching, then pull back when I catch Stacia watching me.

"I drew a picture like this the other day," I say by way of explanation. *Drew a picture*—it sounds like I'm in Kindergarten.

"I didn't know you were into art."

I shrug. "Just a hobby."

"Can I see? I mean, do you have any on your phone?"

I feign indifference, though I know my entire camera roll is filled with snapshots of my work. "Yeah, sure."

She comes to sit beside me. I pull up a charcoal portrait, flick through a couple more colored line drawings.

"These are really good," Stacia says. "And you're not an art major?"

I give a single laugh. "Long story."

Another picture, then another, but then my finger flicks one too far. The screen fills with a photo of Trina and me, a poorly-posed, poorly-lit selfie, both of us trying too hard. I try to swipe past it, but Stacia grabs the phone.

"Aww, who's your friend?"

My face burns. As if Stacia needed proof that I'm from the unpopular side of the tracks. "Trina. An acquaintance, really," I say, taking the phone back and holding it face down in my lap.

"She's pretty."

No, she's not. Trina's plain, mousy even, with her thin hair and long nose. Probably what drew us together in the first place. Trina's nowhere near Stacia's level of pretty. I don't need her thinking I'm friends with such average people.

She goes back to the closet, holds up two more tops, one in each hand. "Ok, my turn. Which one?"

My insides glow—she's asking my opinion.

"I like the white. With those black jeans, the ones with the rips at the knees."

Stacia grins. "I knew you had amazing fashion sense."

She changes into the outfit I chose, then checks herself out in the full-length mirror leaning against the wall, turning her head so that her ear nearly touches her shoulder.

"C'mere," she says, and I slide off the bed. She links her arm in mine, holds up her phone toward our reflections, and I try to mimic her easy confidence. For a moment, I feel silly, making pouty faces to the camera, but Stacia's natural lead is assuring. Where she goes, I'll follow—for as long as she'll have me.

She posts the picture to her Instagram stories, adding the dancing twins emoji for good measure.

I'm soaring.

Joss

Christine's flushed when she returns from Kerry's office.

"All good?" I say.

"Fine. Just needed a couple signatures."

"Tenure stuff?"

"Just stuff. Nothing really. Ready?"

Testy. I grab my purse.

She's quiet on the way to the doctor, which makes me think she's either overanalyzing or not telling me something.

"You can breathe, you know," I say.

"What?"

"Tenure. It's going so smoothly, you don't have anything to worry about. Not all faculty can say that."

She gives her head a little shake. "Oh, right. Yeah, I know. Still just a stressful process."

"Of course it is—you're staring in the face of job security." I remember being on edge the year I was up for tenure—my scholarship was top-notch, but I didn't have all the student love she does. But that was fifteen years ago, and things have changed. Student opinions matter so much more now.

We pull into the parking lot. It's a modest building, the type that easily converts from one business to the next through the decades. Small town life—I'm quite sure it was once an embroidery shop.

"Are you nervous?" Christine asks.

"For what? It's not like I'm going for a pelvic exam." I laugh, but she looks unconvinced. "I'm probably just overworked and under rested. He's going to tell me to have a break from my research for a bit, that's all."

"Nice Gary could get you right in."

I mumble in agreement.

We've known Gary Dillard for years, not just as a family physician, but all the way back to when his daughters joined Abbie as little bedazzled peacocks in the year-end dance recital. We've served on community boards together, will bump into each other in the grocery store and ask about each other's spouses. The familiarity is comforting.

A nurse in pale blue scrubs ushers Christine and me to a small exam room where she takes and records my vitals. We wait. I sit next to Christine in a chair and stare at the exam table, not wanting to sit on it lest I feel like a real patient with a real problem.

Christine doesn't like doctor's offices. Too many appointments with her mother, then Fisher—she associates it all with death. It wasn't until Abbie was born, when visiting the doctor became just another tick in the job description of Parent, that she learned to deal with it. Still, she's edgy, and I'm grateful she's here with me.

Gary enters wearing khakis and a white button down. His mustache is bushy, even though he has a bald spot in the back of his thinning hair.

"Joss, Christine," he greets us warmly. "What brings you in?" His eyebrows pinch, and I decide it's probably not often that spouses attend each other's appointments.

"Oh, it's probably nothing," I start, but then Christine looks at me. I guess I have no choice but to be honest.

"I've had a few forgetful spells lately," I say with flippancy. Despite being terrified after the conference ordeal, I've convinced myself it was a coincidence. There's nothing *actually* wrong with me.

"She put her purse in the microwave," Christine inserts, taking a sledgehammer to my levity.

Gary jots a few notes on his computer. He nods. "Anything else?"

"This is going to sound ridiculous," I say. "One day I couldn't remember how to use my phone. Picked it up and knew I wanted to make a call, but couldn't figure out how."

"Mmhmm."

"And then last week." I pause, the feelings and memory rushing back. "I was in Atlanta for a conference." A small laugh escapes my lips at the absurdity of it all.

"Mhmm."

"Well, I guess it actually started before that." I let out a breath. "There was a slight mix-up at the airport."

"She tried to get on the wrong plane." Christine finishes it for me.

"The wrong plane?"

"It was the strangest thing," I explain. "I knew what gate I was supposed to be at and genuinely thought I was there. I'd checked the boards and everything. When my boarding pass wouldn't scan, I was gobsmacked. Like I honestly didn't realize I was at the wrong gate the whole time." My voice is losing its fortitude, threatening to crumble. "I missed my flight. And then when I finally did make it to Atlanta, I completely froze on stage. Couldn't remember a thing. Not the research, not even what I was doing there. This wasn't a panic attack, if that's what you're thinking. This was something else."

Gary types away. His brow is furrowed, creating several deep creases on his forehead. When he purses his lips, his coarse mustache hairs stick straight out.

"Definitely unusual," he says. "And you've never had any of these things happen until recently?"

"I mean, I suppose there's been small things here and there, but nothing like this."

He removes his glasses. "I'm not going to lie, it's concerning, Joss. You're young. Too young for this to be considered normal. I'd like to refer you to Neuro. But in the meantime, let's get a workup to check your thyroid and other nervous system concerns."

I nod along, though the word neuro is like a dagger through my core. Neuro. As in a brain specialist. As in there's something wrong with my most prized possession.

"Any family history of Alzheimer's or dementia?"

"Wait a minute, Alzheimer's?" My fingers go numb. He can't be serious.

"It's not out of the realm of possibilities, I'm afraid. Early-onset can start in your forties, believe it or not. I'm not saying that's what this is. But let's get as much information as we can, okay?"

He rattles off a list of questions I only half hear. Christine answers most of them. Alzheimer's? How is that possible? My brain is my greatest asset. I've worked it and trained it like an athlete trains his arms or legs. It can't leave me now. I won't let it.

"Have you been withdrawing lately?" he asks, but I'm still wrapped up in my thoughts. "Pulling away from family or things you like to do?"

"She has," I hear Christine say, and my defenses spring up. I can speak for myself, thank you very much.

"It's just my research. I'm busy. It takes a lot of my time."

"Yes, but there's been other instances," my wife says. "You haven't been yourself for a while."

I stare at her, wondering how this could be happening. Sure, I've been focused on my work for almost a year. But have I really been *that* different? That disconnected?

"One of our first courses of treatment should be an antidepressant," Gary says.

I raise my hand. "Already on one."

"Oh."

"Aren't we all?"

The comment does what I intended it to, and we each let out a laugh, though there's nothing funny about this situation. And the anti-depressant to which I think he's referring is most likely a much higher dosage than the teeny pill I take every evening to keep the clouds from descending.

"Well, then, keep taking it. A lot of people become depressed or anxious when their minds start slipping."

"My mind's not slipping, Gary. These were isolated situations. Completely freak incidents."

He gives Christine a look. He doesn't believe me.

"I'll make sure she keeps taking them," Christine says, and all of a sudden I feel like a child whose parent is listening to instructions on her behalf.

We wrap up the appointment with a referral to a bigger hospital in the neighboring town.

"Is this really necessary?" I whisper to Christine.

"Take it easy, Joss," Gary says. "Don't beat yourself up. Wait and see what the tests say."

His words are meant to comfort me, but instead they do the opposite. There's nothing anyone could say that would make going mad sound any better.

Abbie

Stacia corners me after practice. I'm slogging to the bench, sweat forming rivers down my temples. My lungs hurt from sucking late October air.

"Hey," she whispers. "I got an A on that test." A crooked smile crosses her face. I know the truth behind that smile. It should make me scream with guilt, but it doesn't. Being in her orbit is intoxicating. And with Stacia comes the rest of the "in" crowd. The ones who'd never notice me if I weren't part of her clique—including Cody Marshall, football star and all-around hottest guy on campus.

Stacia is close to me now, so close I can see little opalescent rainbows in the beads on her forehead. Her eyebrows arch. "Think you can get the next one?"

"Next one?"

"The next exam. It's in a couple weeks."

I guess I should have seen this coming. Why would I have assumed it would be a one-time thing? The high of getting an A without putting in the work—who wouldn't want a second hit?

A calm settles in my core. Maybe I did see it coming. Maybe I wanted it to come.

"I don't know, Stacia."

As soon as she asks, I know I'll do it, but want to drag it out, make her sweat a little. She's at my mercy now. I want to hear her beg.

"Oh c'mon, Abbie. I'm swamped with work. Graduation is getting closer and closer and I'm seriously just up to my eyeballs with the stress of it all. Please?"

I scrunch my face, like her request is painful. "I'll try," I finally say. "But I can't promise anything." This isn't true. I'll do whatever it takes to get that next exam off Mom's computer.

"You're freaking amazing." Stacia hugs me and we rock there for a second, our sweat mixing into a cocktail of fraud. "Thank you. You don't know how much this takes off my shoulders. I owe you, girl. Now c'mon, let's go grab dinner. The football team should be there, and you know they're wild for our short shorts."

***

I've become a hawk. Tracking Mom's movements is my new mission. She only brings her laptop home on the weekends because she says weeknights are meant for family. Email will suck a professor in twenty-four seven, she likes to say, which is why she removed email from her phone a couple years ago.

Which means afternoons in her office, before we head home for the day together, are the only chance I have to drop nonchalant comments about her classes. I dig for info like a dog searching for its bone.

"Whatcha working on?" I ask a week after Stacia's latest request. Mom is hunched over her computer, clicking away on the keys with her newly painted nails. We did them together last night while we watched *13 Going on Thirty*.

"Why would anyone want to wish themselves older?" Mom had said, as we rifled through a basket of rainbow bottles. I picked my color.

"Black?" she grimaced.

"Yeah. It's cool."

She'd shrugged and then copied me.

Now, against her computer, the color blends into the dark keys. "Oh, just emails," she says.

My questions get more pointed in the following days. *What do you have going on in class this week? Students working on any cool projects? Finals are coming soon, got your exams written?* Mom answers each one without a second thought. I'm the good kid—always have been—never given either of my moms a reason not to trust me.

With Mom, it's even more obvious. She loves that we're tight. "Daughters are often distant during these years," she once told me. "They go away for a while before coming back and reconnecting with their mothers as adults. But not us. We're different, Ab. We'll always be close."

I swallow those words now. They taste bitter.

Stacia's asked me twice if I've been able to get the next exam, and I continue to tell her I'm working on it. Finally, with only two days to spare, my "whatcha doin'" question to Mom gets the response I've been waiting for: "Working on my Theory exam."

Bingo. My senses fire awake. Stacia's exam.

I need to get it.

I perch on the edge of the chair for the next hour, desperately willing something—anything—to pull Mom from her office for five minutes so I can make a copy of the test. But nothing happens. No phone calls, no heads popping in asking for a word, no spontaneous meetings.

It's four-thirty now. Campus is draining of people. The workday is just about over.

"Okay, let's go. I can't stare at this another minute." Mom shuts her laptop and reaches for her bag. I realize I've been clenching my teeth. My jaw hurts.

Fuck.

I search my brain for an excuse. Something to get her out of the office. But she's got her jacket on and is at the door before I come up with anything. I won't be getting the exam today.

Instead, I follow Mom to the car. She's rambling about what to make for dinner, but my mind is somewhere else, thinking—no, planning—how I'll get my hands on that exam tomorrow. I cannot let Stacia down.

* * *

Our schedules are opposite this semester, so when Mom's giving a lecture on cultural kinship (I know this because she gave me an unsolicited overview in the car this morning), I'm using my key—the key Kerry willingly requested for me—to slip into her office. The dean never questioned my having access to Mom's space. Abbie, the good girl. Daughter of two respected faculty members. What harm could she do?

Mom's computer sits on her desk like the genie lamp in Aladdin's cave of wonders. Forbidden. Tantalizing. The brains of it hum louder as I get closer. *Do not touch. Do not touch.*

I open the laptop and the screen comes to life. Instantly, my stomach drops. Login password required. Shit. I hadn't needed it last time since Mom was already logged in and just stepped away for a moment.

My fingers hover over the keys. I close my eyes. If I were Mom, what would my password be?

I try Abbie. No luck.

I try my full name, AbigailGrace. Nothing.

Three more shots, mixing my name with hers. Adding birth years once I remember passwords require numerals. Trying combinations with Uncle Fisher's name. I start to worry I'll try too many attempted logins and get locked out, sending an email prompt for Mom to reset her password.

Shit. Shit. Shit. My stomach is churning now. I throw myself back into her oversized chair and it rocks against its axis. I thought for sure she'd use me as her password. How many more times should I try? Maybe I should abort mission. This password roadblock is giving me major red flags. If this is a sign, it can't get any bigger.

But then I see Stacia's face, twisted into a pleading appeal. I hear her calling me "bestie" and introducing me to the Cody Marshalls of the world. Does our friendship hinge on me getting this test? Will she still invite me to parties if I refuse? I don't want to find out.

I sit up with renewed resolve, back straight, fingers extended out over the keys. I have to think. What's something memorable? Something Mom would never forget? Ma's face flashes through my mind. I type in Joss112669—Ma's birthday.

Attempt failed.

This isn't good. There's probably only one more chance to get it right.

I close my eyes. *Think, Abbie.* I type in Joss061899—their wedding date. The login prompt dissolves and I'm staring at the computer's desktop. I let out a little gasp. I'm in. It worked.

It was Ma all along. I should have known.

Folder icons litter the screen. They're arranged alphabetically—no surprise—so it's easy for me to find one labeled Theory of Gender Studies. I double click. The folder opens. There's a list of documents— PowerPoints, case studies, then finally, exams. I open the file called ANTH450_FinalExam. Within a second, it blazes in front of me, and my heart rate thumps in my ears like a bass drum.

The speed with which I hit Print—without a second thought—surprises me. No Jiminy Cricket on my shoulder tugging at my moral conscience. I know exactly what I'm doing and what I'm risking. And for a split second, that scares me.

How can I do this to Mom?

I sit for a second to consider what Mom would think of this unrecognizable daughter. She wouldn't understand, she couldn't relate. Mom's always had friends, has always been well liked. She'd never get the lure of doing something so wrong. She's perfect.

I log out of the computer, close the lid, and hurry to the printer a few doors down. Last thing I need is someone else to grab it off the tray and question what I'm doing. I smile at a passing faculty member. Everyone knows me here, my presence never questioned.

The exam is there waiting for me, still warm. I slip it in my bag. As I walk past Mom's office on my way out, I check her door to make sure it's locked. The room is just as she left it. My being here will go undetected.

* * *

The hand-off comes at the beginning of practice that afternoon. I slip the folded papers into Stacia's hand like a drug dealer passing a powder-filled baggie. She smiles, then mouths "thank you" and presses her palms together in grateful prayer. I nod, pleased to be her helping hand.

This should be enough. I've done it twice, and all the while I've gotten in with a group of friends everyone wishes they had. I'm going to my first frat party this weekend, and Stacia even loaned me a low-cut halter.

As I watch her shove the exam in her bag, I tell myself it's the last time. My stealing days are done. The semester will be over in a few short weeks, and I vow to myself not to do it again.

Sometimes the lies we tell ourselves are the most dangerous.

Christine

Our faculty development committee meets once a month in a boardroom on the second floor of Avery Hall. I've served on numerous committees during my teaching career, but faculty development is by far my favorite—it's where I excel. Joss proves her skill on paper, but I demonstrate mine in action in the classroom. Promoting collaborative learning, strengthening my delivery approaches, creating a meaningful experience—it's what makes me tick.

The five of us sit around the oblong table eating lunches served in reusable takeaway containers from the dining hall. We're cruising through the meeting agenda, until Sam Archibold gets hung up on a policy surrounding classroom observations. He's on a heater. Tenured faculty ought to be observed just as frequently as those on the non-tenure track, he thinks. He's adamant, his pin-point of a head turning red as he talks, and his hand, finger pointed, stabbing the air with each assertion.

I fiddle with my watch clasp, repeatedly unhooking and hooking it. This topic comes up nearly every year. Why should tenured faculty not be held to the same performance standards as everyone else? I should have a voice here, having spent the first two decades of my career on the non-tenure track. But once I decided to make the leap—to finish my Ph.D. and go for tenure—the fight in me dwindled. Soon, I'd be one of those protected ones. Not that I'd let it shape me. The classroom is my happy place, and I can't imagine that ever changing.

My phone vibrates.

Where R U?

Micah. Damn this meeting for running long. Damn Sam Archibold and his obsession with hearing himself talk.

Still in this meeting. Can't leave.

Where?

2nd floor, Avery.

As soon as I hit Send, I regret it. Micah better not come here. I can't be interrupted. Plus, how would I explain to my colleagues a student happening upon our meeting for the sole purpose of finding me?

I'm *this close* to writing back as much, but something stops me. A fire grows inside my chest, travels down my core and settles between my legs. I secretly want him to come. I want to see him walk past the glass door, unsuspecting to everyone else, just a student walking by, but I'll know the truth: he's here for me.

Sam Archibold blabs on, but my focus is gone.

"We can bring it to Senate and put it to a vote," Maria, a long-standing math professor says. "Christine, you agree?"

I snap to attention. "Huh? Oh. Yes, I agree." I have no idea what I just agreed to, but I'll vote in favor of anything to get Sam to shut his mouth.

"Great. It's decided. All right, let's wrap up. We've already gone over on time. I have class in ten."

They close their notebooks, pack up their briefcases, and stand. At the same time, the door opens. For a split second I think it's Micah, and my heart does a little dance, but it's just a uniformed man, a staff member here to take away our lunch.

"Oh, not finished," he says, taking a step back. "Figures."

"We are," Maria says. "Thanks." She steps away from the table to give him room.

"My pleasure." It's laced with sarcasm, and his bulging eyes give a roll. He must hate his job, cleaning up after other people all day.

"See ya, Christine," Sam says, following our other colleagues out the door. "Off to shape the next generation of leaders." I give a half-hearted wave, though I can't tell if his words are genuine or if he's really that jaded.

Turning back to the table, I reach to stack the empty food containers. "Here, let me help."

"Don't bother," the man says, and at the same time a trill *cha-ching* echoes from his pocket. He yanks out his phone, just as I'm thinking how odd a ringtone it is. Even from where I stand a few feet away, I can see his pupils dilate and a flush come over his sunken-in cheeks. He taps the screen with a hasty finger, and as quickly as he retrieved the phone, he tucks it back into the folds of denim.

I'm momentarily fixed by the strangeness of this weaselly man, until two faculty pass by the open door, clucking about flipping their classrooms. I gather my things. I need to get back to my office. The number of emails I've probably received in the last hour alone—I don't even want to think about it. They're like a never-ending flood no dam can block.

I'm slinging my bag over my shoulder when a new voice breaks the silence.

"*There* you are. You really like to keep me waiting, don't you?" Micah's tone is like butter, the warm melty kind that's drippy and delicious. The kind I usually lap up. But not here. Not now. I freeze. We're not alone.

Micah realizes it a second later when his eyes land on the man cleaning the table. "Er, I mean...Do you have time to talk about our term paper, Dr. Graham?"

It sounds so formal after weeks of him calling me Christine, I want to laugh. Want to give his hard stomach a playful punch and call him Mr. Johnson in return, like we're role playing as mere strangers instead of two people who've seen each other naked.

A nervous laugh escapes my lips, as I look back and forth between Micah and the stranger who has found himself smack in the middle. He halts for a second, mid table wipe, taking Micah and me in, before returning to his job.

"Sure," I say, "Let's meet in my office, ok?" I give Micah eyes that scream *Get out of here*. He gets it, and retreats into the hallway. I turn back to the man.

"Thanks so much for taking care of this—" I notice a name stitched onto his shirt and I strain to read it. "—Lester."

He doesn't respond, but his buggy eyes watch me leave, and I can't shake the jitters that have made my limbs tingle with warning.

Joss

Neurology is on the fourth floor of a large brick hospital. I scheduled the appointment for eleven since Christine said she couldn't miss her freshman class this morning. As humiliating as everything is, I don't want to do it alone. I need Chris here with me.

I'm already in the waiting room when she comes in wearing a camel-colored trench coat, the collar popped ever so slightly. She can always get away with things that would make me look like a frumpy bag lady.

"Hey," she says, sitting down next to me. She grabs my hand, and though it's freezing, a surge of warmth grows inside me at her touch.

"New coat?" I say.

She frowns.

"What?"

"Joss, you got this for me."

My cheeks burn. "I did?"

She gives my hand a little pat that makes me feel like I'm her grandmother instead of her wife. Like we're four decades apart instead of four years.

The receptionist calls my name and a nurse takes us back to yet another exam room. Only this time, it's nothing like our hometown doctor's office. Dr. Kaur is all business. No pleasantries, no catching up on local town updates like we do with Gary. He's serious, much like this cold, sterile space.

"Tell me your symptoms," he says.

I give Dr. Kaur the same rundown I gave Gary a week ago. He takes notes. When I'm finished, he grabs a clipboard from the counter.

"I'm going to have you take a Mini Mental Exam. Don't worry, it's just some basic questions that help to establish a diagnosis."

Diagnosis?

He rolls his chair closer to me. Clicks open his pen.

"What's today's date?"

I freeze. It's the simplest question, but suddenly I feel like I do when they ask Abbie's birthdate at the pharmacy.

"November eighteenth."

His pen checks a box I can't quite see.

"Where are you right now?"

"In a hospital exam room."

Check.

"I'm going to name three objects and ask you to repeat them. I want you to remember them because I'm going to ask them again later. Okay? Apple, Table, Penny."

I'm still hung up on listening intently to his instructions, I'm not sure I was paying full attention to the words. "Wait, can you repeat them again?"

"Just do the best you can."

I look down, thinking. Then, slowly, "Apple, Table, Penny." A breath in between each one.

Check.

"What is this called?" He holds up the thing he's been writing with.

"A pencil."

Christine shifts in the chair next to me. I glance over at her but her eyes are downcast. Wait, did I get it wrong? It's a pencil, right?

122

"I'm going to hand you a card. Read it and do what it says."

He hands me an index card printed with large black letters: CLOSE YOUR EYES. I close my eyes.

Check.

"What were those three items I asked you to remember?"

I open my mouth to say them, but nothing comes out. My mind is blank. I look around the room. Were they things in here? Was one a chair? No, I think it was a car.

"I...I..."

"It's okay," he says. He waits another moment, bestowing on me a sense of humanity and grace, though I suspect he already knows I won't come up with the words.

Think, I force myself. *You just said them a minute ago.*

Nothing comes.

I look up. When my eyes meet his, my vision is clouded by tears. "I can't remember."

***

The diagnosis comes the first week of December, after my CT and PET scan results come back. Early-onset Alzheimer's, just as Gary Dillard feared. The neuro department confirms that while my tests were inconclusive, there's not really much else to explain why I'm doing these things.

"We don't know the cause," Dr. Kaur says. "You have no family history, so it's just one of those completely random occurrences. You'll likely continue to see effects to your thinking and behavior. I'd like to bump up your antidepressant," Dr. Kaur says.

I don't argue. Numbing myself sounds amazing right now. I don't want to feel the ache that's tearing my heart apart. Don't want to shed any more tears in the shower when no one can hear me. Take my emotions, take them all.

"Then what?" I say. "Lock me in a padded room so I can't hurt myself or someone else?"

"It's not to that point, Joss."

"Yet."

123

"It might never be. It could progress slowly, or stay the same even."

I know he's humoring me, but it doesn't help. I've already spent more time than I'd like to admit scouring the internet as an explanation for my symptoms. I've read all about this disease. The prognosis is terrifying—two to six years life expectancy. Two years? Abbie will barely be twenty? I'll miss her wedding. I'll miss everything.

My soul is crushed. I can't even bear to walk past my computer without thinking about my research going unfinished. I'll never see the fruits of all my labor. My name will get lost among the other millions of college professors who amount to nothing. I'm nothing, just like my Dad predicted.

Dr. Kaur clears his throat. "I know this is scary. But go on with your life, knowing this is a new normal. Staying cautious. You and your wife should talk about things moving forward. Ways she can look out for you. Things to double check safety-wise. You'll need to rely on family and friends more than ever—don't try to do this alone, Joss. There's medication that can slow the progression. I'll call it in for you."

It's all a blur. I concede and we hang up. What else is there to say?

***

I give Christine the news first. We cry quietly together. She holds me against her chest, her arms wrapped tightly around my shoulders while my tears leave a wet mark below her collarbone. I melt into her familiarity, trying to remember the last time we embraced with such intimacy.

"It's supposed to be me," she says, and all I can think about is a time in the future when I no longer know who she is. Will she still love me? Will she be the one to take care of me?

Do I even want that?

An image flashes in my mind: Christine, helping me to the bathroom, pulling down my trousers, helping me wipe.

I'd rather die.

"We should tell Abbie together," I say.

Our daughter's in the kitchen raiding the pantry. Christine would normally snap at her since it's so close to dinnertime, but today's not a normal day. Rules don't matter when your wife's mind is drifting away.

"Hey Ab," I say. "Can we talk to you for a minute?"

She stops the flow of pretzels mid-pour. "Why? I didn't do anything." She's jumpy, but I can't even bother to ask why. We've got bad enough news to deliver. Her face goes long when she sees our expressions. Christine's eyes are red. I'm sure mine are too.

"What's wrong?" she says.

"Let's sit."

I pull stools so we're in a triangle around the bar—Christine on one side, me on the other, and Abbie on the end. The Three Musketeers. That's what we've always been. I'm crushed to think of our family turning into a twosome without me.

"I got a call from my doctor today," I say.

"A tumor, right? It's cancer, isn't it?" Abbie cuts me off. There's fear in her voice.

"No, it's not cancer." I pause. "It's worse."

"What can be worse than cancer?"

I look to Christine. I can't even get the word out.

"Alzheimer's," she says for me.

There's no time to mince words. "Cancer you can treat. Alzheimer's is just a slow, soul-sucking bastard." I lay it out there—the truth. None of this is fair. None of it is fun.

"So the purse thing? That was part of this?"

"Yes, as well as some other things we haven't told you. We didn't want you to be worried. I wanted to figure it out before telling you."

Abbie's face is blank. "But you're so young. So...smart."

"Doesn't matter." I bite my cheek. Her words pierce my heart because they're true. I *am* young (relatively) and I *am* smart. But this disease doesn't care.

"Nothing's going to change," I reassure her. "Not yet. I'm going to start taking some medicine, and we'll just have to be on the lookout for me doing weird things." I roll my eyes in a self-deprecating way. Saying this means I have to swallow my pride; I want to minimize it as much as I can for Abbie.

"Ma might just need you to help with her work instead of the other way around, that's all," Christine adds with a laugh, picking up on my attempt to lighten the heaviness of the conversation. Diffusing with humor is usually my role, but in this moment I'm grateful she feels very much on my team.

"Yeah, this is one way to get out of being homework helper." It's a lame joke because I was never the one to help with Abbie's homework. Too busy. Now, that realization is like a gut punch. Still, the farce lands because we all smile. Abbie gives a small laugh. She's using our reactions as a guide. If we pretend it's not too serious, maybe she'll continue to believe it.

We spend the evening making tacos and eating in front of the telly. Even Christine, who's been so wrapped up with her phone lately, is present. The elephant in the room eats with us too, sucking the life from the house. It's not going away any time soon.

As we make our way upstairs for bed later, my body feels heavy. I'm left with one lingering thought: How long will I be able to keep up this façade of strength?

Abbie

My philosophy professor is so ancient, I've started to think he might actually be Aristotle himself. His voice is as soft as his white, fluffy hair, and I have to strain to hear him. Even then, I don't understand what the hell he's talking about—none of us do. We're all only here for three credits. Besides, I can't stop thinking about Ma. I'd be distracted even if Zac Efron were sitting in front of me.

At one point, I look around the room, wondering if it's just me who's lost. A kid in a chunky stocking cap is fully asleep. Half the class is on their phones. I make eye contact with a guy two rows over. He puts a finger gun to his temple and pulls the trigger. I smile, not just because it's funny but because the guy is Cody Marshall.

Cody. Marshall. Hottest, most popular guy at MacAmes, Cody Marshall. I think he's a marketing major. Actually, I know he's a marketing major. And that he's from Boston. And he has a French Bulldog and two sisters.

My social media stalking skills are on point.

Aristotle drones on to the point I'd rather stab myself with my number two pencil than suffer through this agony any longer. I check my phone for the time. Class ends in five minutes. And I know he'll use every second possible. I zone back out.

When I hear shuffling coats and zipping bags, I realize class is over. I head to the door, thankful for the forty-eight hours before I have to sit through this torture again.

"Hey," a voice behind me makes me turn. "Abbie, right?"

"Yeah, hey—"

"Cody."

"Cody. Hi."

Holy shit. The star of the football team is talking to me. I hope my breath doesn't smell. Damnit, I should have put on mascara this morning. He's beside me now and we walk side by side out of the building.

"Talk about painfully boring, huh?" he says.

"Yeah it's pretty bad. I was debating on whether a puncture wound via pencil would be more appealing."

Cody chuckles. "Your mom is Dr. Graham, right?"

The floor of my stomach opens. I know where this is going as soon as he says it. "Yep," I say, picking up the pace. Of course he didn't want to talk to me because he was interested. I'm such an ass.

Cody stays in line with me. "I'm taking her Anthro 300 this semester," he says.

"Cool."

"It's a wicked hard class."

It's raining and I pull my hood tighter. Maybe he'll think I didn't hear him.

"I'm friends with Stacia," Cody continues when I don't give him a response. "We're super close. You're on the soccer team with her, right?"

He already knows the answers to these questions, but I give him an *Mmhmm*. We're nearing Ross Hall where my next class is. Cody has followed me all this way even though something tells me he doesn't have a class in the same building. As I'm about to climb the short steps toward dry shelter, he grabs my arm, stopping me in my Hunter boot tracks.

He lowers his voice. "Listen, I know about the exams you gave Stacia."

My legs go weak. I try to pull away but his grip is tight over my jacket. "I don't know what you're talking about."

"Don't worry, Abbie, I'm not going to tell anyone." He leans in closer. Our faces are inches apart. "Your secret is safe. But would you consider helping me, too? I mean, everyone knows your mom's tests are killer. Our final is Monday. It would stay between you and me."

We stand there for a long minute, staring at each other. A few students hurry past into the building. Nearby, a maintenance man unloads boxes from the back of a van. I catch him giving us side eye as he works.

The wind whips angrily around us, like it's trying to push me inside and away from the temptation of Cody Marshall's gorgeous face.

"Cody, I—"

"I'll pay you," he blurts. He reaches into his pocket and pulls out a fifty. I look at the crisp bill, wondering what college student walks around with cash like that in their coat pockets. "Here," he shoves the money in my hand. "Take it now. There's more where that came from if you're willing to help me. Think about it."

Before I can refuse, he turns and shuffles away. My lips are frozen in an open gape. A girl walks past and gives me a weird look. I cram the fifty into my bag, *down down down* until it settles at the bottom under the textbooks as if that alone would make it disappear. A bell chimes. It's eleven. Class is starting without me.

Christine

I have a problem. I can't stop thinking about Micah. I know, I'm a terrible person. My wife just got diagnosed with a horrific disease, and all I care about is the next time I can see my lover.

Lover. Is that what he is? What a strange word. It feels like so much more than that. He cares about me, wants to know me, my passions. The things Joss used to care about.

But now Joss isn't quite Joss.

And I'm the worst kind of person out there.

I can't help it. The stress of the last few weeks has been unbearable. My paranoia about my impending death has morphed into guilt for it being my wife instead. I should want to hold onto Joss and never let her go. Hug her and kiss her and cherish every minute we have together. But it's almost like her diagnosis has pushed me farther away. I don't crave her. I crave the escapism Micah gives me. For the few moments I'm with him, Joss's illness doesn't exist. I'm young and free and not facing a future that scares the shit out of me.

Fisher's face occasionally materializes in my mind, his floppy ginger hair, piercing eyes—the eyes that understood me more than anyone in the world. Would he even recognize me now?

It's the last day of final exams, and the thought of spending a month of holiday break without seeing Micah makes me want to crawl into a cave and hibernate until spring semester.

Faculty offices are packed with professors scrambling to finish up their grading. A few students linger, hoping to plead their cases as to why their grades should get rounded up. It's way too risky to be in my office with Micah today.

We meet up behind the football bleachers instead. He's waiting for me as I get closer. The thought crosses my mind how cliché this is. Really, Christine? Making out under the bleachers? But I don't care. I don't care about anything but his touch. I need to see him one more time before he leaves.

"I've got a present for you," he says when I'm just a few steps away. My body tingles. He bought me a gift. See? I think. This isn't just about sex.

He reaches down and grabs his crotch, gives it a shake. "It's right here, baby. Who needs Santa when you've got this?"

I laugh, though my mouth has gone sour. "Classy, Micah."

He pulls me toward him and we lock against each other.

"You could stay, you know," I say against his ear. "The dorms are still open for students who can't make it home." The desperation in my voice is thick like molasses. I don't like molasses.

"But I *can* go home."

"Yeah but, Richmond? What's so great about Richmond? If you stayed, we'd still be able to see each other."

"Christine, I'm going home for Christmas. Besides, my mom would kill me if I tried to stay." He laughs as he says it, and it's then I realize this...this *thing*...is nowhere as serious for him as it has become for me. He's a kid. With a mom who's waiting for him to open presents on Christmas morning.

I bite my lip. My mouth feels dry. "Okay."

"It'll go fast," Micah says, tucking a piece of hair behind my ear. All I can do is nod. He has no clue. No idea that he's become the one thing I look forward to. That my home life, my marriage, is fading away quicker than a passing breath.

"It's getting cold," I say.

"Well, let's warm up then." The ground is wet, so he spins me around and takes me standing.

* * *

We've just returned from our neighbor's annual holiday party and I'm officially buzzed from three chardonnays. Joss suggests a movie. We flick through the channels and land on *It's a Wonderful Life*. Even Abbie agrees. Joss pops two bags of popcorn, burning the first round, and I keep my mouth shut about all the calories in the Extra Butter variety.

The movie plays, but only Joss is watching. Abbie's on her phone, as usual, and is probably only appeasing us with her presence because it's Christmas Eve.

If she's not watching, then why should I? I stare down at my phone. The lock screen shows a picture of Joss, Abbie and me four summers ago at Yellowstone. Before Abbie withdrew into herself, before dementia entered our lives. Before I began an affair with a student.

We look so absurdly happy. The photo is almost unrecognizable. Who are these people?

I hover over the Messages icon. The urge to text Micah overwhelms me. Should I really bother him on Christmas Eve? He's probably with his family. Like everyone is. Like I am—at least physically.

Joss sits on the far side of the sectional, her feet propped on the ottoman and a bowl of popcorn in her lap. Between us is Abbie, watching dumb TikTok videos. My phone is by my hip, concealed by the plush folds of the blanket that covers my legs. I could easily text without them noticing.

I peek over at my wife and daughter. Neither seem overly concerned with me.

Screw it.

My thumb taps the icon and I compose a new message. I have his number memorized. The rules of our communication are clear: 1.) no saving each other as a contact in our phones, 2.) always delete incoming and outgoing messages, and 3.) clear the deleted folder every day.

Merry xmas...17 days to go. I add a winking emoji, even though Abbie tells me emojis are no longer cool.

Messages between Micah and I are intentionally vague. Nothing incriminating. Always a way to create a false narrative.

I hit Send.

The status quickly changes from "delivered" to "read." My heart flutters and heat spreads across my chest. He was waiting to hear from me. I watch the screen, anticipating the three little bubble dots of an imminent response.

One minute. Two minutes. Three.

It doesn't come.

Joss gives a boisterous laugh, making me jump. I instinctively flip my phone face down. She's grinning at the actors on screen—a couple doing the Charleston then falling into a pool. Joss shovels another handful of popcorn in her mouth and crunches away. The chomping makes me crazy. I ball my hands and dig my fingernails into the flesh of my palms, leaving little half-moon marks.

Micah doesn't reply that night, nor the next day, or even the week after that. The message sits there in my outbox, growing more and more pathetic by the day. I don't delete it. Each time I open it, I hope there will be a response. A message of longing, telling me he's counting down the days as much as I am.

I'm left disappointed.

SPRING 2022

Joss

It's Wednesday, the first week of spring semester, and I'm re-checking my schedule for the hundredth time. It's giving me major airport vibes, and I do not want to re-live that experience. At least this time the biggest thing I can mix up is a classroom, not a flight.

10:05 Organic Chem. 10:05 Bio Chem. No, Organic Chem. 2:05...wait, that's not right. I look at the sheet I've printed for reference. 10:05 Organic Chem. Organic Chem, 10:05.

I repeat it six more times.

It's been a month since Dr. Kaur put me on meds and instead of getting better, I'm getting worse. Maybe it's that damn once-you-know effect. I'm hyper aware of things, trying extra hard to concentrate on my every move to make sure nothing's amiss. Yet, the effort is moot.

Yesterday I searched the house top to bottom for my car keys, only to finally find them exactly where I always keep them on the hook by the door. A few days before that, I started making myself scrambled eggs and must have wandered off midway through. I was sitting at my desk when the burnt aroma made its way to my nose. The eggs were brown—the pan charred. I didn't even try to salvage it before throwing the whole bloody thing in the garbage.

These mental lapses keep coming even when I'm consciously on the lookout. Like the Alzheimer's is backhanding me across the face.

To hell with you, Joss. You're mine.

Christine was reluctant for me to return to classes, but as I told her, sabbatical doesn't last forever.

"It'll be good to get back into a routine," I'd said.

We met together with my department chair and Ken Redwood, Dean of Faculty.

"Looks like I'm losing my mind, fellas," I said, but not even my attempt at being cheeky could cover the torture behind my words. There'd been lots of hugs, and even a few welled eyes. And after a few more discussions, the powers to be decided I could fulfill my classes this semester.

Relief was an understatement.

Christine and Abbie took turns walking me to my office the first couple days when we arrived to campus, after which I finally put my foot down, telling them it was ridiculous.

"I'm a grown woman, not a child," I said.

"But—"

"The doctor hasn't *officially* said I shouldn't be left alone, so I see no reason I need to be babysat." The forgetfulness is more of an inconvenience at this point—a burnt frying pan.

It's not like I've hurt anyone.

Abbie scrunched her nose.

"God you look so much like," I said before quickly adding, "nevermind."

* * *

My laptop shines as I lift the lid. A familiar sense of comfort warms my insides. I've missed my research these past few weeks. Richard and I decided to have a break over the holidays, but I'm itching to get back to it. I promised him I'd be able to finish my part. That I am fully capable, despite my diagnosis. I refuse to disappoint him—or myself. Only now, I'll have to balance it with teaching again. The thought overwhelms me, but I steady my resolve. It's okay, I can manage. I *will* manage.

Before I open my latest file, the phone rings. I see Dr. Kaur's name, and I answer on the second ring.

"Let me guess," I say with not so much as a hello first. "You're calling to tell me there's a new breakthrough treatment and I'm first on the list." I laugh because the alternative is to cry and I don't like to cry.

"What are you, some sort of psychic?" His tone is light, much different than when he branded me with the Big A in his office last month.

"Can't hurt to dream, right?"

"Joss, I'm not kidding. That's exactly why I'm calling."

My mouth goes dry. "What?"

"It's very new. Just got FDA approval. They're calling it a 'wonder drug.' I thought of you immediately."

A crack in my tough exterior widens and something escapes. "But I thought you said there wasn't really much to do in the way of treating Alzheimer's. That it's more about addressing the psychological effects."

"I did, because that's always been the case. The meds you take now help some people, but not all. This drug is a whole new classification. Early reports show really great signs of it being a major barrier for the disease's progression."

It's silent on my end. The phone is light in my hand.

"Joss?"

"I'm here."

"Are you interested in giving it a try?"

I see a vision of the old me. I'm standing on stage at a conference to present the study I've worked so hard on. The audience roars. I receive a standing ovation. My research makes international news.

"Yes, absolutely. I'll have a go."

"I figured you'd say that." I hear his smile through the phone. But then his tone changes. "There's just one thing. The treatment is not covered by insurance at this time. It would have to be completely out of pocket."

The hairs on the back of my neck bristle. "Okay. What are we talking?"

"Thousands."

"C'mon, doc. Shoot it straight. Thousands can mean two or five, or thousands can mean seventy. Which is it?"

"Twenty grand per round. Recommended for five rounds over the course of a year."

It doesn't take me long to do the math. A hundred grand. I sink into my chair, my shoulders rounding forward, as though even they are drained. We do not have that kind of money laying around.

He must sense my hesitation because he chimes in before the silence gets any more awkward. "I know that's a hefty price tag, but I wouldn't have proposed it if I wasn't confident."

"Sure," I say because my brain's in a haze of dollar signs.

"Maybe take some time to talk it over with your family."

"Sure. Okay."

"There's something else. I'm obligated to notify the Department of Motor Vehicles whenever a patient begins a course of treatment for conditions like Alzheimer's."

"You mean I can't drive anymore?"

"It's probably not the wisest decision. I know things may not seem so severe yet, but you never know."

Yet.

The buoyancy with which we started this conversation is gone. Only gravity remains.

I'm the one to hang up first. The phone slides from my ear and I tap the red icon with my thumb.

The no-driving idea seems paltry compared to the main point of our conversation. But, a hundred thousand dollars?

Possibilities flash through my mind. A second mortgage. Credit card debt. None of it sounds logical. Is there a payment plan for Alzheimer's treatment?

***

The rest of my day is pointless. I can't focus on work when the possibility of something so huge hovers within my reach. I couldn't tell you what I taught in my last two classes.

How unfair for there to be a potentially life-saving treatment that the majority of patients can't afford? Christine and I consider ourselves lucky. We make decent salaries—nowhere near our state school counterparts, but still. Our life is comfortable. Abbie gets spoiled every Christmas and birthday. If we can't afford this treatment, what about the little old lady working the register at the dollar store?

It's cruel.

Christine and Abbie meet me in the parking lot at four-thirty.

"How was class?" I say to whomever feels like answering.

"Riveting." Abbie slogs past me, opens the back door and heaves her backpack-clad self in.

"Don't be so enthusiastic."

I round the car to the driver's side.

"I can drive," Christine says, but it sounds less like a casual offer and more like insistence.

I flash her big eyes. "So can I."

I've been driving for over thirty-five years, I highly doubt I'll forget how. Christine's hesitance puts a serious damper on my mood. We drive home in near silence, save for the breathy sing-talk coming from the radio.

"What is this?" I grumble.

"Billie Eilish," I hear from the back seat.

"Well, he's terrible. This is not music." I flip the station.

"She's not a—oh *forget it.*" Abbie groans and puts in her ear buds. I use the rest of the short drive to hype myself back up for what I need to discuss with my wife. When we get home, we file in through the garage, dropping our bags on the kitchen counter.

Abbie sits on a barstool, flicking through her phone. I sway on my feet and bite my thumbnail like a rabid animal. Christine gives me a look that says, *Are you having some sort of episode or something?*

"Abbie, would you mind giving Mom and I a minute alone?"

Our daughter looks up from her phone and her eyes dart between Christine and me. Then, as though it takes tremendous effort, she hoists herself from the stool with a huff and steps from the kitchen.

"What is it?" Christine says when Abbie's out of earshot.

I lock eyes with her like my life depends on it. "We need to talk."

Abbie

I climb the stairs loud enough so they know I'm gone. In my room, I crank the music like I always do, but instead of staying, I quietly creep back downstairs and sit on the bottom step, just around the corner from the kitchen.

"That's good news, right?" I hear Mom say.

"Well, sort of," Ma replies. They're speaking in hushed tones, which makes me nervous. I already know Ma has Alzheimer's, what else don't they want me to know?

"How can a promising new treatment be anything but good?"

"It's not covered by insurance. Too new. Too experimental."

"So that means..."

"It means we'd have to pay out of pocket. A hundred grand."

Mom's silent and I can picture her face. It's probably the same one she gave me when I told her I spent a hundred dollars on clunky sneakers she claimed she owned thirty years ago.

I don't pay my own bills yet, but I'm no dummy. A hundred grand is a shit ton of money. Like four-years-of-college kind of money. I have no idea how much my moms have in savings, but I do know Mom puts back a pack of chicken breasts when she finds one that's fifty cents cheaper. And that Ma makes excuses why she always takes the budget airline even though I know it's just because it's less expensive.

"But how?" Mom finally says.

"I've been brainstorming. What if we sold my car? Drop down to one vehicle. I could get one of those, those..."

She doesn't finish the sentence, but I imagine she's twirling a finger trying to come up with the word. This has been happening more and more lately. The other day she struggled to remember the word "granola," and instead called it "that crunchy stuff."

"One of what?" Mom prompts her.

"Oh, you know, those..."

I inch forward and peek my head around the corner just enough to see what's going on. Ma's sitting at the table and even in profile I can tell her face is wrinkled in frustration. Mom sits opposite her, leaning forward slightly as though she wants to reach in and pull the word from Ma's cobwebby brain.

"Damnit!" Ma shouts, as she slams her palm onto the table. "I can see it in my head perfectly! The thing with two wheels that you can ride."

"A bike?"

"Yes, thank you. A bike."

Ma crumbles forward, lays the side of her head against the table. I can just barely hear what she's saying now, so I strain my eyes to try to read her lips.

"Fuck this," she says. "Fuck this whole thing."

Mom scoots across and puts a hand on Ma's shoulder. I haven't seen them this close for a long time.

"It'll be all right," Mom says.

"I can't live like this, Chris."

The moment feels too private, too intimate, so I crawl back up the stairs without making a noise. My limbs feel heavy. I fall onto my bed as though all the energy has been sucked from my body, and grab my sketchpad like I always do when I need to work something out in my head.

Ma is really sick. This doesn't look good. If this new medicine is her only hope, we've got to find a way to get it.

And that's when it hits me.

I can help. Mom won't let me get a job—she says I have the whole rest of my life to work and I should just enjoy being a kid—but that doesn't mean I can't find another stream of income.

I grab my phone but stop short of dialing. A knot in my stomach makes me hesitate. I said I wouldn't. I said it was over. If I make this call, put this all into motion, there's no going back.

A text pops up, startling me so much I drop the phone. Jesus, fuck. The message is from Trina. Not now, Trina. I swipe it away, refocus.

I bite my lip, weighing the choices.

Don't do it, my gut says.

But Ma, my heart says.

My fingers tap the key pad. The phone rings against my ear. When she answers, my heart leaps. I keep my voice low, though my music makes it impossible for my moms to hear me from downstairs. Still, I'm not taking any chances.

"Hey Stacia. Do you know anyone taking my mom's classes this semester?"

143

Christine

Sneaking off campus with Micah is harder in the winter. I have to drive slower on the snow-covered roads, and then when we finally make it to our spot, we have so many layers of clothes to remove, we're left with fewer precious moments together.

"Why can't we just stay in your office," he said last week. "Guys aren't big fans of the cold, if you know what I mean." He'd looked down then gave me a wink.

The car *was* getting a little cramped, so I agreed—with one condition. It would have to be after everyone left for the day. There'd been too many close calls with my fellow faculty. One too many students walking past my closed door while Micah's face was between my legs. It freaked me out.

That's why this new evening arrangement is perfect. No one around. I can give him my full attention.

Micah's meeting me here at six. I told Joss there was a speaker on campus I wanted to see. And Abbie? She's been hanging out with friends lately, even getting rides home with some of them.

I'm drumming my fingers on my desk when the clock strikes six. A few minutes later, I'm just starting to consider he's bailed on me, when there's a quiet knock on the door. I practically leap across my desk to get there. The anticipation of our meetings makes me feel uninhibited and light, a younger version of myself. Before the ticking clock of life got closer and closer to The End.

"Hi," he says in that voice that makes my heart thump.

I snatch his hand and pull him in, locking the door behind us.

* * *

We're laying side by side on the floor, him on his back, my head on his chest. His skin is so smooth I want to dissolve right into it.

"How old are you?" he asks, breaking the silence I had been enjoying.

"What? Why do you ask?"

"I know you have a daughter here, so I have a guess."

I lift my head to look at him, then put it back down again. Sometimes seeing his face so close makes me realize just how much younger his is than mine.

"Age is just a number," I say, because I'm definitely not telling him I'm fifty even though his guess is probably close. "Why, do I seem old to you?"

"This gray hair does."

I whip up and press my hair back. "Hey," I say. "Not nice." He's laughing so I laugh too despite the flame I feel in my cheeks. "I don't have any gray and you know it."

The truth is I would be almost completely gray if it weren't for Nicolai who does my color every month. My mother had a head full of silver hair before she turned forty. Ten years later, she was dead.

I give him a playful punch. Now that I'm sitting up, my boobs don't look so good. Gravity and age sucked all the life from them, and they just sort of hang there, like two empty socks. I pull on my blouse, leaving the top two buttons open to still feel a little sexy. Micah lays there, fully confident in all his youthful glory.

"I brought something," he says and reaches for his coat. He pulls out a flask, hands it to me.

"Great, so now I'm drinking with students too?"

145

"Not students, just me."

I consider it for a moment. What the hell. I twist off the cap, take a swig, and wince as the liquid stings my throat. "What is this?"

"Tequila."

"Perfect." I hand him the flask. He takes a long pull.

"So, how long have you been married?" The question catches me off guard and my heart skips a beat. We've never talk about my family. I wear a wedding band, but nowadays people wear all sorts of jewelry on whatever fingers they want.

I'm still processing the question, when Micah continues. "I took Dr. Matson's organic chemistry class sophomore year but dropped it after the first week. Fucking insane."

"So, not only do you know I'm married, but you know I'm married to a woman."

"Small school."

"And you still pursued me?"

"I'm pretty sure you were the one pursuing me."

"Whoa whoa whoa. Absolutely not. You came onto me. Kept getting closer and closer, til the day you finally kissed me."

"You didn't stop me."

This flirty banter is getting me excited again. It's all so...wrong. I know it but can't help not egging him on.

I run a hand through my hair. "It doesn't matter. We're here now. So..."

"Have you ever slept with a guy before me?"

Jesus. This is getting deep. I'm not sure I'm ready to lay out my entire sexual history. Hell, I'm not sure I even understand this new turn of events. I hold out my hand toward the flask. "Gimme that." The alcohol is like fire in my mouth but I take a huge gulp, then shake my head to swallow down the burn.

"One in high school. Couple in college," I say. "Lots of girls. Women know women's bodies better than men."

"So you're bi."

I consider it for a second, this label. I've always thought of sexuality as a spectrum, and knew I floated along it. I just didn't realize how much closer to the middle I was—it's been a while.

"I guess. But I've been married to Joss—to Dr. Matson—for twenty-three years, so I haven't really thought about it."

The mention of Joss makes my ribcage constrict. I quickly flip the script to Micah. "What about you? Always going for older women?"

"You're the first."

"What would your parents think?" I murmur, not really wanting an answer. I sure as hell know how I'd feel if Abbie were—no, I can't even go there.

"Parent. Singular. It's just my mom."

"What about your dad?"

"Never knew the bastard." He shakes his head. "But it's cool. My mom, she'd do anything for us."

I get it. I'd do anything for Abbie, too.

"Us?"

"Me and my sister."

My chest tightens. There's a long pause. "I had a brother...before cancer took him."

"I'm sorry. What was his name?"

"Fisher. We were twins."

"Fisher," he says, wistful.

"Why do you ask?"

"I think names are important. If you say them out loud, the person's not really ever gone."

The statement is so profound, I bring a hand to my heart as though I'm physically holding it inside my body. My eyes glisten, so moved by his depth—I'm not sure I've ever heard such a beautiful truth about death. My head swims with memories. "He was a good man."

The quiet is mutual for a few long minutes, then I take another swig of liquor and change the subject back to something less painful and soon we're laughing again.

We finish the contents of the flask. My body is warm, my eyelids heavy. I wish I could lay down on Micah and sleep for the night, but I know that's impossible.

His phone beeps from inside his coat. "I should probably get going," he says. When I glance to the little clock on my bookshelf, I'm shocked to see it's already eight-thirty.

Micah stands first, then offers a hand to help me up. My legs feel weak, and I giggle a little when he finally gets me to an upright position.

"Someone's a lightweight," he says, and I slap his arm.

We get dressed. I don't bother to fix my hair or tuck in my shirt. Campus will be empty at this hour. We're just about to leave when a noise makes us both jump. It's a key in my door. Micah flies behind my desk and crouches into a ball. I don't have time to do anything before the door flies open.

A man in a worn long sleeve shirt and jeans stands there, one hand on the knob. He practically jumps out of his skin when he sees me not two feet in front of him.

"Christ, you scared me," he says, taking a step back.

I recognize him. It's the same man from a few weeks ago—the one who'd cleaned up our lunch meeting. I try to recall his name, but can't, until I see the script font on his shirt: Lester.

"I was just coming to change the garbage," he says. There's a cart behind him, stocked with a bucket of cleaning bottles, a mop, and trash bags. I exhale, knowing it's not a serial killer. But that does nothing for the fact that there's a student—a student I was just fucking—hiding behind my desk.

"Of course. Sure. Sorry to have startled you. I'm not usually here this late." I move back to let him in. His teeth point in every which direction, and his eyes are just as buggy as before. There's a certain creepiness to him, the scrawny frame, the long fingers. I don't know this man beyond our two interactions, but I instantly don't trust him.

The whole time he's changing the garbage bag, I'm thinking about Micah huddled mere inches away, separated only by the side of my desk as a shield. I break into a cold sweat and everything slows down.

Just change the damn bag, I want to scream.

When he's done, he goes back to the door. My body relaxes. We're almost in the clear.

But then Lester stops. My eyes follow to what he's looking at. I'm smacked with a sudden dizziness.

"That your coat?" he says, pointing.

Of course it's not, and we both know it, because my coat is slung over the crook of my elbow. Plus, Micah's coat is clearly a man's style and is much too big for me.

"Oh," I stutter. "A student left it here earlier." I take a step toward him, hoping it will be a signal for him to leave. I need him out of this office *now*.

He looks at the coat again, then back at me. I smile and hold eye contact to establish dominance. This is *my* domain, not yours, sir. Lester does a final scan of my office before stepping back through the doorway into the hall where his cart waits. He lingers for a beat. I can tell he doesn't believe me. But what's he going to do, ransack my office?

I close the door, as Lester pushes his cart away. Micah climbs out from behind my desk, eyes wide and a goofy smile on his face.

"That was intense!" he says, grabbing my face and kissing me hard.

My tequila buzz slipped away the minute Lester's key entered my door, but now I can taste the liquor on Micah's tongue, so I let it bring me back.

"Imagine what the school would say, you bad, bad girl," he says between kisses.

"That's not going to happen."

I let him feel me up one more time before I pull away. "It's almost nine," I say. "We really should go." I have to be back to this very spot—in professional mode—in less than twelve hours.

Micah goes for the door, but I intercept. "Me first."

I poke my head out and look both ways. The hall is dim with only half the lights on. It's filled with shadows, but appears empty. I cross my fingers.

We leave and I lock the door behind me. Micah goes one way and I go the other. I keep my head low.

Joss

The rabbit's foot is gone from my desk. The spot in which it lives is empty, a gaping hole in my neatly-arranged workspace. I notice it right away, as I go to stroke the silky brown fur but come up empty. For a split second I think maybe I left it on campus, and bemoan the task of driving there on a Sunday. But no, the rabbit's foot travels with me, to and from, just like my laptop. Only now, I have a laptop and no rabbit's foot.

I stare blankly until it becomes clear.

It's Christine, I know it is.

She's always hated my rabbit's foot, and now she's taken it upon herself to dispose of it, thinking my forgetfulness will extend to missing personal possessions, too. Damn her. How ballsy to try to slip this past me. I'm not that far gone that I wouldn't notice a key piece of my writing routine missing.

I stomp to the bedroom and rifle through her nightstand, whipping open the drawer and tossing its contents onto the bed. A spiral journal flops on the comforter, followed by a pen, a couple cough drops, an old prescription bottle.

Where did she put it?

I whisk to the kitchen next. Christine's at the counter grading. I fly past her and pull open the garbage, reaching directly into a layer of plate scrapings from last night. I grab hold of a Lean Cuisine box and whip it out of the can and onto the floor, a slew of food remnants trailing behind.

"What in the hell are you doing?" Christine shouts, jumping from her chair. She's on me in a second, reaching over my shoulders to grab my hands that dig through the waste. "Stop! Joss, stop!"

"I know you threw it out," I shout.

"I don't know what you're talking about!"

I'm elbow deep now, but haven't found the rabbit's foot. Maybe she didn't toss it after all. She hid it.

I move to the silverware drawer, yank it open and rummage through, leaving food droppings atop the perfectly polished utensils. Not there. Onto the next drawer. I reach into the mass of spatulas and serving spoons, pushing this way and that, frantically searching. I'm like a rabid animal. That rabbit's foot is here and I will find it.

Another drawer comes up empty.

"Where did you put it?" I hiss.

"Put what?"

"Just because you don't like something doesn't give you the right to steal it. You know what that means to me. It wasn't yours to take." I'm rushing out of the kitchen now, Christine hot on my heels.

"Joss, calm down. What are you missing? I didn't take anything."

I go to the bathroom, yank open the medicine cabinet, clear the shelves in a single swoop. I'll tear this house apart if I have to.

"Joss!"

"My rabbit's foot! I know you took it. Give it back!"

"I didn't take it, I swear." She's trying to get my hands, to reign me in, but I push her away. She fumbles into the toilet.

"Joss, you're bleeding. Stop, please!"

Her words go in one ear and out the other, not stopping in the middle for processing. I round the corner, using the doorframe as a slingshot. Where to next? Abbie's room? Would Christine really hide it there?

I fly down the hall and burst through Abbie's door. She bolts up when I come barreling through. Her music is so loud, she must not have heard our elevated voices.

"What the—" But she doesn't have time to finish her sentence because Christine tackles me from behind and we fall onto Abbie's bed like a football player being sacked.

"Enough!" Christine hollers. Her arms are wrapped around me. I wriggle to try to get away, but she has some sort of inhuman strength even though I have thirty pounds on her.

"Ma, why are you bleeding?" Abbie says.

It's then that I feel the sharp sting and look to its source. My hand is covered in bright blood, the cuff of my sleeve turning rusty. The gash runs down the outside of my pointer finger, stopping somewhere before the crease of my thumb, though I can't be exactly sure because of the blood.

I tremble. Christine loosens her grip.

"I'm bleeding," I say, trance-like.

"I tried to tell you," Christine says, reaching for a T-shirt on Abbie's dresser. She wraps it tightly around my hand. "You sliced it on something in that drawer. Didn't you feel it?"

"No."

I didn't feel a thing, but now I do. Almost as though a hypnosis has worn off, taking with it my inability to feel pain.

"How do you not feel yourself cutting your finger?" Abbie says. She's staring, horrified, and I'm not sure if it's my hand or the fact that the T-shirt Christine grabbed was one of her favorites.

"I don't know, I just didn't." I glance toward the door from where I came just moments earlier, replay the last five minutes in my head. There's blood on the doorframe and a few drops across Abbie's carpet. My body's shaking now, shock settling in.

"C'mon," Christine says, getting to her feet. "We need to clean this up."

We retrace our steps to the kitchen, following a trail of blood along the way.

"I'm sorry," I choke. "I didn't know."

She doesn't respond, just pulls me along like a toddler, my hand elevated to squelch the throbbing. We get to the sink and Christine unwraps the shirt. The cut is long, but doesn't look deep enough to require stitches.

"What the hell was that all about?" she says, running my hand under the faucet.

"My rabbit's foot. It's gone."

"And you immediately assume I took it?"

"You hate that thing. You think it's stupid."

"That doesn't mean I would throw it out. Why would you jump to that conclusion?"

I don't have an answer—it's just what made logical sense. I cast my eyes down, feeling bad for blaming her, and also for the blood stains that now form a trail through our house.

"But that still doesn't explain where it went," I say.

Christine gets a butterfly bandage from the box that landed on the floor of the bathroom during my rampage. Two strips cover the slice. It pounds when she presses the adhesive, a heartbeat in my finger.

I follow Christine to my office, Abbie meeting us at the top of the steps. The three of us enter and approach my desk. Without a word, Christine steps forward and lifts the papers and notebooks that scatter across the top. I normally wouldn't let anyone touch my work, but I feel like I'm a child being scolded, and something tells me I shouldn't open my mouth at this exact moment.

She checks another stack of folders, moving the pile to the side, peering behind. She reaches for something out of sight, retracts her arm and holds her findings up for Abbie and I to see.

My rabbit's foot.

"But... How did it get back there?"

"I don't know," she says, "But it was there the whole time. I told you I didn't take it."

Christine extends it out to me and I take it with my good hand. She brushes past me.

"Excuse me," she says, "I have some cleaning to do."

153

Abbie

I've done the math. Mom's teaching four classes. Each class averages about three exams each. That's twelve exams over the course of the semester. Her classes usually fill up, which means there's at least forty students per class. If I charge a hundred bucks a pop, and get a roster of clients, I'll be well on my way to helping pay for Ma's medicine. Turn around and do it all again next fall, and *boom*: treatment covered.

"Hey Eeyore, start the car, will ya?" Mom tosses me her keys, and I give her a look from where I've been waiting on the bench by the front door. I yank my hood over my head and grab my bag. The wind assaults my face.

"Fuck, it's cold," I mutter to myself.

Mom's car is parked at the end of the driveway, trapping Ma's in since she doesn't go many places now anyway—shouldn't at all, really. Normally, we'd play a game of who-has-to-leave-first. But lately, Ma's car sits mostly idle. They're still debating whether to sell it.

The wind howls. I hate how it's called spring semester when there's a foot of snow on the ground. Nothing about below-freezing temperatures and scraping ice from a car windshield screams spring. I should be used to it by now, but every morning I have to slip my feet into my duck boots, a piece of my soul dies.

The other reason winter sucks? No more soccer. The world is a bit smaller without my sport. But that's okay because I have something new to focus on: getting as many people as I can to buy Mom's tests.

Stacia said she'd "pass along the info" to a few of her friends. She owes me—she'd said so herself. Knowing her, she'll choose just the right people, who will then tell a couple more, and the offer will spread.

The car is freezing, and I sit on my hands to warm them up. Mom comes out the front door a few minutes later. She's wearing a puffer coat that belts at the waist and black boots with shearling at the top.

"Brrr!" she says, tossing her bag in the back and doing a little shiver-shimmy in her seat. "Ready?"

I nod. She's been unusually cheerful lately, especially given the circumstances. I mean, her wife is facing an involuntary shove into dementia, but Mom's walking around with a shit-eating grin on her face most of the time. What gives? I think it's all an act. I bet she cries every night in bed.

"Mom," I ease into it, "Are you okay?"

"What do you mean? Okay with what?"

"With Ma. The Alzheimer's. It just seems like you're putting on a brave face, when I have to imagine it's got to be pretty shitty."

She gives me a quick glance, but then keeps her eyes on the snow-covered roads. Our town's not known for its excellence in snow plowing.

"I'm trying to stay optimistic, if that's what you mean."

"Yeah, me too." My voice trails off. I look out my window and watch the houses go by. Then, after a stretch of silence, "Do you think she's going to die?"

Mom reaches a hand to my leg. "Oh, Abbie, no. I mean, we're all going to die eventually, but Ma's a fighter. She's not going to let this take her down. Don't let yourself think like that. We have to rally, to support each other, okay?"

155

"Okay," I mumble. But there's something else that just occurred to me and it brings a sour taste to my mouth. My stomach feels like it's trapped in a vice. "Am I going to get Alzheimer's, too?"

"Why would you think that?" Mom says, her mouth turned down into a frown.

"You know why. We all know why."

She stares at me, but doesn't acknowledge what we're both thinking.

"It's a hereditary disease, Mom. Even I know that," I say. She's silent. Refusing to confirm nor deny. "Why won't you guys just tell me? Don't you think I have a right to know what genes I carry?"

Her lips are pressed into a thin line, and I can tell she's thinking. Maybe this is finally the moment. If a life-threatening disease isn't enough for them to come clean to me, then I don't know what is.

"You're nineteen, Abbie," she finally says. "You don't need to be worrying about Alzheimer's right now. What we need to do is focus on Ma and move forward with this new reality we're facing, okay? I can't take an added layer of stress right now. We're both your moms and that's the way we want to keep it."

I huff and cross my arms. She's being so selfish. If I had any lingering guilt about stealing from Mom, it's gone.

***

Getting the exams has been easier than I expected. I know Mom's password, I know how she organizes her folders. I can walk around the faculty hall so freely, given who I am. Everyone knows me—the sweet, quiet daughter of one of the school's favorite teachers. It's almost too easy, really.

My phone is now crammed with numbers of students looking for my "services." They text me things like, Count me in and I've got cash. I reply with a meeting date and time. Give them a set of folded papers, and pocket a Benjamin.

It's only been two weeks—only three of Mom's classes have had an exam—but I've already made close to five thousand dollars. It feels like gold in my hands. It feels like Ma's future.

Now I just need to get it to her.

Christine

We had a particularly bad night. Joss kept waking with nightmares, saying she was lost in a forest and couldn't get out. I tried my best to calm her. Placed my hands on her shoulders, hoping the weight would ground her. Told her she was safe. Eventually we'd lay back down, only to have her repeat the same cycle again an hour later.

The neurologist had explained sundowning, but I'd rejected it as just another thing that wouldn't happen to my strong, resilient Joss. Now I get it. It's like the lower the sun dips in the sky, the more agitated she becomes. Nighttime is our new hell.

She's sweat through her night shirt, so I get a new one from the dresser—the striped ones with contrasting piping at the collar. I got all three of us matching sets from Old Navy years ago—back when Joss and I still touched and talked. Back when we'd put aside $100 every month for a babysitter fund because date nights were something we valued.

What happened to us?

I'm exhausted. The Alzheimer's is wearing on me too. Over the last few weeks, I've found myself nodding off during meetings, unable to keep my eyes open much past the seven o'clock news. I'm slipping in my work. Between worrying about Joss, and spending time with Micah, my classes have become my last priority. When I get tenure, it won't matter anyway. My job will be secure.

But Joss's—that's another story.

"This isn't working," I say to her as we're getting ready for work. I dab concealer under my eyes but it's doing a shoddy job of hiding my dark circles. We're side by side at our double-sink vanity—one of the things we quickly realized after marriage that would be a must-have. "Don't you think it's worth asking about an extended sabbatical? Or a medical leave?"

"I'm fine. My classes are going great."

I give her a deadpan look, one set of lashes painted black, the wand extended to the other. "Your classes are not going great and you know it." *Does she though?*

"I was late twice."

"You missed an entire class. Forgot how to use the projector. You're behind on all your grading." I place a hand on her arm. "Joss, it's okay. You don't have to be the hero here."

"I'm just doing my job, Chris. Try letting someone tell you to quit. See how you like it."

"I never said quit. Maybe just a little more time. Until this treatment works." I add in the last part purely for optimism—for both of us.

Joss bristles. She swipes on a thin layer of pale lip gloss and leaves the bathroom.

Our drives to and from campus are becoming more and more tense. No one wants to talk about the obvious, the fact that Joss is no longer capable of doing her job. It's a false reality we're living in, yet every time I bring it up, to try to show I care, she instantly shuts down. I'm in a lose-lose situation, a fight I don't want to have but one I know needs to happen.

We're walking from the parking lot, about to split to our own respective buildings, when Dean Redwood approaches, as though he's been standing in the cold waiting for us.

"Just the two I was hoping to bump into," he says with a wan smile I don't quite believe. In fact, I don't believe it at all, because as we all turn to walk together, he flashes me a look Joss doesn't see. It's a look of concern: hooded eyes and a pained gaze.

* * *

Dean Redwood fights my battle for me.

The chemistry department has pulled in adjuncts to finish Joss's course load.

"Take some time," Ken says in his gravelly voice. "Let us worry about the rest of the semester. You just rest up. Then we'll all be raring and ready to go for next fall. Hmm?"

Joss can barely meet our eyes. When I try to give her a hug, she pulls away, mumbles something about going home. I let her go.

When I get back to my office, I text Micah.

Need to see you.

He doesn't respond even though I know he's not in class. I should forget about it. Should do a final run-through of today's PowerPoint. But I don't. Instead, I text him again, fingers fast and sure.

Bleachers?

We don't have time to take my car somewhere. It's not even sex I want. Just the comfort of his presence. The temporary relief of his hug. To talk to someone about something other than my wife turning into a ninety-year-old.

No response.

My chin quivers, spurred by a sudden wash of emotion that takes me by surprise. Please, Micah. I need to forget.

I grab my bag and leave on foot, heading God knows where, but just hoping I'll bump into him in the next twenty minutes before my class starts.

Campus is bustling with students in between classes. I scan their faces as we pass each other. None of them are Micah. I check my phone again. Still no response from him. Why isn't he answering me? Something I want to call anger, but what feels like embarrassment, bubbles inside.

After wandering around a bit longer, the throngs of students dissipate. Soon it's just me trudging up a sidewalk between buildings. I peek at the time and see it's already five after the hour. I'm late for my own class, and I still have to go back to my office to get my things.

Great, not again.

Each time, I fly into class with a cheerfully apologetic excuse, and the students are all too happy to forgive—that, or they just don't care. Today should be no different.

I break into a light jog, as I round one building and see mine up ahead. By the time I get to my office and then to class two floors up, sweat drips down my back. My face is flushed, and I'm struggling to catch my breath when I enter the lecture hall. I'm twenty minutes late to a fifty-minute class.

The seats are half empty. A girl near the front lowers her phone and looks at me. "The rest of them left. Fifteen-minute rule."

"Oh," I say, embarrassed. Professors can be late, but not *this* late. I've never had students actually leave because they'd waited so long. Now my lectures will be all messed up. "I'm sorry, I—" But I can't even think of anything good on the spot.

"It's cool," she says. "I would have left too, but I'm just waiting here til my next class." A couple of the other students nod in agreement.

"All right. Well, I guess we'll just pick up next time." I spin on my heels back toward the door, then stop. "Sorry about that, folks," I add, because these people are going to be evaluating me at the end of the semester and I can't afford for them to be annoyed. I've never had anything but stellar evals, so I'm hoping this little blip won't come back to bite me. I'll bring them donuts next class to make up for it.

Back in my office, I text Micah again.

Hello? Why aren't you answering me?

Three little dots appear, and my heart skips.

Sorry, busy.

"Busy?" I say to my phone. A burning sensation prickles my chest. Too busy to respond to a simple text? A word floats into my head, one I've heard Abbie use, but didn't understand fully until now: Ghosted.

Nausea rolls in my stomach. I put the phone down and bring a hand to my mouth. Whatever's in there is threatening to come up. I barrel out of my office to the bathroom, making it to the first stall just in time to vomit. Not much comes out though since I haven't had anything to eat, so it's more dry heaves than anything. My body clenches, angry at the force with which it repels the contents of my stomach. I'm glad there's no one else in here to listen to these boorish sounds.

When I'm finally able to breathe, I go to the sink, cup my hands under the faucet and bring the water to my mouth. I swish and spit any foul remnants. My hands are shaky. I feel as though I've been run over—totally depleted.

It's then, as I stare at my sallow face in the mirror, that I see it. The reflection of it in the mirror: a tampon dispenser hanging on the wall. My vision blurs, my breathing goes shallow, and I try to answer the question that's just hit me in the face. When was my last period?

Joss

Our mail is not usually very exciting. Bills, direct mailers, Abbie's *Seventeen* magazine she says she's outgrown but that Christine keeps renewing. No one sends letters anymore. Life's too busy to hand write notes, I suppose. Not that I can really talk—I haven't sent a letter to someone in ages. Still, it's nice to find a short, fat envelope in the mail instead of the long, skinny ones you know are just bills.

I pull the handful from the mailbox and flip through it as I walk back to the door. More of the same. That is, until I come to a small blue envelope addressed to me in a messy scrawl that either belongs to a child or a centenarian.

My nose wrinkles, and I tilt my head, wondering who on Earth it's from. Then I stop in my tracks. Is it my birthday? Have I forgotten my own birthday? I gaze up, thinking. No, it's February. My birthday was in November.

Curious, I slip a finger under the back flap and tear it open. Inside, there's a folded piece of paper. I remove it. It feels thick in my hand, like there's something inside. When I unfold it, a handful of cash floats to the ground. There's an assortment: mostly twenties and fifties, but also tens and fives, and even a couple hundreds.

A gasp escapes my lips, as I stare at the pile of money. "Blimey," I whisper. A gentle breeze uplifts two of the bills, sending them rolling, and I bend down and gather them into a pile. I have no idea what this is for or who it's from, I only know I don't want a bunch of cash tumbling down the street.

At first, I think it must be a mistake. This must have been intended for someone else. A neighbor perhaps? I turn the envelope over again. Sure enough, my name's there, front and center. There's no mistaking it: this money was sent to me.

The bills stacked in my hand, I hurry into the house, as though I've done something illegal. I don't know exactly how much money is here, but it feels like a lot, and having a wad of cash out in the open seems wildly suspicious.

I put the money on the bench inside the door and open the folded paper all the way. Two short sentences appear in the same messy handwriting:

For your treatment. More to come.

I draw a sharp breath. My eyes go from the note to the money and back again. I walk to the window and peer through a slit in the curtains, hoping to see someone—anyone—on whom I can accredit this letter. I half expect someone to jump out of the bushes and yell "Gotcha!" like I'm on that *Punk'd* show from years ago.

This can't be real. But it is.

It's real, but I can't accept it.

Who would give me all this money? We don't have rich friends. Hell, we haven't even told many friends about my diagnosis—at least I don't think we have. Maybe Christine has told more people than I realize. But still, I can't think of anyone who would randomly send anonymous money.

I grab the envelope again and realize it's not even postmarked. There's no stamp, which means it must have been hand delivered to our mailbox. Whoever sent this money must live in our town.

My brain is reeling now. I go through every friend, relative and neighbor I can possibly think of. None of it makes sense.

My legs have gone weak, so I have a seat on the bench next to the cash. I touch it. It's beautiful. Full of promise. Should I keep it? Even if I didn't want to, I wouldn't know who to return it to.

So, I let myself daydream about the possibility. The new medicine with all its hope. And myself, returning to the woman I once was.

***

"You guys aren't going to believe this." I practically attack Christine and Abbie when they walk through the door. I hold up the money.

"Where'd you get all that?" Christine says, eyes like saucers.

"It came today in the mail. With this." I show them the letter. "Addressed to me, but with no return address and not even a postmark. I have no idea, you guys, but talk about a blessing. Someone's a good Samaritan. Someone wants to help."

"Whoa," Abbie says, fanning the cash, "that's a lot of dough."

"Enough to get my first dose started." I'm smiling so hard my cheeks hurt.

"That's incredible, hon," Christine says. "But aren't you a little curious? I mean, it feels strange to just accept this much money out of nowhere."

"Of course I'm curious. I've been sitting here all day thinking about where this money came from and whether we should keep it. But I keep coming to the same conclusion. Whoever sent it wants me to have it and they don't want any recognition for it. It's an anonymous offering."

"I'd totally keep it," Abbie says.

"Thank you," I say, giving her a nod of approval.

"I mean, it's not like you're going on a shopping spree or something. You're using it to stay alive."

I drop my head, giving her a sidelong glance. "I'm very much alive, thank you, but I understand your point. The money is for treatment, and that's exactly what I'd use it for."

Christine's staring at me like she doesn't know what to say. I get it. I didn't know what to say at first either.

"Chris, this is a gift. Let's accept it."

"Of course," she says, seemingly snapping out of her daze. "It's a wonderful gift and whoever it's from is an angel. We should call your doctor."

"Already did. I can pick up the first dose tomorrow."

Abbie claps, and I'm so happy I join her. Soon the three of us are jumping up and down in a circle. I pull them into a group hug. My heart bursts with joy, a faith I haven't felt to this point. Only when I make eye contact with my wife, when our faces are mere inches apart, and when she quickly darts from my gaze, does the light inside me dim just a little.

December 2001

*G*et over here, quick!"

"What?" she says, jumping up from where she's bundled in a thick fleece blanket. She dashes to me, plops down on the couch, eyes frantic. "What is it?"

"You've gotta feel this," I say. "Baby's going nuts in there."

Her face relaxes. "Jesus, you scared me."

I lift my shirt, then take her hand and put it on my swollen stomach. My belly button popped last week, something I had no idea was even a thing. I've been self-conscious of it—there's absolutely nothing sexy about the end of pregnancy—but she says it's cute.

The baby kicks so hard we both jump. "Feel that?"

"That was a big one," she says with a giant smile.

"Just imagine what it feels like on the inside!"

We laugh and she curls up next to me, leaving her hand on my belly. I move it around when I feel the baby reposition. I want her to feel just as involved in this pregnancy as I am.

She shivers. "I need my blanket," she says.

"It's not even cold."

"You insist on making this house an icebox." She gives my leg a pinch before returning to her chair and burrowing under the throw again. The glow of the Christmas tree casts the room in a soft glow.

It's true—growing a human has increased my body temperature by a thousand degrees. If I could walk around naked in the snow I would. Well, maybe not—that wouldn't be a pretty sight with these extra pounds.

"I wish you didn't have to start spring semester," she says, even though we've been over this. I'd rather get my classes going before someone takes over in six weeks when the baby comes. "You're going to be exhausted waddling around campus every day in a coat and boots."

"Excuse me, waddling?" I throw a pillow at her face.

"You know what I mean."

"Get back over here," I say, reaching my arms out. I don't want our lazy holiday to end.

"I'm not leaving this blanket."

I wink. "I'll warm you up."

She slithers toward me and our bodies cocoon together, big belly and all. Our intimacy has waned these last few months, but the pregnancy books say that's normal—it'll return.

Bing Crosby croons in the background. I look to the tree and picture another set of presents under it next year. Presents for our child.

She intertwines her fingers with mine. I love us. I hope we stay like this forever.

Abbie

I've never seen Ma so happy as when she got the first chunk of money. A smile so big, I thought her face might crack in half. Seeing her reaction made stealing the exams worth it and only fuels my determination to get more.

I'm supposed to meet a guy tonight for a handoff. I've been trying to do all the trades during the day, since there's not an easy excuse for me to go back to campus in the evenings like there was in the fall when I had soccer practice. Still, I've had to make nighttime runs twice now, and neither Mom or Ma seem overly concerned.

"I'm going to campus for a study group," I tell them, as we finish dinner.

"You are? What about *The Voice*?" Mom says.

"You can watch it without me."

"Aw, but that's no fun."

"Sorry, Mom. School comes first," I mock and give a little shrug.

When I get to campus it's dark, with only the snow and a few scattered lamp posts lighting up my path. I haven't printed the exam yet—don't like to carry around too many copies on me at once—so I head to Mom's office, where I use my key to sneak in.

I leave the light off, so as not to attract suspicion, though I doubt there will be anyone in the halls at this time. Her laptop sits in the middle of her desk. I round the corner and roll the chair close. I open the lid and it fires to life.

The password's still the same as earlier, thank goodness. It will be changing soon, as the school requires everyone to update their passwords on a regular basis. I'll cross that bridge when I get to it. Right now it works, and that's all that matters.

The background of Mom's computer is a picture of the three of us. My gut twists, so I raise a hand to cover the picture. I don't need my moms staring at me while I'm in thief mode.

I open the folder and find the exam file. Double click. It opens. I do a quick scroll to make sure it's all there. Yes. This is almost becoming too easy. Coach's voice rings in my head, warning not to get too cocky when we're winning by a landslide.

I'm not cocky—am I?

Just as I'm about to hit Print, a noise makes me flinch. I look up to see the doorknob turning. I don't have time to exit the screen before the door flies open.

Joss

The house is quiet without Abbie. Even when she's glued to her phone, there's still the presence of her—the hum of her music, the footsteps in and out of the kitchen.

Christine and I wander to the living room. She flips on the TV.

"We don't have to watch this if you don't want," she says, as a young country-singing wannabe sings in front of four superstar judges.

"I don't mind."

Christine loves this show, likes to give her opinion as though she has some sort of musical repertoire even though I know better—I've heard her sing. This hinge-your-fame on others is all smoke and mirrors to me. Success doesn't just happen with the snap of a finger—or the turn of a chair. It's earned. It's worked for.

I should know.

I glance over at Christine. She's changed from her office clothes into black yoga pants and a long sleeve tee. This is the Christine I love, the cozy kind, the kind that curls her legs up on the couch and doesn't care that her hair is frizzy from the late afternoon mist coming home. The kind who hasn't shoved her body into constricting shapewear that claims to make you drop two sizes.

"Oh come on," she says to the screen, arm out in protest. "No one's going to turn for him? That was so good." She catches me looking at her. "Don't you think? That guy's got talent."

I agree, though I wasn't watching. I couldn't really care less about tomorrow's next big singer. I might not even be here tomorrow.

Christine looks back to me. "What?" she says.

"Nothing."

"You're staring."

"Sorry." I don't know how our interactions became reduced to single, clipped words. I spin my ring around my finger. There's an indentation from where it's sat for a quarter of a century.

"Chris," I say. She doesn't respond. "Chris." My voice is louder this time, and she turns. "Do you love me?"

Her brows draw together to touch at the center. "What kind of question is that?"

"Exactly what I said. Do you love me?"

She gives a little huff. "Of course I love you. Where is this coming from?"

"Will you still love me if...if I turn into someone else?"

There's a pause, and Christine looks to her hands. On screen, a new singer, a young girl in tight leather trousers belts out a Whitney Houston hit. Even I know you should never attempt Whitney.

"Don't think like that," Christine says.

"I can't help it. I already feel like I'm changing. I know I'm changing. And I'm scared, Chris. Proper scared. Remember that movie we watched about the old lady losing her mind and the husband's struggle to care for her? What if that's going to be us? I don't know if I can handle the thought of it."

She slides toward me on the couch, puts her hand on my leg. The singing continues—a shoddy version—and the lyrics feel serendipitous to the question I just posed.

"Everything will be fine," Christine says. And because I trust those eyes, I believe her.

But that's not enough. It's not just Christine I need. My family is only part of what makes me whole. The study—the research with my name on it. I have to finish.

Christine's sitting so close, our pulses begin to beat in rhythm. When was the last time we touched? I miss this—I miss her.

An email comes through on my phone. I shimmy away from my wife, and she gives me a supremely effective look that says everything I need to see.

"Sorry," I say. "I'm so close to finishing the section I've been working on." I stand. "You get it, right? Besides, this is yours and Abbie's show. I don't even know what's going on."

She's small there on the couch now that I've left, like the sole survivor of a shipwreck, waiting to be saved. Only I'm leaving—I *have* to leave. Time is ticking away, taking my study and all the accolades along with it.

"Sure," she says, and it's so small I barely hear it.

When I retreat to my office, half of me stays behind in the living room with my wife. Snuggles up next to her and begs her understand, to wait for me. I don't know if she will. She might be already gone.

Abbie

"Well, well, well. What do we have here?" A creepy dude with hair plugs and nasty teeth stands in the door. "I came here expecting to catch someone, but it certainly wasn't you."

"Who are you?" I say, although I know perfectly well who he is. It's Mo, one of the maintenance guys. Well, his real name's not Mo, but that's what all the students call him. Mo-Lester, because he looks like the type you wouldn't want to leave young kids alone with.

"I work here, sweetheart. I'm allowed to be in these offices at night." He holds up his key ring. "But you, I suspect you're not supposed to be here right now, are you?"

"This is my mom's office." I'm trying to sound confident, but there's panic in my voice. "I have a key."

"Your mom, huh? The one sneaking around here with her student?"

Huh? "I don't know what you're talking about."

He walks closer to the desk, and I instinctively push back in the chair to keep distance between us. He's looking at the picture frame on her bookshelf. The one of me and my moms. He squints, but even then, his eyes are so big I can still see all the whites.

"That one there. Her, with the red hair." He points to Mom. He's come around the side of the desk now to get closer.

"Yes, that's my mom."

"And who's that other woman?"

"My other mom."

I didn't think it would be possible for his eyes to bug out any further, but they do. His mouth forms a wide O and he lets out a hearty laugh. "Two moms? She's a lesbian? Oh, this is good. This is too good."

I have no clue what's so funny, but his laugh alone has a sinister tone that makes the hair on my neck stand up.

"You should leave," I say. "I'm doing work in here."

He spins to face me. "Work, you say?" He leans toward the computer, where Mom's exam fills the screen and the mouse hovers over the Print button. Without warning, it's like the lightbulb goes off in both of our heads. I scramble to close the laptop, but he's too fast. He grabs my arm.

"Hold on a minute there, girlie. Let's have a look at what you're working on." He yanks me out of the chair and takes my place. I'm breathing hard, not sure whether to scream for help, gouge at his eyes or just cower in the corner. Is this a fight I want to fight? Or have I just been defeated?

"Ho ho. I can't believe my luck," he says, then spins in the chair to face me. "So *you're* the one who's been stealing the exams."

"I don't know what you're talking about," I lie again, but my stomach hits the floor. How the hell does he know?

"Kids think they're so smart. But you're just a bunch of babies playing dress up. None of you can keep your damn mouths shut. And the faculty? Don't get me started on those hoity-toity snobs. Heads so far up their asses they'd never see any of this. But me? A little old janitor? I hear everything. And guess what, sweetheart? Your friends have been talking. I've heard about this little ring you've got going on, I just didn't know who you were. I'll give them that, they're careful with names. But what are the odds I stumble in here tonight at just the right time. Thought I was catching someone else, but this might be even better."

There's no mirror in here, but I know my face has gone completely white. If Lester has heard rumors, who else has? I'm sick at the thought that my scheme hasn't been as fool-proof as I thought.

And what does he mean about catching someone else? The only other person who'd be in here is Mom. What would he catch her doing? For a moment, I consider he's in the wrong office altogether and I've just experienced the worst possible case of bad timing in the history of bad timing.

"Don't worry, little chickie," he continues. "I'm not gonna turn you in. Not unless you refuse my request."

"What request?" It's barely a whisper because that's all the breath I have.

"You're going to split your profits with me."

My body goes cold and I feel dizzy. I reach out to the bookcase for stability. What he's asking is impossible. There won't be enough for Ma's treatment.

"No," I say, sounding firmer than I feel.

"What'dya mean no? You'd rather I turn you in?"

"I...I..." I have no response because of course I don't want him to turn me in. I'd be expelled. Humiliated. The world's most disappointing daughter, and friend-less on top of that.

"That's what I thought," he says, a smug grin stretching across his face. "Meet me here on Thursday evenings. Eight o'clock. If you don't show, I go to Student Affairs."

I'm too stunned to argue with him. Pleading will do no good. I can tell this is not the type of guy to be swayed by a few tears. Refusing is equally bad. It's a lose-lose situation with no hope of coming out on top.

Lester slinks back through the door, chuckling as he goes. I slide down the wall to the threadbare carpet below, put my head in my hands and cry. I'm totally screwed.

175

Christine

K erry pokes her head around my door as I'm Googling "Likelihood of pregnancy at age fifty."

"Chris, do you have a minute?"

Her expression is serious and instantly my throat tightens, thinking about the note that was under her door a few weeks ago. What if there's been another one? Or worse, what if someone spotted us? Impossible. We've been so careful.

"Sure, Ker. Everything all right?"

"Let's talk in my office, okay?" Her lack of direct response doesn't help the sinking feeling in my bones. Something tells me this isn't going to be a positive, tenure check-in.

She vanishes from the doorframe, and I obediently follow. In her office, I take a seat on the same leather loveseat and cross my ankles. My houndstooth blazer feels constricting all of a sudden, and I want to take it off, but only have a sleeveless camisole underneath, and that too seems inappropriate.

I wring my hands in my lap. "What's up?" I aim for a carefree tone, but it comes out much more concerned than that. Relax your face, I tell myself.

"Listen Chris, this isn't easy to say." Her eyes are darting all over the place, and I can tell she's nervous. "Your midterm evals came back, and they're not great. Actually, they're pretty bad."

"Really?" I say, though I'm aware my performance this semester has been less than my best. "Bad in what way?"

"A lot of comments about you being distracted during class, showing up late—or not at all. One student said you don't even seem like you know what you're talking about when you're teaching. Another said you let them out early half the time."

My face is on fire. I want to slide under this couch and literally die. "Wow, Kerry. I mean, I'm shocked."

I'm not shocked. Not in the least. It's all true. I just didn't think it would catch up to me.

"These are all very out of character allegations for you. You're one of our best teachers. So, I was taken by surprise when I read these reports. Your scores are much lower than the national mean, and that's never happened with you before."

"Yeah, I mean, I have no idea." I hold my hands palms face up, feigning complete innocence.

"How do you think your semester's been going?"

"Well, it's no secret we've got a lot going on at home," I say. "There's been a couple times I might not have been on my best game. But this sounds much more severe than I think is warranted. I'm a good teacher, Kerry."

Kerry nods along with me. "I know you and Joss are up to your eyeballs with stress, and I feel awful for that. This really couldn't come at a worse time, you know. Tenure year? What are the odds. But Chris, this is serious. The administration will not just sweep these evals under the rug. You'll get another set at the end of the semester, I just hope they're not more of the same. Because truthfully, I worry about them awarding tenure to someone with this kind of feedback from students."

It's everything in my power not to let my mouth hang open. The thought of not getting tenure is like a stab wound to the jugular. They might as well put me in front of a firing squad, because that's what it will feel like. Mortification aside, I'll lose my job. That's how this works. Get tenure, or find another place to teach.

I can't speak. Kerry hangs her head, and I can feel her empathy from where I sit. We're friends. She knows my teaching history, knows how much I value my job. I respect the institution of education—or at least I did.

"Listen, try not to beat yourself up over it. I just wanted to give you a heads up is all. I know you've got a lot going on in your personal life, but you're so close. Only two more months until they make their decision."

"Okay," I say. "Thanks for letting me know. I really do love my job, you know."

"I know that. Some choose a career of teaching, but other times, teaching chooses the person. Teaching chose you, Christine. You're brilliant in the classroom, and you deserve tenure. Just remember, I'm not the only one making the decision."

"Got it. Thanks, Ker. I'll be on my toes from now on, I promise."

I leave her office with a sick feeling churning in my gut. How have I let this happen? I make a pitstop in the bathroom, where I can't even look at my own reflection. I'm too embarrassed. My dream is within reach, and nothing but my own bad choices stand in my way.

Back in my office, I remember the Google search. Pregnancy. Diminishing eggs. Highly unlikely but not impossible. I frantically read the search results, then laugh, putting my head in my hands. This would happen to me. Pregnant at fifty. Death by geriatric childbirth. Of course. Why not? A punishment for my sins.

My phone beeps. It's Micah.

Can't meet today, sorry.

My teeth clench. I want to throw the phone across the room. Instead, I slam my laptop shut and squeeze my hands into two hard fists. Everything is falling apart.

I need to talk to Micah. He's been distant lately, and I don't know why. What I do know is I don't like it. He's the only good thing I have going right now, the one that lets me forget about all the other shitty things that are happening.

178

I stand and grab my coat. I'll find him, wherever he is. But first, I think I better make a trip to the drug store.

Abbie

Hey girl, want 2 hit up Henry's after class?

Every time I hit send on a text to Stacia, I get a little thrill. I know she and some of the girls go to the diner on Friday afternoons—a mid-afternoon meal, leaving plenty of time for their stomachs to empty in prep for the onslaught of alcohol that will enter their bloodstreams by eight. No one drinks on a full stomach. What's the point?

She doesn't respond to my text. In fact, she's been a bit dodgy for the last couple weeks, even when I know she's on her phone 24/7.

I decide to up the ante.

Need 2 talk about something. Important.

It's not a lie—I've been considering whether to tell her about Lester, see what she thinks I should do. The stress of it all is weighing on my shoulders like a dozen bricks. It's heavy. And it would be nice to let someone in on what's going on. It's not like I can talk to my moms about it.

Hey, sorry. This week is nuts. Maybe next time?

My breath hitches. I was really getting used to not spending every weekend at home.

I look to the ceiling, twiddle my thumbs. The wheels in my head turn, until I land on something that feels solid.

I have a fifth of V from my mom's liquor cabinet. Was hoping 2 share!

Three dots.

Just one?

My fingers can't type fast enough. I can prob grab two.

There's a brief pause. I grin when her response comes through.

Perf! Meet you at my place at four!

See? My lips pull into a smirk. All is fine. Nothing a little vodka can't fix.

Christine

Want to know what's embarrassing? Buying a pregnancy test when you're fifty years old. I can't make eye contact with the man behind the counter, so I slide it across, and then fiddle with my debit card while he rings it up. *It's for a friend,* I want to say, but that's just stupid because why wouldn't a grown woman buy her own pregnancy test.

There's no time to take it on campus, and I'm not sure I really want to wait out those results in a public bathroom anyway. Plus, I need to talk to Micah, need to figure out what's going on between us. So, I shove the test to the bottom of my purse, and put the impossible thoughts out of my mind until I get home later.

I pull back on campus and check the time: an hour until I have to be in class. This is supposed to be my lunch break, but the thought of eating only adds to my nausea. Come to think of it, I haven't had an appetite in days.

I have no idea where Micah could be right now, but I know he's not in class because I memorized his schedule. Since he lives off campus, it's not like I can go stake out his dorm and wait for him to magically appear.

The Student Center is my best bet. It houses a grille and an a la carte stand where most of the upperclassmen prefer to eat. I vaguely remember him mentioning something about eating burgers there three days a week, to which I'd made a joke about the metabolism of youth.

It's packed when I enter at the height of the lunch rush. Students form lines at the various food stations, buffered further apart by bulky backpacks. I don't usually go to the dining areas like some of my colleagues do. Too busy. I'd rather eat a yogurt in my office and take a chunk out of the endless grading that plagues me.

I find an empty table near the window and use a napkin to brush off the layer of crumbs from the surface. A group of giggly girls pass, their salt-stained combat boots squeaking on the tile. Their lightness makes me think of the night I shared the tequila with Micah and became giggly myself.

I open my laptop to appear busy, and scan the sea of faces. He's not here. At least not yet. I could be early. There's still time. Or maybe he won't be here at all today. Two girls walk past and say hello. I smile.

Then there's a man approaching—Tobias Fletcher from the music department—and I let out a quiet groan. He's always flirted with me, even though I've made it abundantly clear that I'm married. And even if I wasn't, the man couldn't be further from my type.

"Don't see you here often," he says, putting both hands on his hips. He's got a Forrest Gump feel, with that goofy smile and high-hiked pants, though I was the first one to pass the motion to appoint him to our Senate's executive committee last year.

"How's your semester going?" he says.

"Oh, hi Tobias. Great, just busy as always." I gesture to my computer. Now is not the time for small talk. I have to watch for Micah and I don't want to miss him just because Music Man sees an opportunity to drop some pickup lines.

He rattles on another minute—something about the upcoming production of *Into the Woods*?—but I don't look up from my computer. He gets the hint pretty quick.

"Well, guess I'll see ya around," he says, looking slightly dejected.

"Yep. See ya."

Now that poor Tobias is gone, I'm back to searching the room. I look out the window to where students traverse the walkways. And that's when I spot him. Micah is in the middle of a group, hands shoved deep in his pockets, shoulders raised against the bitter air. I'm off my seat and slamming my laptop closed in a second. I hurry out of the Student Center, half jogging toward him. He stops when he sees me. The others stop, too.

"Micah," I say, now a few feet from the group. "Hi."

A few of the boys snicker. One brings his hand to cover his mouth. I think I hear someone mumble, "Aw, shit."

"Hey, Dr. Graham," Micah says with a jerk of his chin, as smooth and sexy as always.

I suddenly don't know what I planned to say if I hadn't caught Micah alone. It's not like I can discuss our relationship in front of other students. "I, uh," I stammer. "Can I talk to you for a minute?"

"Oh, shoot. I'm actually running a bit late to class."

I know he's not. The next class time doesn't start for half an hour. I know because I teach it. Why is he avoiding me? I take a deep breath. I can't let him—or the others—see me flustered.

"Sure, no problem. Maybe swing by my office afterward? I wanted to go over something for class." This, of course, is ridiculous. He's not even in my class this semester. As soon as I say it I feel transparent, like they can all see right through me.

"Yeah I can probably do that." He starts walking again, his friends joining back in line. I hear muffled laughter. One of them gives Micah a hearty nudge. My insides shrink. Has he told them about us?

I stand in the middle of the sidewalk and watch them go. He doesn't look back.

* * *

Waiting for Micah to show up is worse than waiting for the last student to finish an exam. If I could pace in my office I would, but it's too damn small, so all I can do is stand and sway nervously. Every time there's a knock, I think it's going to be him, but so far it's only been other students. *I don't have time for you right now,* I want to scream.

A little after three his head pops in my doorframe. I shoot up from my chair, and it glides back from the motion of me standing.

"Good time?" he says.

"Yes." My heart is racing and my fingertips tingle. I don't have to tell him to close the door behind him. He stares at me with his big, brown eyes. "Feels like forever," I breathe, and immediately push aside the thought that I sound like a clichéd juvenile. "Why didn't you respond to my texts?"

"I've been busy."

"Too busy to send a simple text?"

He cocks his head. "Christine."

I step forward and grab his hands. "Never mind. Forget it." I don't want to have an argument. And I don't want to think about the weirdness I've felt between us lately. I lean in to kiss him, but he pulls back.

"What?" I say.

"Christine, I don't know if—"

"Don't say it," I cut him off, not wanting to hear what he was about to confess. He can't end this; I'd die. Not the way I've been anticipating lately—but still. I press my lips to his and within a few seconds, his hands are grappling for my blouse buttons. The sex is hot and fast. Time apart has turned me into an animal. We're breaking our not-during-the-day rule, but I don't care.

When we're done, I'm on the floor, leaning against the wall and trying to catch my breath. My pants are around my thighs.

"God, I missed this," I say. Micah's quiet, save for his ragged breathing and the sound of his pants zipping. "Did you?"

"Yeah. But—"

"But what?"

He runs a hand across his hair. "Things are crazy right now. My classes are intense, and graduation is literally right around the corner."

"I know all that. It's fine. We'll still find time."

"I'm just saying, I might not be as available."

I pull down the cup of my bra, revealing a hint of brown nipple. "If you want this, you will be." As I say it, I cringe a little inside. I've gone from a juvenile to a complete whore.

Micah bites his bottom lip, leans down and gives my boob a little smack. My insides fire up again. I'm not sure I've ever felt this alive. At least, not for a long, long time. When he leaves, I'm left with only one question: How can something so wrong feel so right?

Joss

Richard has been taking over more and more of our research study. I just can't seem to keep up. Either I'm too knackered, or I can't concentrate long enough to get any substantial amount of work accomplished. I'll stare at the screen, type a few words, and then have to go back and re-read what I just wrote multiple times for it to sink in. It's like I can see where I want to go, but my brain won't let me get there.

I've been sitting at the computer all morning. An oversized water bottle is on the desk—one of those ones with the progress lines and motivational phrases like "keep chugging!" There's not much I can do to stop the progression of this disease, but maybe it's finally time to give Christine's healthy lifestyle a chance. This morning, I tossed the Goldfish and dumped what remained of the Coke bottle down the drain.

It's been four hours and I can already say one thing for certain: clean eating is terrible. Everything tastes like cardboard, and I'm left salivating for sugar immediately afterward.

I shift in my chair, trying to appease my new overactive bladder from all the water I've drank this morning. Finally, after I feel like I'll burst, I head to the bathroom. I'm going through so much toilet paper, it's insane. The roll is empty, so I reach toward the vanity door for a new one, but instead I knock over the trash can in the way. Its contents spill out onto the floor.

"Damnit," I grumble, stretching for the crumbled tissues and dirty Q-tips.

I grab a handful of garbage, but something feels hard under all those fluffy tissues. It's long, like a stick. When I look closer, I see the tip of whatever it is sticking out. My blood turns to ice. I recognize this pink cap, even though it's wildly out of place in my home. It's wrapped in toilet paper, and I hurriedly unroll it, letting the plastic stick fall to the floor. It lands face down.

A pregnancy test.

Abbie.

My mind immediately jumps to my daughter. I know she's been more social lately, and has even had some friends over to our house to hang out. But she's never mentioned any boys, never talked about being interested in someone special. Certainly not told us she's having casual sex.

Scenarios spiral through my brain. She's dating someone secret. She got drunk at a party and hooked up with someone. Then my stomach falls. What if she was hurt? Taken advantage of. Raped, even. My eyes water thinking of her scared and alone, not wanting to tell us what happened.

If my daughter is pregnant, that means I'm going to be a grandma. A grandma at fifty-four. Is that common? I can't be old enough. There's only a sprinkle of gray at my temples. I haven't even hit menopause.

Or, maybe she won't want to keep the baby. Maybe she already has other plans. I'm a firm believer in a woman's right to choose. I'd support my daughter in whatever decision she makes. A vivid image flashes before my eyes: accompanying Abbie to an abortion clinic. I feel sick.

Then it occurs to me: Just because someone takes a pregnancy test doesn't mean it's going to be positive.

My mind's getting away from me, taking me down a rabbit hole of what-ifs. I'm still sitting on the toilet, for Christ's sake.

I wipe and refasten my jeans. I squat down, hovering over the test like I can see through to the result on the other side. Do I want to confirm this? It could set our family on a whole new trajectory.

Yes, of course I need to know. We're talking about Abbie here.

My hand shakes as I reach down and turn the test over. A solid blue line crosses the little box in the middle. My eyes move frantically, trying to interpret the result. Does one line mean positive or negative? The symbols to the right verify it.

Negative.

She's not pregnant.

Relief washes over me, and I fall back onto my butt and lean against the wall with the test in my hand. I study it to make sure I didn't misread. It's still a single blue line.

At once, any feelings of sympathy turn to anger. My body tenses. What is she thinking being so careless? Does Christine know? Everything in me wants to drive to campus, yank her from class, and give her a good tongue lashing.

But I don't. I'll wait for her to get home, then the interrogation will begin.

Abbie

Everywhere I go on campus, I'm looking for Lester, but he's never there. Maintenance workers sprinkle the campus doing everything from fixing flooded toilets in the girls' dorms from flushing too many tampons, to excessively icing the sidewalks so the school doesn't get slapped with a lawsuit if someone were to slip. Every time I see that drab uniform, my stomach drops. But it's never him.

By the time I get home with Mom, my head is pounding. Lester's ultimatum is like a boulder behind my neck, weighing me down under its pressure. I have to meet him tomorrow, and the anticipation is killing me.

I walk into the house with my head down, wanting nothing more than to go straight to my room and bury myself under the covers. I'm so distracted, I practically run right into Ma, who's standing in the kitchen with her arms crossed.

Ugh, what now?

"You have some explaining to do," she says, as Mom comes in a few steps behind me.

I stop in my tracks. My arms go tingly. She knows. But how? She hasn't even been on campus since they stuck a nail in her grave (her words, not mine).

"What's the problem?" Mom says.

I just stare, unable to form words, but thinking of how I can possibly avoid blame.

"This." Ma holds up something that takes me a minute to recognize.

"A pregnancy test?" Now I'm completely confused.

"Yes a pregnancy test, Abbie. Imagine my shock when I found it rolled up in the trash can today. Do you have something you want to tell us?"

My eyes grow. "It's not mine," I say incredulously.

Ma's face turns red. I'm waiting for steam to blow from her ears. There's only three people who live in this house, and I know two things for certain: It's not mine, and Ma wouldn't be accusing me if it was hers. The thought alone of my moms being pregnant right now is so disturbing I could gag. But if it's not me, and it's not her, that leaves one person.

"Christine, help me out here," Ma says.

I turn to see Mom, whose skin has gone ghostly pale. And that's when Lester's words ring in my ear.

I came here expecting to catch someone, but it certainly wasn't you.

Was he hoping to catch Mom? Doing what exactly? If this pregnancy test has anything to do with it, I think I know what he was implying. But it can't be true. It's impossible—on so many levels.

"Ma, I swear that is not mine," I say again.

"Well if it's not yours, then whose is it, huh?"

If Lester was telling the truth and Mom is messing around with a student—I can't even wrap my head around that—then I should shut up right now and let her do the explaining. Why should I take the blame?

But Mom's not saying a word, and Ma wouldn't believe her anyway. I think on the spot and remember Stacia and some of the soccer girls who'd come over last weekend. "It must be one of my friends," I say. "No one said anything to me when they were here, but someone had to have gone into the bathroom to take it. I swear, Ma. I'm not lying. I'm not even having sex anyways."

Ma recoils a little when I say the word sex, like I'm nine instead of nineteen. It's true, I'm not having sex with anyone, and even if I were, and even if I thought I might be pregnant, I wouldn't be stupid enough to leave the test in our joint bathroom garbage.

Ma sits on a stool, her body shrinking as though all anger she'd built up suddenly burst and shriveled. She puts the test on the counter and we all stare at it. Mom hasn't said a word.

"Don't you have anything to say?" Ma says to her, reading my mind.

"I believe Abbie," she finally whispers. "I don't think she'd lie to us about this."

My moms lock eyes in that way parents do when they're communicating telepathically. I wonder what they're each thinking. After a minute of awkward silence, Ma speaks again.

"Well, tell your friends to keep their pregnancy tests at their own houses." It's snarky and cutting, but then the redness fades a bit. "And you better check to make sure whoever it was is okay. It's not that hard to use birth control, you know."

"Okay," I say to appease her, though I'd rather be doing just about anything else than listening to Ma talk about birth control methods.

Mom steps forward and grabs the pregnancy test off the counter, then swiftly drops it in the kitchen garbage. I eye her. The color has returned to her face, but now it's overly red, as though the flame transferred from one parent to the other. Splotches creep up her neck that even her collar can't hide.

Ma disappears, presumably back to her study, leaving Mom and me in the kitchen alone.

We stare at each other in a way that says we both know the thorny truth—or at least some version of it.

I go to talk, but Mom stops me.

"Don't, Abbie. Just don't."

She brushes past me, and all I can do is bite my tongue. I don't know what the hell is going on, but it's something. And it's not good.

As I stand there in the kitchen, my gaze drifts to the refrigerator covered in pictures. Our annual Christmas card hangs next to a bunch of candids. Happy Holidays from the Graham-Matson family. My eyes narrow. Was I about to get a sibling?

Christine

Just because the pregnancy test was negative doesn't mean I feel any better. First of all, I'm an idiot for not getting rid of it somewhere else. What were the odds the trash can would spill and Joss would find it? I guess that's a consequence I deserve for my stupidity. I've never believed in karma, but there's a first time for everything.

It never occurred to me Abbie could take the fall. She came up with a good excuse—or at least I think it was an excuse. I'm not confident she believes it herself. Not the way she looked at me. I was in her crosshairs for sure.

This is getting dangerous in ways I'd never considered before. I don't want anyone else to get hurt. It has to end, this thing—I can't bring myself to say the word *affair*. I need to break it off with Micah. I don't want to, but, like putting down a suffering animal, I know I have to.

Tears run down my cheeks as I get dressed in our walk-in closet. I think back over the past six months and how alive I've felt. How young he's made me feel.

But that's not real life. Real life is living in the moment, not in the past. Real life is being loyal and fair and doing what's right. This has been nothing but wrong.

Micah is supposed to meet me in my office this evening. We'd planned it days ago—a time when our busy schedules finally lined up. My body aches for him, even more so now that I know I'm going to cap it with a firm hand, a period at the conclusion of a very run-on sentence.

Getting through my first two classes is torture. All I can think about is this evening and what I'll say. Will he be hurt? Will he try to talk me out of it? I picture his deep eyes pleading for me to reconsider.

Will I be able to hold my ground?

By lunchtime, I can't handle the anticipation any more. I'm so nauseous with nerves, I can't eat. Tonight can't wait. I need to clear my mind—and my conscience—*now*.

I head toward the Student Center where I'd seen him before at this time. If I can get his attention and talk to him privately this can all be over and done with. Right here, right now. I'm fueled with a sudden surety that not even this public setting discourages. He'll be graduating in mere weeks, and then I'll never have to see his tempting face again. Our lives can go back to normal—or at least whatever sort of normal Joss's illness will dictate.

The tables are full, so I wait outside. I wrap my arms around myself, pretending to be engrossed in my phone. A few people walk by and give me a look. I'm sure they're wondering why I'm lingering in the cold instead of just a few steps through the door where heat blasts from the ceiling.

I slink back around the corner of the building. Occasional peeks come up empty—lots of students, but no Micah. When my toes are officially frozen and I'm about to give up, I peek one last time and see him approaching, flanked by two other guys. My knees wobble. I jerk back, waiting to grab him at the last second. Their voices get louder. They must be only a few feet away now. I lean to hear.

"Sigma House tonight?" one says.

"Nah, can't dude. I'm busy." It's Micah. I could recognize his voice anywhere.

"Are you seriously still hittin' that? The bet's over, man. You won. You proved your point."

My lungs constrict, making it hard to breathe. I sink back a step, the words a blow to my core.

Micah laughs. "What can I say? The sex is good."

"Yeah, but she's old."

"Pussy's pussy, dude. Mom pussy hits different."

Their voices fade, as they enter the building. I lean against the cold brick, attempting to swallow the lump that's formed in my throat. My chin quivers. I'm nothing more than a bet. A passing amusement between a bunch of testosterone-fueled boys. I wrap my hands around my middle and bend forward, feeling suddenly light-headed.

It can't be. It all felt so real.

Micah's confession stings more than a swarm of bees. I emerge from the shadows and do a quick scan to make sure he's gone before bolting back to my office. I shut the door just as the tears start to fall.

How could I have been so blind?

I run to the bathroom and scrub my hands under scalding water. My skin turns bright pink, but I don't care. The pain feels good. I rub so hard, my knuckles start to bleed. A line of red winds its way down the drain, but even that's not enough to make me feel less dirty.

I catch my reflection in the mirror and let my eyes idle there for a moment. *Who are you?* I think. My eyes are hollow; heavy bags have settled underneath them. Age spots mix in with my freckles as though they're playing hide and seek. Maybe some people wouldn't notice, but I can tell the difference. My lips have crevices at the center, where lipstick settles into the grooves. They're no longer silky like Abbie's.

Did I really think Micah desired me on his own? That he honestly found me attractive?

The more I stare in the mirror, the more I hate myself. How stupid can you be, Christine? What a fool. My mouth curls into a snarl. I lift a hand and slap myself across the face. The pain burns, and when I look there's a mark that's already starting to welt.

I deserve it.

A feeling of certainty settles inside me. I was already planning to end it, but now I'm sure. It's over. Only instead of feeling bad about it, sorry for him, I'm angry. Heated breath hisses through my teeth. I'll confront him tonight when he comes to my office. Let him see what it feels like to be on the receiving end of a lateral blow you didn't see coming.

Joss

I used to love being alone, spending days with just my thoughts. But now my thoughts don't make sense half the time. I barely get through an hour of writing and I'm completely whooped. So, I end up sitting here, staring off at nothing, wishing I actually wasn't alone.

Lately, I've found myself waiting by the door for Abbie and Christine to get home. Seeing their faces grounds me in the present. Reminds me of who I am—who we are. When we're together, I'm reminded there's still something to fight for. I've come to cherish our evenings together—even though there always seems to be something one of them is heading back to campus for.

Christine used to be adamant about leaving work at work. Home time was for family and our life, not MacAmes. Which is why it's been odd to see her picking up so many evening functions on campus lately. I suppose it's an extra push for her tenure portfolio—showing how engaged she is in campus life and all that. I'm glad for her, even if it means I've been spending more time alone.

Tonight there's another something or other she's attending. I've thought about telling her I'll tag along, but the truth is, I don't feel like being around a crowd of people. What if someone starts talking to me and I don't recognize them? I know just about everyone on campus, down to the admissions counselors and payroll accountants, but the thought of this disease robbing me of long-time friends makes me stay rooted to the recliner in our living room.

We eat dinner together—the one thing we've been able to keep up through this whole ordeal. Christine pokes at her food, and when I try to engage in conversation, she's distracted.

I give up and turn to Abbie. "Want to watch a movie later?" I say.

Abbie holds up a finger as she finishes chewing. "I'm heading back to campus for a study group. Stacia's picking me up in twenty."

"You too?" My shoulders slump. "You both are quite social lately, aren't you?" I try to hide my disappointment, but I must not be very convincing because Abbie quickly counters.

"We can watch one tomorrow?"

"It's fine," I say with a wave, though there's something blocking my throat.

Christine takes our plates to the sink. I come up behind her and put my hands on her waist. We used to sway like this all the time, our bodies pressed together as one. I miss the closeness.

"I can do these," I offer, knowing full well she'll say no. Christine never takes my offers when it comes to housework.

She whips her head around. "Would you? I need to get to campus." She shimmies out of my grasp and speed walks to the door, grabbing her coat and purse on the way. I'm left standing there with my hands outstretched as though they were still resting on her waist.

"Oh. Sure."

"Shouldn't be late," she says, one foot out the door. The screen shuts before I can say goodbye.

I finish the dishes and go to dry my hands. The towel is slippery and not at all absorbent. I pat my hands on it, but the drips just fall to the floor. What is wrong with this towel?

"Ma, what are you doing?" Abbie's voice startles me and I look up to see a concerned expression on her face. "That's not a towel." She crosses the kitchen and pulls the dish towel from the oven handle. Extends it to me. "Here."

But if that's the towel, what am I—

I look to my hands. The thing—the not-towel—takes shape. I've been trying to dry my hands with a bag of hamburger buns. Water droplets cover the plastic. Inside, the bread is smashed.

I freeze in place, trying to wrap my head around how I could have thought a bag of hamburger buns was a dish towel. A car horn gives two sharp beeps outside.

"Stacia's here," Abbie says softly. "Are you sure you're all right to be alone? I can stay."

"Don't be silly. Go. You shouldn't miss study groups. I'm fine."

She eyes me carefully, but at this point I want to shoo her out the door. I don't need my own daughter babysitting me. The thought is more humiliating than drying your hands on a plastic bag.

"Abbie, I'm fine," I say again, this time with more force. I turn her around by the shoulders and walk her to the door.

"If you're sure."

"I'm sure. Off you go. I'll see you when you get home."

She leaves. I go to the window and watch her climb into the passenger side of a cherry red car. When she drives away, a hollowness settles in my chest. The aloneness swallows me. It feels like the walls are closing in, inch by inch, my world getting smaller by the day.

My throat constricts. I still have so much life I want to live. I'm not ready to give up my independence.

I sit for an hour. Move to the office and try to type, but it's no use; I can't remember how to spell. I snatch my rabbit's foot and squeeze it so hard I feel a tiny bone on the inside crack. What a farce, such a childish notion—an animal part bringing good luck. It's probably not even a real rabbit's foot.

"Rubbish," I say, tossing it onto the ground. It bounces twice before coming to rest on its side a few feet away, all worn and used, a piece of junk no reasonable adult would have put so much faith in. Still, after a minute, I slide from the chair and crawl toward it, cradling it in my hand and stroking its length, as though this apology will mend the broken little girl inside me.

We sit there on the floor, the rabbit's foot and I, my shoulders hunched so far forward I feel like I might fold in half. When I can't take the solitude another second, I get up, grab my keys and toss on my coat. I've got to get out of here. I need a drive. Fresh air. Something to clear my head. Sitting alone at home is starting to mess with me. I grab the keys from where they hang by the door.

The sun has officially set, leaving the sky edged in blues and pinks. There must be clouds up there somewhere because there's not a star in the sky. Just a blanket of darkness.

I don't know where I'm going, only that I want to feel the energy of being behind the wheel and charting my own course. Maybe I'll just drive around town. Maybe I'll break my clean eating and go get myself ice cream.

Our street merges into a busier road, leaving our quiet neighborhood behind. Up ahead, restaurant signs and businesses light up the small downtown strip. I see the sign for Jolly's Ice Cream. My body goes warm, and I smile. Yes, a little sugar therapy will do the trick.

I merge into the left lane. Jolly's is just past the intersection. The light ahead turns from green to yellow. My brain signals a reaction. I'm supposed to do something with my foot here, I know. But instead of coming to a stop, I'm speeding up. The intersection is coming fast. Too fast. In my peripheral, I see a car coming from the left. Their light is green. They're not slowing down. Neither am I. Why am I not stopping?

The red light whizzes overhead and out of sight. A horn blares, long and steady. The last thing I hear is the sound of crashing metal. I'm whipped around, my head hitting the window, before I'm plunged into black as dark as death.

Christine

My office feels small. I mean, it is small, but now it feels even smaller.

I look around and wonder how Micah and I managed to do all we did in such a cramped space. When we were together, the world felt huge, even if we were no more than tangled limbs on the floor of a tiny faculty office.

He should be here any minute. I check my watch. Almost eight. I've practiced what I'm going to say, but I'm scared that when I see him, it'll all come out in a blob of anger and hurt. Or worse—I won't be able to follow through at all.

I hear those boys' voices again. *You won the bet. You proved your point.*

How could he use me like this?

Everything inside me wants to put on a suit of armor and act like I'm not bothered in the slightest. Oh, you were just using me for sex? That's fine, because I was doing the same. But it's not true, and I'm afraid we both know it. I formed feelings for him—real feelings, however bizarre the circumstance. For the last seven months, he's been the first thing I think of when I wake up and the last thing I think of before I fall asleep. We've shared secrets. I've told him my dreams.

But it was all a lie. All based on a bet to see whether he could get in my pants. And would you look at that—he won.

A soft knock on the door makes me startle, and when I turn, he's already coming through.

"Hey," he says with a smile. His eyes are soft—they always are when we're together. He licks his lip as he comes closer.

I take a step back, fold my arms across my chest. "Don't," I say, as he reaches for me.

He stops. His face scrunches. "What?"

"I heard you with your friends today."

He shakes his head a little and turns his palms up. He doesn't know what I'm referring to. Part of me wants to laugh. These cocky kids think they're so invincible. I'm sure he never thought twice about who was around when he spoke so openly.

"Outside the Student Center," I continue, hoping this will jog his memory.

It doesn't. He's still just staring at me, which makes my blood boil even more.

"I know about the bet," I blurt.

Realization crosses his face in the form of a clenched jaw. I see it go from soft to hard in a second. A vein pulses at his neck.

I nod. "Yeah. I heard it all." It feels good to throw it back in his face, but at the same time my insides are sobbing.

"Christine, that was all a joke," he says, stepping toward me again. His hands are on my face in a second, and even though I lean back, he pulls me in. I could break away. I could push his hands away, but I don't.

"But it's true," I say. "This was all a bet you made with your friends? To see if you could sleep with me?" Our lips are nearly touching.

"It was never just a bet for me." He kisses me, and I melt into his soft mouth.

"You used me."

"No."

"Tell me the truth."

"It might have started out like that, but it turned into more." Our kisses are hungry, and he's unbuttoning my blouse. I'm falling. Down, down, down. Back into the world where Micah's touch means nothing else matters.

Don't do this, a voice in my head says. I see the red flags. They're waving with gusto.

I don't listen.

But then there's another sound. I've heard it before, in a situation just like this. Something inside me plummets into a river of cold. I look to the door, see the knob turn. It flies open.

Not again.

But it's not the same.

Abbie's mouth hangs open. "Mom?"

Abbie

"**M**om?" I'm so stunned at first, it's like I don't even know what I'm seeing.

She's supposed to be at some presentation. At least that's what she told Ma and me. But she's not. She's very clearly here in her office. And Micah Johnson is, too. They're standing so close. Too close. Hold up, why is his hand in her shirt? Her bra's exposed. That can't be right. And, wait a minute, I've never seen that bra before. It's black and lacy and Mom only ever wears those plain cotton ones.

She pushes Micah in the chest and he takes a step back, avoiding eye contact with me. "Abbie," Mom says, "It's not what you think." She's buttoning her blouse with flustered fingers.

"Are you kidding me? What the hell, Mom." I mean it in so many ways: What the hell are you doing making out with a student, and what the hell are you doing making out with a *guy*. My brain's exploding. I feel like I'm going to throw up.

"Listen, I can explain."

My body's shaking. I lift a finger and point it at her. "I knew something was going on. You've been acting so weird lately." Then I remember the pregnancy test. "Oh my God, the pregnancy test. You were going to let me take the blame? That's a new low."

At that, Micah comes alive. "Pregnancy test?" He looks to Mom, whose face is the color of a tomato. "Fuck no. Tell me you're not."

"No, I'm not pregnant. The test was negative." She reaches to him in what I assume is a comforting move, but he dips aside.

Micah rolls his head back in relief, then raises his hands, like an old-fashioned stickup. "This shit's too heavy. I'm out." He comes toward the door and I move out of the way, not wanting to be anywhere near his radius.

"Micah, wait," Mom says, but he keeps going.

"You're seriously trying to stop him?" I hiss. Her eyes are sad, and that's when I realize this is more than just a casual hookup. She might actually have *feelings* for him. I feel like I'm in an alternate universe. Wake up, Abbie, this nightmare is getting weird.

I grab her shoulders and give them a shake. "Mom, are you freaking crazy? You're a teacher. He's a student. Do you realize how fucked up this is? You could get fired."

"I know all that. But—"

"But? Are you fucking kidding me? You...and him. Him? What the— I mean, I can't even..." The words are fractured, twisted with my runaway thoughts, it's like I'm speaking another language. Spit collects at the corners of my mouth. "How long has this been going on?"

She lowers her eyes. "A while."

"A while, like two weeks? Or a while like two months?"

"Since the beginning of the year."

"The whole school year? You've been sleeping with a student for," I count on my fingers, "for seven months?" I officially explode, but there's no one here so I don't care. Hell, let them hear.

"Yes."

She doesn't even try to deny it. There's no point. I caught them, saw it with my own eyes.

I pace the small space in front of her desk. "This is...this is just un-fucking-believable," I say, and Mom doesn't even scold me. My throat has gone dry from rushed breathing.

The picture on the bookcase grabs my attention and I stop, fling a hand out toward it. "What about Ma?" I say, suddenly filled with sadness for my mom who—I assume—is clueless that she's being cheated on. "She's not completely gone yet, you know. Nothing like kicking a dog when it's down."

Her head is lowered, her whole body somehow so much smaller now than it's ever seemed—like a role reversal I never asked for. "You're not going to tell her, are you?"

"Oh, so that's all you're worried about? Ma finding out?" I shake my head. "This whole thing"—I swirl my hand in front of me like I'm washing a window—"is disgusting." I fumble toward the door. "I have to get out of here."

"Wait, what are you doing here in the first place? Abbie? Why were you coming to my office at night?"

I don't answer. I can't stay any longer, staring at Mom and thinking about what she's been doing. The hallway is dark, but that doesn't slow my speed. I hurry from the office, hearing Mom call my name once more. She doesn't follow me, and I'm glad. My mind is still reeling with questions I'm not sure I want to know the answers to. Who started it? Where? What? Ew, no. I can't go there.

My eyes blur by tears I didn't expect. Our family's not perfect, but we're still a family. The three of us. I've always considered myself lucky to have parents who love each other. At least I thought they did.

I round the corner to the stairwell, fueled by adrenaline, needing to get outside to inhale some fresh air. My foot doesn't make it to the first step. I run smack into a body that stops me dead in my tracks. Because it's dimly lit, I don't recognize who it is at first, and I'm about to apologize and keep going, until I hear his voice.

"Where you going in such a hurry?" The whites of his eyes are visible through the darkness.

With all the distraction of my mom, I completely forgot the whole reason I'm on campus.

"Aren't we supposed to meet in your mom's office?" Lester says, pointing in the direction from which I just came.

I stutter, not sure what excuse to give. That she's here and I didn't know, or that I forgot my key? I've got enough of my own problem with Lester, I don't need him knowing about Mom, too. Then again, it sounds like he already knows.

"Outside," I say because it's the only thing I can think of, and because I might choke on this stale air if I don't get out.

He reluctantly agrees. We descend the stairs in silence and make our way into the cold night.

"How much ya got?" Lester says when we come to a stop. There's a lamp post overhead, and its light gives me a clearer view of him. His pupils are massive. He leans forward and licks his lips like a rabid animal.

"Only five hundred."

"Five hundred? Don't lie to me. I know you're bringing in a lot more than that, girlie."

"There's only been one exam."

He squints like he doesn't believe me even though I'm not lying. I hold the bills out to him.

"I expect more than this next time," he says, swiping the cash and shoving it in his pocket. I swallow hard, thinking how that money is supposed to be Ma's.

"Why are you doing this?" I say, unwanted emotion rising in my throat. "I mean, why not just turn me in?"

Lester laughs, pulls out his phone. "You ever hear of a little game called poker? Well, let's just say it's easy to rack up a debt, if you know what I mean. This here will buy me a little time until I get my winnings back up."

I've never played poker in my life, but I know a guy from high school who got sucked into the world of online gambling and lost thousands. As if on cue, Lester's phone makes a *cha-ching* sound.

"Thank you for your business," he says, giving a little bow. "Until next week." He slithers off into the shadows, leaving me dazed.

I consider going back inside to find Mom. Coming clean about what I've been up to and the trouble I'm in. But then I see her hands tangled in Micah Johnson's hair, the way she looked at him. All the times she's acted sketchy lately. I don't want to hear her explanation. At least the cheating I'm doing is for a greater good. I'm putting myself at risk to save Ma. All Mom's doing is thinking about herself.

My own ringing phone interrupts my thoughts. I pull it from my pocket. Ma's name flashes on the screen. Talk about timing.

"Hello?" I say.

But it's not Ma. It's a man—a man with a voice deep and regimented. "Is this Joss Matson's daughter?"

"Yes." My veins turn to ice. Where is Ma, and who has her phone?

"This is the Danville police department. We've been trying to get ahold of Christine Graham but haven't been able to get her. Your mom's been in a car accident."

I fly back into the building, screaming Mom's name, and thinking only two things: This is all my fault, and please don't let her be dead.

February 2002

*T*he contractions come swift and angry. We've been pacing the
house—up the stairs, down the stairs—all night.

Midway through our route around the kitchen, she stops
and leans into me, rests her head on my shoulder. I follow the second-
hand on my watch.

"Just breathe," I say.

She moans.

"Breathe," I say again. "Breathe through it, like the teacher showed us.
That's it."

We thought we'd been so proactive, taking those birthing classes. As if
watching a video and seeing an old, hippie woman demonstrate breathing
techniques meant we'd know what to do when it became our turn.

She stands again, releasing her weight from me. My arms ache from
supporting her, but I refuse to say anything. I wish I could take her pain
and put it on myself.

"How long?" she says.

"About sixty seconds."

"That was a bad one."

I smooth the hair from her face. "Let's keep walking."

We're only a few steps further when she clutches her belly and bends forward again.

"Already?" I say, but her moan is the only answer I need. I check my watch. When it passes and she meets my face, her eyes are glazed over.

"Those were only two minutes apart," I say. "I think we should go."

She doesn't have the energy to disagree.

***

"I can't do this!"

Sweat drenches the hair around her face. She grimaces as another wave crashes into her body. I look to the monitor. The line keeps climbing, and I wonder how much further it can go before it breaks her.

"Yes you can," I say into her ear. I'm standing next to the bed, watching my wife writhe in pain and I can't do anything about it. "You're doing it. You're so close."

The nurse walks around the end of the bed and taps a few buttons on a screen. She's ridiculously calm and I want to scream: Do something! Can't you see my wife is hurting?

Another contraction. Then another.

"I think I need to push," she says, her eyes suddenly going wide.

"You feel the urge to push?" the nurse says.

Yes, she just said she needs to push, you dimwit.

"I need to PUSH!"

I look to the nurse. "Let me get the doctor," she says, and then she leaves. It feels like hours until the door opens and a man in teal scrubs enters.

"Sounds like there's a baby on the way," he says, much too casually, before slipping into rubber gloves. He slides over on a stool, stopping right in between my wife's bent legs. "Let me check you." And then his hand disappears inside her, and I try not to gasp.

"Fully effaced. Ten centimeters," he says. "You two ready to have a baby?"

"Yes," I say, but my wife doesn't reply because she's wincing in pain again.

"I'm pushing!" she hollers.

"Go ahead," the doctor says. "When you feel the next contraction, I want you to take a deep breath and bear down." He glances at the monitor. The line starts to spike again. "Okay, here it comes. Ready? Push!"

Her face turns scarlet as she yanks back on her legs. I hold my breath too, though it does nothing more than add to my already lightheadedness.

"Great job," the doctor says. "Now, breathe. Ready? Do it again. Right down here in your bottom. Big push. And one, two, that's it, five, six, keep pushing..."

She pushes and pushes and twenty-five minutes later our baby is born.

"It's a girl," the nurse says, wiping blood and goo from the little head.

I lean into my wife's face and we cry. "A girl," I say. "She's so beautiful."

"What should we name her?"

We settle on Abbie.

Christine

A bbie's voice penetrates the sound of my own sobs. I bolt upright from where I'd collapsed on the floor after she left.

Silence. I must be hearing things. Wishful thinking for her to return, for me to fix what I've done.

"Mom!" It comes again. I'm *not* hearing things. There's panic in her voice. I know that sound, the same one she had when she broke her arm jumping off the swing set in our back yard and came running in to find me, arm dangling at all the wrong angles.

I hoist myself from the floor and rush into the hallway where we collide not five feet later.

"What? What is it?" I say, my tone already frantic. I search her face for an answer.

"It's Ma."

She's holding her phone out at me, as though that explains everything. But I don't know what she means. Is Joss on the phone?

"The police," she says, out of breath. "They called me. Said Ma was in an accident."

"An accident? What? You didn't take the keys?"

"I forgot! I'm sorry. It was, it was Stacia, she was waiting, and I just, I just left."

"Fuck, Abbie. Is she, did they say she's okay?"

"They wouldn't tell me. Just said they couldn't get through to you, and that we should come to the hospital right away."

I'm already back in my office grabbing my stuff. I snatch my phone and realize it's still on silent from earlier. There are three missed calls from the same number—the police, I assume. A wall of guilt crashes into me.

"Let's go," I say to Abbie, who's swaying slightly in the doorway.

We race across town. I'm not even worried about getting pulled over for speeding. The age-old excuse—*my spouse is in the hospital!*—would actually be true this time. Maybe we'd get a police escort, though at this hour there's hardly any traffic on the streets to warrant one.

I fly into the emergency room lot. Our hospital is small but reputable, and I'm comforted knowing she's here. If her injuries were critical, she'd likely have been transported to the bigger hospital an hour away.

Abbie and I hurry through the wide, automatic doors. A woman in braids sits behind the desk reading a magazine. She looks up as we enter.

"My wife was brought in a bit ago," I say, the words coming out more like a question I'm looking to confirm. "Car accident." This last is like a squeak.

"Name?" she says, and I wonder how many people were recently admitted from a car wreck.

"Joss Matson."

She flips a couple papers. "She's in triage. Let me page the doctor. Have a seat, she'll be right out."

"Is she okay?"

"I'm not at liberty to disclose information, I'm sorry."

"All I want to know is if my wife is okay. Please."

"Ma'am, I'm sorry. I really don't know. The waiting room is just there."

How am I supposed to sit? How on Earth can I wait? But that's what I do because Abbie leads me to a group of chairs not far from the desk. I perch on the edge, bounce my foot so my knee is bobbing at rapid speed. Abbie puts a hand on my leg.

"She'll be okay," she says.

I want to believe her, but what does she know? Joss could be on the brink of death behind those doors. Or worse—she could be dead already.

I think I might vomit. I try to slow my breathing. The last time I was in a hospital, my brother was losing his battle against an evil disease. It's safe to say, hospitals aren't my favorite place.

In what feels like hours, but in reality is less than five minutes, the double doors swing open. A doctor in baggy scrubs approaches us. The first thing I notice are the blood smudges on her shirt. Is that my wife's blood?

"Is she alive?" I blurt. I'm standing now, but my legs threaten to give out at any second.

"Mrs. Matson?" the doctor says.

"Graham. Christine Graham. I mean, yes. I...we're married, but I kept my name." I hate that I'm rambling.

She nods. "Mrs. Graham. I'm Dr. Bashir. I treated your wife upon arrival."

Answer my question, damnit.

I stare at her, studying her expression. Does she look sad? What does a doctor who's about to give devastating news look like? There's an image in my head. Too many episodes of *Grey's Anatomy*. Dr. Bashir's face is stoic. I can't read it, and I don't know if that's good or bad.

"Is she alive?" Abbie demands. I'm thankful she's here to back me up.

"Yes. Your wife, your mom," the petite doctor looks between us, "is alive. She's pretty banged up, but she's stable."

I exhale and bend forward. Abbie grabs my hand. Tears crest both of our eyes.

"Can we see her?"

"She's getting moved to a room upstairs. We want to keep her overnight, run a few more tests and keep an eye on her breathing. The airbag saved her life, but also collapsed a lung in the process. Give us a couple more minutes, and I'll have a nurse take you up, all right?"

"Thank you," I manage. I realize I'm crying. The tears are extra heavy, what with my guilt mixed in.

214

Dr. Bashir leaves us. Abbie wraps her arms around me and we lower to the seats as one.

"Abbie, I'm so sorry about—"

"Not now, Mom, okay? Let's deal with Ma first."

I respect her request. I can't expect instant forgiveness. It's going to take more than an apology to make up for my betrayal. Sitting with this shame is part of my punishment.

A creak, and we turn to the door again. A nurse emerges.

"I'm assuming you're Joss Matson's family? I can take you to her now."

Joss

It feels better to keep my eyes closed, though the doctor said they may swell shut soon anyways. When the airbag deployed, it blew my hands right into my face. I quite literally punched myself in the eyes.

I haven't seen myself in a mirror, but I can feel the tightness in my skin. There's a burn going down my neck that the doctor covered with gauze. A line of stitches across my forehead will be a new look for me. What's the term? Avant garde.

But I'm not complaining. I'm lucky to be alive. Things could have been much worse.

The door screeches open, and I pry my eyes apart. It's blurry for a second, but then the room comes into focus. My heart leaps to my throat. Christine and Abbie are here. They rush to my bed, one on either side.

"Joss, oh my God," Christine says. "Are you okay? What happened? Why did you— You know you're not supposed to drive."

She's hurling questions at me I don't know how to answer. The truth is, I don't remember what happened. Only that I was going for ice cream. Not supposed to drive? What is she talking about?

Abbie's crying. I lift my hand to wipe away her tears. "Don't cry, darling. I'm okay."

We're not alone for more than a minute before two uniformed police officers enter.

"Hi there," the female says, and I wonder if she's the boss of the two, or if they decide who's going to do the talking based on the gender of the patient. Woman to woman—maybe I'll feel more comfortable. "I'm detective Naples and this is detective Arujo. We're here to ask you a few questions about your accident. Can we speak in private?"

Christine squeezes my hand, and I know what she's thinking. I don't want them to leave, they just got here. I don't want to be alone.

"Can't they stay?"

"That's up to you," Naples says. "If you're comfortable with that."

"Yes. They're my family. They stay."

She nods. Detective Arujo pulls out a notepad and pen, but Naples is the one to speak. "Can you tell us what happened?" she says.

"I don't know, really. I was driving and the next thing I knew there was a horn and a loud crash, and I woke up here."

"Where were you going?"

"Jolly's. For ice cream." It sounds pitiful now, and I think if my face weren't already red from my injuries, it'd be flaming of embarrassment. An overweight, middle-aged woman going for ice cream alone. All because I felt sorry for myself. Pathetic.

"I honestly don't remember what happened," I continue, when really what I'm trying to get at is the question that's been burning in my chest since the doctors told me where I was and why. "Was it my fault?" I can barely get it out because I suspect I already know the answer.

The detectives look to each other. Naples' face softens. "You went through the intersection when it was a red light. The car coming the opposite direction had the green. You didn't stop."

The room spins. I close my eyes.

I caused the accident.

"And the other driver?" I whisper.

Naples looks down. "I'm sorry," she says, and my whole body goes numb. "The other driver didn't make it."

Abbie gasps.

"Oh my God," Christine says. She squeezes my hand harder. My mouth hangs open.

I killed someone. I'm a murderer.

But, no. It was an accident. I was alert, I wasn't distracted, wasn't drunk. It's not like I was on my phone. Jolly's was right there, I could see it. How did this happen?

"A witness says she saw your car speed up as you approached the intersection. Faster, instead of slower."

It hits us at the same time because Christine and I meet eyes and I can tell she's thinking the same thing as me.

"The wrong pedal," she says. "You stepped on the gas instead of the brake."

I nod slowly. "I think so. I must have."

"How old are you, Mrs. Matson?" Detective Naples says, and I instinctively want to correct her with *Dr.* Matson.

"Joss, please. And I'm fifty-four. But I know what you're thinking. This sounds like something an eighty-year-old would do." I sigh, my body sinking into the white mattress. "I have Alzheimer's. Early onset. Got the diagnosis a couple months ago."

Detective Arujo scribbles on his pad, but Naples just stares at me. Something in her eyes is sad, like she pities me.

"And your doctor said you're not supposed to drive?"

"I don't—" But I can't finish, because I'm honestly that confused.

"We'll give you some time with your family," she says. "But then I'm afraid we'll have to ask you some more questions."

"Is she going to jail?" Abbie says.

Naples extends a hand. "Let's not get too far ahead of ourselves, okay? Joss, you should get some rest. We'll be back soon."

They go, leaving in their place two other domineering figures: Fear and Grief.

Abbie

Mom and I refuse to go home. We both suffer through shallow sleep curled up on chairs in Ma's room, simultaneously uncomfortable and comforting. The doctor comes first thing in the morning to take Ma for another test—an X-ray, or CT Scan, I'm not sure and really don't know the difference anyway.

Mom said I can skip my classes today. She sent a group email to my professors explaining what happened. I don't want to leave this room. If they're coming back to arrest Ma, I want to be here. It could be the last time I see her. She could go to jail. She killed a person, after all, even if it was an accident. What's that charge called? Vehicular manslaughter, I think.

I look at my phone, which has been in my coat all night. Fifteen missed texts. Three calls. All about exams. I'm supposed to be delivering a few today.

I jump on Facebook for a momentary distraction, and a link populates at the top of my feed. It's from our local newspaper. The headline makes my stomach drop.

EVENING CRASH CLAIMS ONE LIFE.

I click on it, and my eyes scan the top paragraph.

Virginia State Police are investigating a two-vehicle crash at the intersection of Route 58 and Evans Park Road last night that killed one driver and sent the other to the hospital. Witnesses said the driver of a 2018 Honda Accord proceeded through a red light at a high rate of speed, hitting a Toyota Rav4 broadside. The Toyota's driver was pronounced dead at the scene by Danville Coroner Mark O'Reilly. Names of those involved have yet to be released, pending further investigation and notification of the families.

My chest is tight as I read, but it loosens when I reach the last sentence. The names haven't been released. Not yet. Ma is safe—for now.

I go back to the texts. Everything in me wants to stay here at the hospital, to write back and say *Fuck it, you're on your own this time.* But then I think about the money. Clearly Ma needs this medicine more than we realized. I have to keep going.

Will they let her continue treatment in jail? Does a criminal deserve life-saving medicine? I shake my head to dismiss such sickening thoughts. I don't know the answers, but until I do, I need to keep the income source alive. She's due for her next treatment this week. Maybe after this second one, we'll start to see improvement. Ma's future is up in the air, but for now, I'm going to pretend nothing's changed.

I reply to the texts.

Be there in twenty.

I turn to Mom. Dark smudges of exhaustion rest under her eyes. She's wearing yesterday's makeup, which has smeared, leaving her looking disheveled and more tired than I've ever seen her.

"I have to run to campus real quick," I say.

"I told you, you don't have to go to class. You're excused."

"I know, but I have to turn in my portion of a group paper. No sense everyone being late just because of me. I'll be quick."

She doesn't argue. I'm not sure she even processed what I said. She simply nods, and lays her head back down. I doubt she slept at all. I know I didn't.

When I get to campus, I keep my eyes low. The news of Ma's involvement will be out soon. Mom might have already even emailed the school to let them know. I don't need any interrogations right now.

I meet Sydney Ambrose outside the Student Center and hand her a folded exam. Next, I walk to the boy's dorm to meet Chuck Pfieffer. All around campus I go: Erin McNair, Callie Bettner, Zane Polanksi. I pass them the goods, they pass me the cash.

I don't think about the fact that my mother is in the hospital and could be facing charges. I don't think about how I could be expelled for what I'm doing, nor the embarrassment it would cause my parents.

What I do think about is saving Ma. That's the only thing. What I'm doing can't be wrong if it's all for the purpose of keeping Ma with us.

Right?

After my deliveries, I hightail it back to the car, thankful I didn't run into any faculty and no one asked me anything about the accident.

It's eight-thirty when I get back to the hospital—twelve hours after the accident. The police are there again. They turn when I enter the room, but Ma says it's okay for me to come in.

They're holding up a map of our town, thick red marker drawn along one road, and blue marker tracing another. The lines come together and meet at the center. That must be the intersection, the point of impact.

The woman detective is tracing her finger along the red line labeled Vehicle A. "So, this is you, Joss. Traveling north. Vehicle B was going west. You hit directly on the driver's side door."

Ma winces, and I wonder if she's reliving it.

"Am I allowed to know who it was yet?" Ma says.

The detectives give each other a look of bald confusion, then the woman steps forward. "We figured you'd heard. The victim's name was released earlier this morning. I thought maybe the school had contacted you."

At the word victim, both my moms take a sharp breath. It's a harsh reminder: someone died at the hands of Ma. But I'm only wondering what MacAmes has to do with it, why the school would call Ma when the driver's name was released.

Detective Naples opens her folder, scans an official-looking piece of paper. "Male, aged twenty-one," she says. "Name: Micah Johnson."

Christine

I hear her, but I don't hear her. The detective's voice swims through thick, brown syrup. My body's on the ceiling and I'm watching the scene unfold. But no, I'm very much here, on the ground, sitting beside Joss, holding her hand, and hearing my lover's name come from the detective's lips.

Micah Johnson. The victim. Dead.

Dead.

I'm not processing. Something's not connecting. How can it be? I was with him just last night, only hours ago. His hands on my face, trailing the line of my bra. When Abbie walked in on us, Micah had fled. I didn't think about where he was going, only that he was leaving me.

This shit's too heavy. I'm out.

But now it's all coming together. He left campus—of course he had—heading where I now suspect was home. Home, not far from Jolly's Ice Cream. Only, he didn't make it there. He drove into the intersection at the exact moment Joss was coming from the other direction. An unlucky chance of fate.

Someone's shaking me. My shoulders rattle, and I come back to reality only to realize no one's touching me. I'm shaking on my own.

I look to Joss. Her hands have flung over her face, and she's sobbing. "Twenty-one," she says over and over.

Abbie's crying too, the knuckle of a finger shoved between her teeth in effort to quell her sobs. Maybe she's trying not to scream.

"I'm so sorry," Detective Naples says. "I know he was a student of yours."

A tunnel forms in my vision. I might pass out. I stand on wobbly legs, holding onto the chair's arms for balance. At the end of the tunnel, there's the door. I narrow in on the knob. Get to the door. I need to get out of here. Need to howl. But I can't do it in here. Not in front of these people.

"Excuse me," I say, drone-like. "I need a minute." I stumble to the door, knocking my knee on the corner of the bed in the process. Am I walking? I can't feel my legs so I can't be sure.

"Mrs. Graham?" someone says, but I keep going.

The cool outside air hits my face and is the only thing that stops me from losing consciousness. I drop to my knees right there next to a stone bench. A sound comes from my mouth that I can only classify as animalistic. It starts in my core, travels up through my throat, and comes out as a long, painful cry.

I'm gutted. I feel as though my insides have been torn from my body. Both for the loss of Micah and for Joss's involvement. A life cut so short. It's not right. It's not how it's supposed to be. I don't think his future involved me—I know this deep down in my gut—but he had a future nonetheless, and the idea of it being destroyed in a split second crushes me.

"Ma'am, are you okay?" There's a hand on my back, and I twist to look up into the face of a man in scrubs. His name tag flops at his breast pocket, but I can't put the letters into any sensible order. I can't read. I'm rendered helpless, like a child.

"She's okay." This voice I know. Abbie squats beside me, replacing her hand where the man's just was.

"Are you sure?" he says.

"Yes, we're fine. Thank you."

He leaves us. Abbie covers her body over mine while I return to my weeping. She doesn't speak, just holds me.

Eventually we're sitting upright, and my head rests in the hollow of her neck. There's a wet spot on her shirt from where my tears have formed a puddle. It feels very much like a role reversal—parents are supposed to be the ones to comfort their children.

"I'm sorry, Mom," she says, and I can't comprehend how she has any sort of empathy for me in this moment. Not after what I did to Joss. She's not sorry for the guilt I feel, but for the fact that Micah is dead. Anyone would be.

"I just can't believe it," I finally manage, once my crying has slowed to a place I can talk again. We're both ash-stricken. It wasn't just me who saw him last. Abbie did too. I can tell by her face that she's just as rattled as I am. When you're in the company of a person, you don't expect them to be dead minutes later.

"Do you think he told anyone?" she says.

I know he did, I heard the proof myself when he joked with his friends. But I don't want to worry Abbie about that. Maybe those boys will keep quiet. What would be the point of spreading it? Micah's gone. And it's not like he wasn't a consenting adult. It was his idea in the first place, not the other way around. If it comes out, I'll deal with it then. For now, I need to protect my child and my wife.

"I don't think so," I say. "I know I didn't."

I suspect she's thinking of Joss at this moment, and the fact that I could hide something like this from her. I'm about to tell her I'll confess. Tell Joss everything. But she speaks first.

"Ma can't know."

I meet her eyes. They're neither warm nor cool. They're flat, vague.

"What good would it do?" she says.

I want to object, but don't. This is a gift she's giving me. She'll keep one mother's secret to protect the other. I don't deserve it, this much I know for sure. It's not fair for her to carry the burden of my mistake.

But what's the alternative? Adding another layer of devastation to a woman who's already at rock bottom seems cruel.

I nod slowly. Abbie is wise beyond her years. In this moment, I'm both proud and guilt-ridden. I go to pull her into another hug, but she keeps me back with a stiff arm. Our warm moment is done.

"It doesn't mean I forgive you," she says, and now her eyes have cooled.

"Understood," I say, because how can I argue?

At that, she stands and walks back into the hospital. She doesn't turn around.

Joss

They release me after forty-eight hours. By now, my eyes have all but sealed shut from the swelling and I have to feel my way to the bathroom. When I'm able to peer at my reflection through the slits, I gasp. I'm bruised every color of dusk. The gash on my forehead is crusted and pinches with every movement. I can't wash my face, only dab lightly, and I haven't yet washed my hair, which makes me feel even more disgusting than I look.

When Micah Johnson's name was released Friday, a dark cloud descended on our town. The campus community received an email with information for grief counseling services, along with an announcement that there would be additional support available. Our campus therapy dog, Buddy, is making rounds through the dorms, offering his nuzzles and slobber in return for their tears.

My heart is broken. I can't stop thinking about that boy's parents. Did he have siblings? I can't bring myself to read the obituary. What if he was an only child like Abbie? Now his parents are alone. I picture them getting ready to bury their son, and I weep.

Christine hasn't gone back to work. The administration gave her a temporary leave. She brought me home and hasn't left the house since. I'm grateful for her presence, though she's walking around like a shell of herself. This morning I heard her crying in the shower when she thought I was downstairs. My heart sinks at the thought of what I've done to my family.

The doorbell rings. I turn from where I'm sitting on the couch, wincing as my torso twists and internal bruises bump up against each other. Sunday basketball is on, not that any of us are paying attention. The background noise helps ease the heaviness in the house.

"I'll get it," Abbie says. She bounds to the door. Her joggers hang loose on her frame, and I notice she looks awfully thin. It's amazing what stress will do to a body.

After a minute, I call to her. "Who is it?"

"Dr. Viotto's here," she says, coming back into the living room followed by Kerry who's carrying a tray covered in aluminum foil.

"Lasagna," Kerry says, lifting the tray a little. "Homemade. Not that frozen stuff. Grabbed your mail, too."

I realize we haven't got the mail all weekend. She lays the stack on the side table. "Oh, Kerry, that's so thoughtful. Thank you."

We've been friends as long as Christine and I have been at MacAmes. There's a special connection between the female faculty. An unspoken thread of support for one another. When Kerry got department chair, we toasted to another piece of the glass ceiling shattering.

"I'll go put this in the fridge," she says.

When she's gone, I flip through the mail with a listless hand. About halfway through, I see the envelope. It's the same one as before—no return address, no postmark.

Abbie's in the chair across from me. "Another one?" she says with enthusiasm, as I rip open the back. Sure enough, a handful of cash sits evenly inside. I don't pull it out, nor do I smile. The sight of it does nothing for me. I lay the stack of mail back on the table.

"Ma, this is good," Abbie says. "Just in time for your next treatment."

"What's the point? I'm done with that. It's obviously not working. They might as well give it to someone else."

"Don't think like that."

Kerry returns. She sits beside me, gives me a gentle hug like I might break.

"How are you?" she says.

Water instantly floods my eyes. I'm like a never-ending waterfall. Just when I've stopped crying for a stretch of time, I realize I've stopped, which makes me feel even more guilty. I deserve to cry for eternity.

"It wasn't your fault." Kerry places a soft hand on my leg. "It was an accident. A complete accident. No one blames you."

"Of course they do." I sniff. "Why wouldn't they? I'm the one who ran the red light."

"But your...condition. There's an explanation for it. It's not like you weren't paying attention."

"My condition isn't public knowledge. They'll crucify me."

Christine walks in then. "Oh, Kerry, I didn't know you were here," she says. Her eyes are red-rimmed.

"Chris." Kerry stands and the two embrace. "This is just awful."

"Yes." Christine's voice quivers. Then, "What's happening on campus?"

Kerry sighs. "I haven't been there since Friday, obviously, but Janet in Residence Life texted me. Said it's pretty somber. A lot of crying students. She said they're planning a vigil for later this week."

I lower my head, picturing hundreds of students holding thin white candles. A beautiful campus shrouded in sadness.

"Are you going to go to the funeral?" she asks.

The idea sends me spiraling. I don't think I could witness such a thing. But even more so, I doubt his family would want me there—a visual symbol of the one who survived, when their son didn't.

"I don't know," Christine says. "When is it?"

She must not have read the obituary either.

"Tomorrow afternoon."

Christine gives a little nod. Maybe she should go as a representative for our family. Show we care, that we're not bad people.

We aren't bad people.

The silence is uncomfortable. As much as I appreciate Kerry's visit, I'm not up for conversation. I want nothing more than to curl in on myself and not come out.

"I'm not going to stick around," Kerry says, reading my mind. "Just wanted to drop off dinner and let you both know I'm thinking of you. You know how much I love you two. I support you, and am here for whatever you need."

"Thank you, Ker," I say.

Christine walks her to the door. I hear it open. I wait for it to close again. Instead, Christine's voice sounds surprised.

"Detectives," she says.

"May we come in? There've been some updates."

Christine

Kerry and I give each other a quick hug before she slips past the detectives on the front stoop.

"Come in," I say. My eyes go to the handcuffs clipped on Detective Arujo's belt and I wonder if they'll shortly be slapped on my wife's wrists. That must be why they're here. To arrest Joss. Now that the dust has settled, it's clear what happened. She caused the accident that killed Micah. I suspect we've all been waiting for this moment.

This is it. Joss will be doing a perp walk out of this very door any moment.

Detective Naples enters first, and I'm glad she's been the leader of this case. Right or wrong, I can't help but feel a man wouldn't have the same compassion, the same softness about it all.

Joss is standing when we get to the living room. She no doubt heard the exchange at the door, and I can read the panic on her face.

"Hi Joss," Naples says. "How are you doing?"

I analyze her words for hidden meaning. Would she be bothering with pleasantries if she were here to arrest Joss? *How are you doing?* How does she think we're doing? Awful, we're doing awful, thanks for asking. Maybe this is just her way of showing a bit of empathy. My body stiffens, waiting for the blow I know is coming.

Abbie's there, too, and even though I know this will be impossibly difficult for her to witness, I'm glad she's here. We're a family, and we need each other. I need her.

"May I sit?" Naples says, though she's already lowering herself to a chair. "I wanted to swing by to let you know the case is closed as of this morning."

I blink several times. Must not have heard correctly. Closed?

"But—" Joss's mouth gapes.

"Do you *want* to be arrested?"

"No, of course not. I'm surprised, is all."

"There will be no formal charges. It was an accident. Everyone agrees on that." She sets her mouth in a thin line that tells me she doesn't necessarily agree with this outcome, and it makes me re-think her loyalty to us.

"Ma," Abbie says, and when I look at her there are tears in her eyes. She flings herself onto Joss, burying her head against the soft pillows of Joss's breasts. She's a child again, a scared child expressing relief in the comfort of a parent. Seeing them like this delivers a pang to my heart. I haven't seen such closeness between them for years.

"Why do you still look like there's more you want to say?" Joss says to Naples, as she pats Abbie's head.

Naples shifts in the chair. "There could still be a civil suit from the Johnson family."

"They could sue?" I ask. I picture Micah's family, rallying together to throw their pain onto the one person who caused it all. I can't say I wouldn't do the same if it were Abbie who was taken away from me so suddenly. Throw them on the fire, make them pay.

"They could."

"Even though it was an accident?" Joss says.

"Your doctor said you shouldn't be driving. You ignored this order."

"I didn't ignore it, I forgot. There's a difference. It's part of my—my disease."

Her face reads pure agony, and my soul crushes watching her try to defend her character.

"The family has made one immediate request, however," Naples continues.

Yes, yes, whatever it is, yes. Anything besides Joss going to jail.

"They're requesting that you surrender your driver's license."

It takes a second, but then Joss's face twitches. "Not drive anymore?"

"Yes."

"Can they do that?"

"They can petition the court to make a ruling. It was already a medical recommendation, but now it'll be absolute."

I can see the wheels turning in her head. I know what she's thinking: another simple pleasure, now denied. Another freedom lost.

"But it was just a freak thing," Joss says. "Maybe because it was dark. Or, I don't know, I was daydreaming. I'll focus more."

There's a desperation to her voice that makes my heart hurt. The detectives look to me, and I sense it's my turn to speak.

"It's not that big of a deal, hon," I try. "Plenty of people don't drive. That's what Abbie and I are here for, right Ab?"

"I'll take you places," Abbie says, though I can see sadness in her eyes, too.

"What am I, a wrinkly old lady? A charity case?" Joss's chest is heaving.

I slide in beside her. "Of course not," I say. "But they're right. It wasn't safe then, and it's definitely not safe now."

Our eyes are locked, and I focus in on the golden flecks that speckle her irises. They're one of the first things I noticed about Joss when we met. It's been forever since I've looked into her eyes long enough to recognize them.

I nod, but it's more like a question. *Okay? Do you agree?*

Her head drops. "Okay," she says quietly.

My breath releases. Knowing her obstinance, this could have gone bad. She could have put up more of a fight. I suppose the alternative is enough for her to give in. The prospect of charges, a trial, jail time—none of that outweighs the truth that's staring us in the face. Joss should not be driving anymore, that much is crystal clear. And while some of my nerves have allayed, it's only half of the weight I'm carrying.

Tomorrow there will be a funeral. And I have a decision to make.

Abbie

Mondays suck in general, but the Monday after your mom is in a car wreck that kills someone is extra fucked up.

Even though my professors said I could take more time, I need to get back to normalcy. Sitting around the house with my moms makes me even more depressed.

A quiet campus is really weird. It's like people are afraid to show any hint of happiness. The sun's out for what feels like the first time in eternity, but no one's taking advantage of it. I get it, though. I mean, playing cornhole and laughing feels a little insensitive when the kid from your English class just died.

I'm walking along a path between buildings when I hear my name.

"Abbie, wait up!"

When I look, Stacia is jogging up to me, her Kate Spade tote bag bumping against her hip. Part of me wants to turn and keep walking. I haven't heard from her at all since the accident. Not an oh-my-god-how-are-you call. Not even a text. Indifference—the worst kind of hurt. I thought we were friends. Now that I think about it, no one reached out to me, not even Trina. The thought of my old friend brings with it a sharp taste to my mouth. I owe her a call, or seven.

Stacia breaks into a light smile as she gets closer. My shoulders relax. I'm sure she'll say something now. Maybe she was just waiting to see me in person. A quick image flashes through my brain—us hugging, her being my support person, defending me against the hate I foresee might be hurled at my family. In the time it takes her to cross the remaining feet between us, I've forgiven her silence.

I flash a closed-mouth smile, waiting for the shower of sympathy.

"I'm glad I caught you," she says, her breath slightly ragged. "You know Maggie, the girl you, uh...helped the other week? One of her friends is looking to get in. I told her I'd let you know. Assured her you'd get the goods." She winks.

I'm rendered speechless. A little cough escapes my mouth. "What?"

"You're on a roll, I figured one more would be like nothing."

"Stacia, I kind of have a lot going on right now." I can't believe she hasn't even said anything about Ma. About the accident. About Micah. Seriously? The first thing out of her mouth is a request to steal another exam?

My tone must have read loud and clear because Stacia crosses her arms. "Hey, you're the one who started all this."

"I did it for you. Once. It was a temporary side-hustle, not a career."

"That's on you."

I let out an exasperated breath. "Listen, I don't really have the mental space for this today."

"Ok, whoa. Someone needs a vibe check. Anyway, Tekes are throwing their spring fling this weekend. I can add a name to the block list with a simple text. You'll never get invited again."

I clench my jaw to prevent it from falling open. The words sting. She could be bluffing, but I don't want to find out. Being against Stacia would be worse than being the nobody I was before this all started.

What's one more?

But it's not just adding one more person to this circus I've created. It's the way she said it. The implication that I don't have a choice—or at least if I don't want to become a social pariah. That it's become expected, an act that no longer requires the shower of praise which fueled it all in the first place.

The alternative hovers close to the edge, and I sense how quick this could all disappear: the friends, the acceptance.

"Fine," I say, and her face lights back up again.

"I knew I could count on you," she says. She puckers her lips and blows me an air kiss.

I watch her blonde locks swing as she walks away. And that's when I realize she never did end up mentioning anything about the accident.

So much for emotional support.

I continue along the path with my head down, avoiding cracks in the sidewalk just like I'm doing with the one that's formed in our friendship.

Christine

Black is not my color. Even though it's the de facto hue of traditional office wear, I've never owned a black suit in my life. When I started teaching, I decided I would only wear suits for things like conferences or days when my class was being observed. I wanted the students to find me approachable, and nothing says *un*approachable than a stuffy, formal business suit.

Warm colors are much more flattering on me. Which is why when I slip into a black dress for Micah's funeral, I feel even more uncomfortable. The color does nothing for my skin tone. If anything, it washes me out.

I'm taking in my reflection as these thoughts come to mind, and then I give myself a mental slap across the face. This isn't about me or my outfit. No one gives a shit what I wear today. I'm disgusted at my own thoughts. But deep down, I realize I want to look good for him. The one person who's not even alive to see me.

I take the stairs gingerly in my heels. Joss is at the kitchen table eating a bowl of cereal. It's four in the afternoon. Our schedule has been completely thrown off the past few days.

"Are you sure you don't want to come," I say.

She shakes her head. "I can't bear to show my face there."

"But everyone knows now."

"Doesn't matter. They still won't want me there. Let his family put him to rest without me serving as a distraction."

Put him to rest. I swallow hard to keep the acid down. It's still not fully sunk in.

The door opens and Abbie enters, backpack flung over one shoulder.

"Hey, sweetheart," I say. "How were classes?"

Her eyes are daggers. I drop the forced cheer. She's not ready to absolve me of my sins.

Abbie rounds the table and gives Joss a peck on the cheek. My belly clenches. I've been dethroned as the favorite mom.

"Are you coming to the funeral?" I ask.

"No."

"Really? I thought a lot of students were planning to go."

"It's not like we were friends. Plus, I have some other stuff I need to do."

She's short with me, offering no further explanation. I wonder whether she feels obligated to stay home with Joss. It's an unspoken understanding that she shouldn't be home alone for long stretches anymore.

"You go," Abbie says. "He was your student."

The dig cuts to my core. Her eyes never leave mine when she says it, and we both know the meaning behind her words.

I imagine it would be hard for her to sit next to me as I watch Micah's casket come down the aisle of the church. I'm sure she's wondering why I'm going in the first place. *I'm* wondering why I'm going in the first place. Why would I put myself through this pain? The only answer I can conjure is cliché: closure.

I don't meet Abbie's eyes when I say, "Okay. I'll see you in a few hours." Then I grab my purse and leave.

***

The line wraps around the funeral home. I fall in place behind a group of boys I vaguely recognize as previous students. Up ahead are several faculty members from various departments who made the trip to Richmond together, and who'd invited me to carpool, an offer I couldn't bear. I drove alone and cried most of the way.

Sorrow drifts through the line, weaving amongst us. One woman dabs her eyes with a tissue. The scene brings me back to Fisher's funeral—one of the worst days of my life. Only instead of being one of the consolers, I was the grieving twin, firmly rooted at the head of the casket, half of my soul laying there in pillowed folds of white, with too much makeup caked on his forty-one-year-old face.

I don't know if I can see another young person like that.

It takes thirty minutes to even get into the building. Once inside, the route travels through a parlor and another side room before leading into where I know the casket is. I fan myself with the prayer card the director handed me at the door. It's suffocating in here. Sweat prickles my face as we move forward. Each step brings me closer to what feels like impending devastation. My knees feel weak, and I'm just hoping I can make it through this line before they give out completely.

Along the way, bulletin boards full of photos sprinkle the path. Pictures of Micah as a baby with fuzzy curls and big brown eyes. One of him standing next to an oversized crayon, in what I presume is a pre-school snapshot. We have one of Abbie like that.

As the images progress, he gets older. A photo with a girl whose caramel skin matches his own. A sister. They're in matching pajamas in front of the Christmas tree. She's alone now, an only child when that was never supposed to be the case.

Just before I cross into the main room, the pictures stop. The last set shows the Micah I knew. Handsome and strong, depicting his last years of life. Throwing a football. Lounging on a couch with a video game controller in hand.

That's it. That's where his life ends.

I've been to viewings before, I've seen these picture collages. But they normally continue into old age. Where's the gray hair? Where's the creases in his face that should have come with time?

The realization hits me: This wasn't a man. This was very much still a boy. Old enough to vote, old enough to buy alcohol, or join the military, but also young enough to live at home and squabble with a sibling, and sit at the table while his mom makes pancakes.

I'm at the front now. Next in line to pay my respects to the family members flanking the casket. The boy in front of me steps forward. I extend my hand toward a woman who looks no older than me. I recognize the lines around her eyes, the skin at her neck that's not quite as firm as I suspect it once was. She could be me. I could be her. Life hasn't been fair to her, yet today she looks beautiful.

"I'm so sorry for your loss," I say, and it feels insufficient. Her hands are soft like Micah's. I see him in her eyes. This is his mother. She wears the pierce of grief like an unmistakable brooch on her collar.

"Thank you," she says. There are salt stains trailing down her cheeks. "How did you know my son?"

My heart blips. She doesn't know me. Doesn't know our connection. "I had him in class." And then I add, because it feels right, "He was special."

The line moves me along and I murmur soft condolences to the others—the sister from the picture, a tall man whose full lips Micah shared. An uncle, perhaps? Or is this the father he never knew, showing back up when it's too late?

Then I'm at the casket. I'm glad it's closed because I don't think I'd have the strength to see his face, sleeping but not really. It's hard to believe he's in there. I trail my hand along the shiny surface.

"I'm sorry," I whisper. And I am. I'm utterly sorry. Sorry for letting it happen in the first place, and sorry for not putting a stop to it sooner. We were both in the wrong, but it should have been me who saw clearer.

"You shouldn't be here." The deep voice startles me, its volume coming off loud in the quiet of the funeral home. I whip my head up to find all eyes on me. Micah's family—the mother I'd consoled—glares in my direction. For a split second, I think we've been discovered, Micah and I.

"How dare you come here," his mother hisses, stepping toward me. "When your wife is the one who killed him. Get out. Get out of here. You're not wanted." Her voice elevates and her once-somber face is now filled with rage. "Get out!"

The sick feeling comes on fast. I shouldn't have come—it was foolish to think I could handle it. I hurry out, not stopping to interact with anyone in line, even when I hear a mumbled chorus of, *Hi, Dr. Graham.* My car is parked at the edge of the lot facing a dense patch of trees. I make it there just in time to hurl into the bushes.

Joss

A week has passed since the accident, but it might as well have happened yesterday. Everything's still dark, the clouds refusing to lift. I've spent the past few days in bed, too despondent, too *whatever*, to get up. My body is a glacier, heavy and slow-moving. I sleep a lot.

Outside, the tulips Christine planted poke through the loose Earth. I wish they'd stay underground. I can't bear to see anything beautiful, anything resembling any sense of renewal. There's no renewal here. I'm going backwards.

I have a neuro appointment at two—at least that's what's written on the giant board that now tracks all my movements. Christine is getting someone to proctor her class so she can take me, now that I'm not allowed to drive. I feel fully capable, and the fact that I have to be chauffeured like a child only adds to my inner rage.

The phone rings, startling me. I roll over, grab my cell off Christine's pillow, and am greeted by Detective Naples' voice.

"Hi Joss. I'm not interrupting anything, am I?"

If you count laying around in days-old pajamas something, I want to chide, but tell her no instead.

"I have good news," Naples says. "The Johnsons have dropped their suit."

The phone slips from my hand and I scramble to bring it back to my ear.

"Did you say dropped? You mean there won't be any punishment?"

Naples' tone is even. She's not one to insert much emotion, I've learned. "Not formally or civilly. I suspect the emotional burden is plenty."

I swallow. That's an understatement. "You have no idea."

"The uncle was pushing for litigation, but the mother declined. We've spoken to her. She's angry and devastated, of course. But in her heart of hearts, she realizes it was a complete accident. What was it she said? 'To err is human; to forgive is divine.'"

The hairs on my arm stand up. I expect a wave of relief to crash over me, but it doesn't. At least not in the way I envisioned. I killed someone. A young man died because of my negligence—medical or not. That's not something I can easily forget.

Naples clears her throat. "Joss?"

"I'm here."

"This must come as a reprieve. I can't begin to imagine what you've gone through, but you can't let blame bury you."

It's the first time I've heard any sympathy in her voice, and something about it is comforting. I mumble a response. My alarm beeps at the same time a reminder flashes across my phone: Time to get up, you have an appointment at 2:00.

I swipe it away, and consider not going at all.

"I'll let you go," Naples says. "I hope this is the last we'll have to see each other. And I mean that in the nicest way possible."

"Thank you," I say, meaning it.

When I hang up, I roll off the bed, deliberately avoiding my reflection in the mirror. I still can't stomach who I've become.

The shower can't scald me enough.

* * *

244

"It's not good," Dr. Kaur says with a sigh. He places his hands on his desk and leans forward, as though the approachability will somehow ease the blow he's about to deliver. Christine reaches for my hand, but I'm too busy stroking the rabbit's foot on my lap. "The latest scan came back showing amyloid proteins in the temporal and frontal lobes."

Christine cocks her head. "In English?"

"Abnormalities." He pulls up two images on his computer. Both brains are rainbowed with ribbons of activity. "This," he says, pointing to the picture on the left, "is a normal, healthy brain." He moves to the right. "This one is yours."

Dark blobs cover portions of the image, as though my brain were being sucked into a black hole, and as I stare at it, I decide that's the perfect analogy. I'm being pulled into a giant black hole.

"So you're saying I'm dying."

"We're all dying, Joss." His voice is kind, but I don't want to accept his kindness. He folds his hands into a steeple. "I want to be honest with you. I'm not a sugarcoat-it kind of person. The treatment's not working. We would have seen a decrease in progression by now, not an increase. How have you been at home? Any more instances you can think of?"

I flash to yesterday and how I had to sign a check but couldn't remember how to write my name. The pen had stayed put, eventually leaving an ink spot when I finally scribbled something illegible.

"Yes," Christine answers for me. "She's misplaced several things recently. Called our dentist thinking it was your office. Things like that."

My cheeks flare listening to Christine rattle off all my shortcomings.

"The other day she thought Norfolk was in Wyoming even though it's only two hours from our house. We go there almost every summer. We've never even been to Wyoming."

"What?" I snap. "No I didn't."

"You did, Joss. We were in the kitchen talking about how summer break will be here before we know it."

I search my memory but come up blank. I don't remember having that conversation, let alone thinking Norfolk, Virginia was across the country. I shrink in my chair. There's a sudden pressure behind my sinuses and tears threaten my eyes, but I'd rather die than cry here.

"Yes," Dr. Kaur says. "These are all common, I'm afraid." His mouth turns down. I wonder how people can navigate such depressing jobs. Doctors, surgeons, therapists. Telling people they're losing their minds can't be fun.

"So, now what?" I say.

"We treat the side effects of the disease. The anxiety, the depression. We try to make you comfortable."

"Make me comfortable? It sounds like you're sending me home to die."

"That's not what he's saying," Christine says.

"Oh yeah? Well, that's easy for you to say. You're not the one facing a future of incapacitation." It's a big word, and it comes out hot. I can tell by her face it stung.

Dr. Kaur runs a hand through his thinning hair. "I'm so sorry, truly."

We leave having agreed to cease the new treatment. Why throw money at something that's clearly not working? It wasn't even our money to begin with, but it still seems futile, like we're opening the trash and tossing the bills straight in.

Right on cue, my phone rings as we pull into our driveway.

"Why is Ken calling me?" I murmur, but Christine still hears.

"Ken, as in Dean of Faculty Ken?"

I nod and accept the call.

"Joss," he says, raspy and strained. "I think it's time we talk about retirement."

Abbie

I've stolen eight exams and made two hundred transactions. Twenty grand. Twenty grand that should have gone to Ma. Then Lester came along and now I've only been able to send Ma half.

It should still feel good—the getting money for Ma part. It's what I set out to do. But it doesn't. Ma's treatment isn't working. She's getting worse, not better. And now I'm stuck in this vicious cycle where both options suck: keep stealing from Mom (even though the cause no longer stands), or throw in the towel and risk being exposed by a creepy gambling addict.

Then there's Stacia.

She's been cool toward me in the last two weeks, despite my continuing devotion. The closeness I thought we had has turned distant and I don't know why. What did I do to her?

I pull out my phone and hold it under the table, away from the eyes of my history prof, and type out a text.

Lunch today?

It's Thursday and I know she has a break from noon to two. Less than a minute passes, though it always feels like an hour when I'm waiting to hear back from Stacia.

Can't, sorry.

No reason. Just a no. I double tap and send back a thumbs up emoji because I don't want to seem disappointed. A second later my phone vibrates and a new message pops up.

Ugh, she's SO clingy. I can't wait to graduate so I don't have to deal w her.

Heat drenches my body. This text isn't meant for me. It's *about* me. I stare at the screen, not sure whether to respond. Do I play dumb? Let it go? What's the less humiliating option?

I play dumb, send a single question mark back as a response.

Three dots appear. She's typing. Is she going to own it?

Oops, wrong person.

That's it. No explanation. At least it's the truth, I think. That text definitely wasn't supposed to come to me. I want to write back and ask who she's talking about, who's the clingy one, but stop short of causing myself even further embarrassment. We both know her slip-up.

Seeing the words on screen makes something click in my brain. This was all a sham, our "friendship." It was never a friendship at all. Stacia used me to get what she wanted, then she continued to use me to help her real friends.

The classroom around me shrinks. It feels like the walls are closing in. How could I have been so stupid? Part of me wants to laugh at myself: *Abbie, you really thought Stacia King wanted to be your friend? How gullible are you?* But there's nothing funny about this because it's not just me losing what I thought was a friend. There's a lot more at play. I've done bad things, and sitting here in this brightly-lit classroom, I suddenly realize just how wrong it all is.

A guy's backpack bumps my shoulder, returning me to the present, and I realize everyone's shuffling from the room. Class is over. I grab my stuff and follow, my mind spinning.

I'm scheduled to meet Lester this evening. I have a handful of cash I'm supposed to hand over to him. I picture the exchange, remember the other times and the sick feeling I got watching the money pass from my hand to his.

The spring air hits my face when I exit the building, a welcome jolt to the senses. Spring on campus is pretty, but I haven't even appreciated it this year, not with Ma's diagnosis, Mom's midlife crisis, and then the accident. I've barely enjoyed my freshman year at all.

I stop mid-stride, as though a new resolve has fixed itself in my core. Fuck this. I'm done. No more exams. No more buying friends. And definitely no more Lester. The decision comes fast and sure, bringing with it a confidence I'm not used to. I'll confront Lester tonight. Tell him his little blackmail game is over. What's he gonna do? To implicate me would mean implicating himself.

I walk with a lightness, feeling the relief of a thousand suns. This whole thing is about to be shoved in the past. I just can't believe I'm actually going to get away with it.

***

Once again, my moms barely notice that I'm leaving at eight o'clock on a Thursday night. Ma's been spending a lot of time staring into space and I can't be sure if she's really even here. Mom's trying to catch up with the days she missed following the accident. She doesn't look good, doesn't have that spark she did before all this. She's lost weight. Her wedding ring spins around her finger freely.

"I'll be back," I say, and am returned with quiet grunts of acknowledgement.

When I get to our designated meeting spot, Lester is waiting.

"Thought maybe you balked," he sneers. "Thought I'd have to march straight to the president's office."

He's trying to threaten me, trying to instill fear, but I'm over it. He's just as guilty as me. I want to reach out and flick him away like the pesky insect he is.

"I highly doubt the president is here at this hour," I say flatly, and I detect surprise in his reaction. His back straightens a bit, as though he expected me to come flying in apologizing how it would never happen again. Turns out I'm not the groveling type.

"Sassy tonight, aren't we?"

He opens his palm, waiting for me to drop the wad of bills into it as usual. But I don't. I stand there with my hands in the pocket of my hoodie.

"What are you waiting for?" he says, looking over his shoulder. Our exchanges have been quick. He doesn't like my lingering.

"I don't have anything for you," I say.

"Cut the crap, girlie. Hand it over."

"I'm serious." I fold my arms across my chest. "I'm not doing this anymore."

A vein pops at his neck. "Oh, so you'd rather me turn you in?"

"You're not going to turn me in."

"Oh really? Why so confident?"

"Because I'll just tell them about how you blackmailed me into continuing, how you took half of the money. You're not some innocent bystander, you know."

It seems to take him back because his jaw clamps shut and his lips purse. But instead of yelling or hissing at me, he breaks into a laugh. His head tips back and his mouth opens. I shift on my feet, wondering what could be so funny.

"Oh, you really are a naïve little thing, aren't you?" he says. "You think you're calling the shots here? Try again."

Now it's me whose teeth clench. I try to hold my ground, but his laugh has an evil edge that makes my limbs tingle.

"Your mother," he says.

At first I think he means Ma. By now the whole town—and extended area—know about Ma's accident and Micah's death. But what does that have to do with me not reporting him?

He looks up and I follow his gaze to a window on the third floor. Mom's office.

Mom. He knows.

"Yeah," he jeers, drawing the word out and nodding. "I know all about your mother's little escapades with that boy. I saw him leaving her office one night when they didn't know I was hiding around the corner. Little hussy, that mom of yours."

Instinct makes my hands ball into fists.

"Whoa," he holds up his hands and takes a step back, though he's laughing the whole time. "You gonna hit me for speaking the truth? Listen girlie, your mom was doing God knows what with a student. I can't imagine that would bode well for her tenure application should it come out."

I can't help it, my mouth drops open. A pleased look crosses his face and I want to punch the smug right off him. I was supposed to have the upper hand in this conversation. How did it twist around so horribly?

My confidence evaporates until I'm standing there in the same predicament, if not worse. Would he really do it? Or is this just a big charade, a big threat to keep me going?

I think of Stacia and her text.

I can't wait to graduate in 3 weeks so I don't have to deal w her.

I think of Ma and hear the words she whispered after that last doctor's appointment: *It's not working.*

There's no reason for me to continue. I can't. I don't want to.

"Fuck you," I say to Lester. His grin only widens. I turn and walk away.

"Suit yourself," he calls.

I stay the course.

Christine

Retirement paperwork is almost worse than a tenure portfolio. Joss is getting more and more confused by the day. Abbie went to campus for something—did she say a study group?—so Joss and I are using the quiet to tackle a couple forms while chicken piccata simmers on the stove. A rich aroma floats through the room, and my mouth waters. My appetite's only recently returned.

Joss props her elbows on the table, lets her head sink into her hands like dead weight.

"It's not that hard, hon," I try gently. "Lump sum or pension."

Normally it would be a no-brainer: take the pension. But normally she wouldn't be retiring at fifty-four. Normally she'd be finishing her sabbatical and returning to the classroom for at least another fifteen years.

There's nothing normal about this situation.

Facing the rapid progression of her disease, the lump sum seems to make more sense. We don't know how much more time she has. We never even made it to Hawaii like we wanted.

Joss traces her finger along the woodgrain of the table.

"Joss, can you focus?" I don't mean it to come out as harsh as it does, and I instantly feel bad. She can't help what's happening to her. But that doesn't mean it's not incredibly frustrating.

After she talked to the Dean of Faculty, we had a meeting with her department chair, then another with HR.

"It's what's best," Ken had said.

We all knew it. There'd be no way Joss could return as an effective teacher. It would be unfair for everyone. She cried that night, and I held her in bed for the first time in a long time. Our bodies curved together, my head nestling into the back of her neck, my arms wrapped around her middle.

"I'm just so scared," she'd said, and tears slipped down my cheek to the pillow.

The truth is, I'm scared too. What does my future look like without Joss by my side? It's never been a question I've had to ponder before. Even with the gray waters of the last year or so, there was never a time I didn't see her next to me. She was supposed to plan my funeral, not the other way around.

The thought hits me: if she knew what I'd been doing, would she still feel the same? I'm sick to my stomach just contemplating it. I'm a horrible, horrible person.

Now in the kitchen, she pushes back from the table, the chair skidding against the floor in a screech.

"I don't know, Christine, okay? I don't know anything anymore."

"That's not true," I say, though it sort of is. I reach for her hand. "Let's take a break from this, huh? What do you want to talk about? Summer's coming. We should go somewhere. How about out West. Remember that trip to Yellowstone? We could pack Abbie up and hit the road. We could—"

"Enough!" Joss shouts. "Don't you get it, Chris? I'm dying. Wasting away. I'm not going to be making new memories. The best years of my life are behind me. And even if we did take a holiday I probably wouldn't remember it anyway."

I feel the blood drain from my face. It's like mine has transferred to her—her face boils, a thin line of perspiration near her hairline.

"Don't say that," I whisper.

"It's true. I'm fucked." Her chin quivers. "You might as well start planning a future without me."

She leaves before I can say something. I should go after her. I should pull her to me and jumpstart her heart with mine. But the truth of it hits hard, and I can't get up.

No sooner does Joss exit, but Abbie enters through the kitchen door. She huffs across the linoleum and I can see anger in her eyes.

"What's wrong, sweetheart?" I say.

"Don't sweetheart me," she snaps, not stopping as she hurls her venom. "This is all your fault."

She stomps up the stairs, leaving me alone in a kitchen that smells of garlic and grief.

Abbie

The following morning, I wake to an email from Student Affairs, CC'd to the Dean of Students.

Dear Abigail Graham-Matson,
The Student Conduct Council has received an accusation of academic dishonesty against you. As per the University's policy and the procedures detailed in the student handbook, the Council requests a meeting with you to discuss said allegations. This meeting has been scheduled for today at 2 p.m. in the Alumni Boardroom. Your schedule indicates a break in classes during this time, but if you're unable to attend for separate reasons, please respond indicating such.
Sincerely,
Ruth Chambers
Director, Student Life and Affairs

Fuck.

Fuck, fuck, fuck. This is not good. Lester did it; he turned me in. That bastard.

Nausea creeps in, and I want to throw the covers back over my head and erase the past eight months. But I can't, because if I don't show up, I know their next step will be to contact Mom. Thank God I signed that FERPA confidentiality waiver. Even if they can't tell her what I did, they can still use her to get to me, and Mom will freak if she learns the disciplinary panel is looking for me.

I'm screwed. What excuse do I have? None. I stole exams and sold them to students, plain and simple. There's no way to sugarcoat it.

I reply to the email even though it didn't ask for a confirmation.

Thank you, Ms. Chambers. I will be there.
Abbie Graham-Matson

I don't defend myself or ask for clarification, but I'm careful to sound polite and respectful like Mom taught me. Maybe it will help my cause.

Black seems like an appropriate choice for the day. It's my academic funeral, after all. I slip on a dark MacAmes tee, hoping my collegiate fondness will be enough for them to not suspend me.

The ride to campus is excruciating—Mom trying to go back to normal even though it's impossible, and me trying to match her ease to avoid suspicion anything's wrong.

"Ma and I were talking about summer vacation plans," she says.

I don't even bring up the obvious: Ma's not going on any trips this summer or any summer after that. And once she discovers what I've done—unless I can still get away with it somehow—I doubt she'll be treating me to any vacations either.

When we park, I can't jump from the car fast enough. The sinking feeling in my stomach only multiplies when I see the smile on her face—the smile I haven't seen for weeks. I'm about to crush her all over again. Any trust I've formed with my parents will be gone. Poof!

I make my way to class, convinced I might as well have skipped. I'll never be able to concentrate.

The room's half full, and I head toward the same seat I always take (it's like college students don't realize there are no assigned seats). As I pass the professor at the front, he motions to me.

"Abbie, this was on the podium when I got in." He hands me a sealed envelope with my full name on the front. I turn it over in my hand, confused. The professor shrugs. "I don't know," he says, clearly not giving a care, and returns his attention to the computer screen.

The envelope burns in my hand and I can't help but think of the ones I slipped into our own mailbox, addressed to Ma. This one, however, is light, definitely not packed with cash. So light, it feels like it could be empty.

I take a seat, lower the envelope to my lap, concealed by the desktop, and tear open the back. Inside is a small piece of lined paper, ragged at the top like it was torn from a notebook. A single sentence, written in all caps:

LEAVE ME OUT OF IT, AND I'LL LEAVE HER OUT OF IT.

I quickly fold the paper then glance right and left. No one's paying any attention. I inch it back open and read it again. My heart's racing. Another threat, another ultimatum. But this time it involves more than just me. Now he's also blackmailing Mom.

The professor starts rambling but I don't hear what he's saying. My brain's whirring, going through all the what-ifs. What if I say no? Tell him to fuck off (again), and then he follows through with revealing Mom's affair? If I agree to these new terms, Mom's spared, but that means Lester gets off, too.

I bite the inside of my cheek so hard I taste blood. Everything in my power wants to hold my pride. If I'm going down, I'm taking him with me.

But I see Mom, her career, her future. Can I do that to her? She screwed up—more than once, I'm afraid—but I have the chance to make it all slip into oblivion with no fallout.

Before I know it, class is over and I've done nothing but think about what I'll do when I meet the Conduct Council at 2:00. I'm still not completely sure.

Joss

My computer sounds like a plane about to take off. I've been leaving it on, email open, because I can't remember my password anymore. Christine suggested writing it on a Post-It next to the computer, and I tried that for a few days but threw out the note thinking it was garbage. So now heat pumps from the vent underneath the laptop, and I'm waiting for it to combust at any moment.

I sit here because it's what feels familiar, not because I'm doing any work. The words don't make sense anymore. My focus is gone, slithered off into the great white emptiness.

An email comes through. Great news to share! the subject line reads. I click on it.

Joss,

Fabulous news. We were accepted for October's edition of Chem Social Review. They're placing us as the feature piece.

This is such a bittersweet moment, as this paper would not exist without you, yet we cannot celebrate its publication together. You're a brilliant researcher, my friend, and your contributions to this world and to MacAmes will never be forgotten. I'm honored to have worked alongside you on this project.

I'd love to clink champagne glasses, but for now, I'm thrilled to share this news with you, hoping it brings a well-deserved smile to your face.

All the best from Florida.

Take care,

Richard

I finish reading with a palm over my heart. My lungs expand. Richard. I know him, right? He feels familiar, yet I can't picture his face. Yes, I know Richard. We worked on something together, that I do remember. Just can't recall the exact details. Still, this sounds like a good email, something to celebrate.

I read it again, trying to piece together the threads that are still a little foggy. Then, with a satisfied smile, I push back from the desk, feeling like there's something urgent I need to do. I leave the computer and walk out the front door on a mission.

Abbie

"Welcome, Ms. Matson. Please have a seat."

I'm instantly irked they've disregarded the rest of my last name, as though half of my identity doesn't matter.

There's six people in total, three men and three women, and I suspect that's intentional. Don't need students accusing them of gender bias. They're seated on either side of a long table whose shiny surface reflects the fear on my face. The woman who spoke gestures to the chair at the head. I pull it out and take a seat, keeping my bag in my lap. My toes scrunch in my boots.

There's little friendliness here. Not only the stern looks on their faces, but also the room as a whole. We're surrounded by wood paneled walls and an ugly paisley carpet that reminds me of a hotel lobby. It feels dark. Even the room is mad at me.

"We've received some serious allegations against your academic conduct," the woman says.

I'm assuming this is the same woman—Ruth Chambers—who sent the email, though I don't know for sure. None of them introduce themselves, and something about that doesn't make me feel warm and fuzzy. No introductions, straight to business. Like their verdict has already been decided. Cut and dry.

"Are you aware of these allegations?" she continues.

Here it is. The moment of truth. Do I lie and dig my hole even further? Who knows the extent of information they have. Did Lester give them names of the students I've helped? Maybe they've already contacted Stacia or Cody, or one of the dozens of other people I've sold exams to. Something tells me any one of them would sell me out in exchange for safety.

Or do I come clean? Sacrifice myself—and only myself—to save Mom. Face the repercussions of my choices, both here at school and at home.

They're all staring at me. One of the men, tall and bald, taps the table like I'm wasting his time.

"Yes," I say. Yes, I'm aware of the allegations. It's not a confession of guilt—not exactly.

"And do you admit to their validity?"

I picture Ma, at home, doing not much more than wandering the house, no longer able to work, struggling to hold onto whatever's left. I see Mom and the pain on her face with Ma's diagnosis.

The woman's mouth is set in a thin line. She's intimidating as hell. Scares me a little, to be honest.

"Did you steal faculty exams for the purpose of selling them to students for profit?" Her tone is stern, and I sense she doesn't appreciate my silence.

The Council's not going to let this go. They'll track down leads until they find the students who are my accomplices in this whole thing. There's no way I can get out of this, and that's when I decide that lying will only make it worse. I might as well give up.

"It's true," I say finally. A few of their eyes widen. Ruth sits back in her seat in what I interpret to be an I-knew-it move. "I stole my mom's exams."

The panel scribbles on their notepads. One of the men speaks up. "And was there anyone else involved in your little scheme?"

I've seen this guy before, an English prof, I think. I imagine his blood is boiling even more than the rest. Faculty exams—they're proprietary. He looks like he wants to reach out over the table and slap me across the face.

"No one else. Just me," I say.

Ruth removes a sheet of paper from a manilla folder and slides it in front of me. "We're going to need you to provide the names of everyone who paid you for an exam."

I shake my head. "No."

"Excuse me?"

"I'm not giving names."

I knew this was coming, but I'd prepared. Giving people up is only going to alienate me further. Protecting them could be the one thing that saves me socially. I'll take the fall—all of it—if it means I come out of this with a few friends intact.

"You do realize we have a source, right?"

"I assumed, otherwise I wouldn't be here."

English prof eyes me, and I think he's the type of guy who'd wash his kids' mouths out with soap when they get sassy.

I place my hands flat on the table, holding my ground. What they don't know I know is that their "source" is anonymous. Lester would never drag himself into this. He might have tipped them off, but he surely didn't give his name.

"This is a big campus," Ruth continues, "but students talk. We'll end up figuring it all out eventually. Your cooperation will save us a lot of time."

"I'm sorry, but I'm not ratting people out."

"So you're willing to take all the punishment?"

I hesitate, and she jumps on it.

"They're not your friends, Abigail," she says with the first note of softness I've heard during this entire interrogation. "Friends wouldn't have asked you to do what you did."

The words cut me, and I think back to Stacia's text. How she can't wait to be rid of me. All those moments together—sharing clothes, taking mirror selfies. The times she linked arms with me like we were a unit, a two-for-one deal. None of it was real. Then I think of Trina, the person who accepted me for me all along. The one who didn't care if I had a thousand followers on Instagram, or if I wore brand-name clothes. She was always a good friend—even when I haven't been.

My pulse turns from a cool simmer to a boil. I set my jaw, lock eyes with the woman who holds my fate.

"Stacia King," I say. "It was all her idea."

She sits back, pleased. Gives a nod to the paper in front of me. I write Stacia's name, followed by Cody—yes, Cody—and all the others I can remember. That's it. Done. My social standing crushed back down to the ground where it started. I'm left with a strange mix of heaviness and buoyancy I can't quite interpret. How can it feel good to lose all my friends?

When I hand it back to her, she slides another in its place. It has a red and yellow symbol at the top—MacAmes' crest. "This is a formal expulsion letter. Given the nature of your actions, the Student Conduct Council has no choice but to proceed with the harshest punishment possible. You're officially expelled from MacAmes University."

Christine

There's an envelope on my desk when I get back from class. MacAmes' red and yellow crest is in the upper left corner. It looks formal.

Kerry must have put it here—aside from Abbie and Joss (who's definitely not on campus), she's the only one who has a key to my office. On closer inspection, I recognize her handwriting across the front. My heart rate quickens. I know what this is—at least I'm pretty sure I know what this is.

My tenure decision. She'd told me to expect it this week, and now here it is.

I consider the appearance of the letter without any other contact from Kerry or the rest of the tenure committee. What does it mean that she dropped it off, knowing I was in class? Wouldn't she have wanted to congratulate me in person?

Instantly, my fingers go numb. It's going to be a "no." It has to be. Those negative evals sealed my fate. The times I was late because I was with Micah, and then with the week off after his death, I've been struggling to catch up.

Tears prickle my eyes. I've screwed this up so bad. Everything I've worked so hard for. Gone. What would Fisher think?

I shove the letter in my purse, not wanting to cry here on campus. I'll wait to let it all out at home.

Then I think of Joss. What will she say? My tenure appointment has been nothing short of a sure thing for years in the making, something she helped me prepare for, something we talked about celebrating together. It would take something drastic for me to be denied. How will I explain it to her?

My heart pings. Maybe I won't have to tell her at all. Maybe she won't even remember. It's a viable possibility. The realization stings like a thousand bees. My wife...my poor Joss.

I sit behind my desk and try to busy myself with emails, but my eyes keep drifting to my purse on the floor. The corner of the envelope pokes out, taunting me. I have to know.

I grab it and tear it open, scan for words that will jump out and ease my foreboding: We're sorry. Regret to inform you. Decline.

Within the first sentence, I go dizzy. I reread it three times.

It is my great pleasure to inform you of the Rank and Tenure Committee's approval of your promotion to the rank of Full Professor with tenure, effective immediately.

A gasp that's sort of like a laugh exits my mouth. I bring a hand to my belly and bend forward.

I did it. I got tenure.

Despite everything.

The guilt comes then, and I place the letter on my desk, as though I don't deserve to hold it. Is this warranted? I've given nearly twenty-five years to this university. Taught overloads when budgets were cut, volunteered to chaperone student trips, attended conferences, led pedagogy workshops.

But I also broke one of the cardinal rules of academia by entering into a relationship with a student. I didn't stop it. I fueled it.

Does one cancel out the other?

There's a knock at the door and I look up to see Kerry, who wears a beaming grin.

"Congratulations!" she squeals, raising her shoulders and doing a fingertip clap. She tiptoe dances toward me, arms outstretched. I hug her.

"Thank you," I say, but it's half-hearted. She must read the conflict on my face.

"Aren't you ecstatic?"

I wipe my brow. "Yes, of course. I'm thrilled. It's just been a bit of a rough year and—"

"Chris, you deserve this."

There's a pause, and I pinch my lips. "Do I?" My voice threatens to break. I don't even care if she thinks I'm crazy. The battle going on inside me has moved to the front lines.

Kerry touches my arm. "Yes. You do." Her voice is firm. "You're a great teacher. You're also human, and no human is perfect." Her eyes penetrate into mine and something passes between us.

Knowing.

All I can do is nod, accepting this act of charity she has no obligation to give me.

"I'm so sorry," I whisper.

She pulls me in again and my body trembles against hers. We don't say anything else. Just stand there for a minute, two women, two friends, two colleagues. The letter stares up from the desk. I let myself smile, though it doesn't feel good. Not yet.

Abbie

"You're awfully quiet," Mom says on our way home.

It's been two hours since my appointment with the Student Conduct Council. I'd left the meeting asking for the evening to break it to my moms. I'm not stupid, this news will travel through faculty faster than a beginning-of-the-year cold. Part of me is surprised she hasn't gotten a text yet.

"Mmhmm," I mumble, looking out the window. I'm waiting til we're home. No sense hashing it all out twice. The swish of the windshield wipers is the only sound between us.

We pull in the driveway. "Can you hang downstairs for a minute when we go in?" Mom says. "I have something exciting to tell you two." She's smiling, and it's not lost on me that I have an announcement too—one that's going to wipe that smile right off her face.

I get out of the car, but something makes me freeze.

"Mom, why's the front door wide open?"

She follows my gaze, and her face falls. We both run into the house.

"Joss?" Mom yells. "Are you here?"

I'm right behind her, echoing her panic. "Ma!"

There's no response. I take the stairs two at a time and fling open her office door. Empty. Mom and I collide in the hall, outside the bedroom from which she's just come.

"She's not here," Mom says, her chest rising and falling.

"Fuck," I say, and Mom's too scared to even give me a look of disapproval.

We dash back downstairs and out the front door into the rain, calling Ma's name, like she's a puppy who accidentally got out. I look up and down the street, but it's deserted. It's only four-thirty, but the sky's covered in gray April clouds that have sucked up any ounce of afternoon sunlight.

"Where could she have gone?" I say.

"Check out back."

I spring around the house, bending down to check under bushes, as though a fully grown woman could somehow hide under a shrub. "Ma!" I call again. When I reach the front, my shirt sticks to my skin. I'm breathing hard.

"Nothing," I say.

Mom moves toward the car. "Get in."

She speeds out of the driveway and heads down the street, the rain playing an ominous percussion on the windshield. I don't even know if we're going in the right direction.

"We should never have left her home alone," Mom says under her breath, though I know she's berating herself and not me. I'm just the kid.

We look both ways at every intersection, trying to spot a semi-frumpy woman with short dark hair walking alone. The sidewalks are empty. No one would be out in this weather willingly.

Mom's knuckles are white, a startling contrast to the black leather of the steering wheel. "We'll find her," I say, and though I think Mom agrees, that's not the thing. The thing is whether we'll find her *safe*.

We've been driving for ten minutes, winding down streets around our neighborhood. Mom turns onto a narrow road, leading out of town.

"You think she'd be this far?" I say. Mom doesn't answer.

The road rolls in soft hills. We come over a crest, and that's when I spot her. I squint. "There!" I yell.

She's a football field ahead, her striped pajamas the thing that stands out the most. I breathe a sigh of relief not only to have found her, but that she's walking on the side of the road, not down the center like I had briefly let myself imagine.

Mom steps on the gas and we're upon Ma in seconds. We pull to the berm. I'm out of the car first.

"Ma!" I scream, and she turns. I run to her. Mom's right beside me.

"Joss! Thank God you're all right." Then, after a beat, "What are you doing out here?"

Ma's face scrunches. "What do you mean?"

"You're over a mile from home. You're in your pajamas. Where are you going?"

"I just popped out for some champagne."

"Champagne?" Mom and I blurt at the same time. There are no stores near here, not to mention the absurdity of the comment—we have nothing to celebrate right now.

"Yes?" Ma says in more of a question than a statement, like *Duh, why wouldn't I be walking to go get champagne?* "To celebrate with Richard."

"Richard is here? In Virginia?" Mom says. Her hair's plastered to the sides of her face now, the rain turning it into red veils that frame her temples. I'm sure mine looks equally ridiculous.

Ma stares at us, and I can see the first signs of confusion settling in. "Well, I— he said—" She's grappling for words that make sense. Nothing does.

"Come on," Mom says with a swoop. "Let's get in the car."

We each take an elbow, as though Ma is a fragile nursing home patient. She doesn't fight us. I get in the back. Mom exhales a long breath, staring straight ahead, and I know she's probably figuring out the right balance of concern and criticism.

"Joss, you can't just leave home like that, okay?" Water droplets fall from the tip of her nose. "It could be dangerous. We didn't know where you were." She stops short of adding what I'm thinking: *You could walk out into traffic and be killed.*

"I just needed champagne," Ma says again. She crosses her arms. Her voice has a childish whine to it, like a toddler defending her actions.

Frustration bubbles on Mom's face. Her jaw clenches. She looks like she might explode.

"Mom," I say, slicing through the tension. She eyes me in the rear-view mirror. It's an unspoken reminder: Remember what the doctor told us. Don't argue with her, it only makes it worse.

"Okay," Mom says. She bites down hard on her irritation. She's patting the steering wheel, when she should be patting Ma. "It's okay. I'm just glad you're safe."

We drive home in silence. Ma stares out the window the whole way. I'm still not sure she understands what she did. Her memories often disappear minutes after they happen.

When we walk through the door, Ma heads to the kitchen.

"Lunch, anyone?" she says.

It's almost six, and we're all soaked.

Christine

I return to the kitchen after changing into the thickest sweats I own. Even then, I can't shake the chill.

Joss is eating a turkey sandwich with mayo because she insists she hasn't eaten yet today, though there's a bowl with cereal and milk remnants in the sink, and an empty Lean Cuisine box in the trash. I buy those for myself—she's always turned her nose up at them—but apparently Alzheimer's can alter someone's taste buds just as easily as the wires in their brain.

I watch her and wonder what's going through her mind. Clearly not that she was just wandering down the road. In the rain. Wearing pajamas. Heading to a store that doesn't exist.

This changes everything. She can't be left alone anymore. The sorrow weighs on me, until I remember my letter. I straighten up. I deserve this one moment of pride.

"I got tenure," I say, looking between Joss and Abbie, who's staring at Joss with the saddest eyes. Joss doesn't look up from her sandwich. She takes a massive bite like she hasn't seen food in a year. But Abbie whips her head toward me.

"Really? Wow," she says. "Congratulations."

I give a little nod. It feels good to say it out loud—even if Abbie's tone is less than genuine.

"Did you hear Mom?" Abbie says to Joss. "Ma?"

Joss finally looks up. "What?"

I lean toward her. "I said I got tenure. Kerry delivered my letter today." "Is that good?"

I look to Abbie. We both shrivel in our chairs. Abbie bites her lip.

"Yes," I say. "It's good."

"Oh, well, great." She finishes the sandwich in two more massive bites without swallowing in between. A piece that can't fit falls from her mouth to the plate. She picks it up and shoves it in, looking more like a messy chipmunk than a poised adult. Once she swallows, she uses her tongue to lick the mayo at the corners.

My lips pull tight. I can't quite pinpoint the sensation in my gut. It's like Joss has lost all humility, all sense of grace that I fell in love with. Then the word comes to me: Disgust. I'm disgusted watching my wife eat. It's ugly to admit.

Abbie clears her throat. Her expression mirrors what I suspect mine looks like. Joss gets up from the table, leaving her plate behind, and wanders out of the room without a word.

I'm at a loss for words. Who is this woman and what has she done with my wife? My heart is bursting in half. Here, on a day I should be commemorating a professional achievement, I'd rather shut myself in a dark room and pretend this isn't my life.

"Mom," Abbie says, breaking me from my thoughts. "There's something I have to tell you." She's wringing her hands.

"Whatever it is, it can't be worse than that," I say, pointing to wherever Joss has gone. It's mean, but humor is all that's keeping me afloat.

"It's pretty bad."

My head lolls to one side. "Great. Now what?"

She takes a huge breath and lets it go. "I really fucked up." Her voice shakes and pink blotches crawl up her neck like the ones I get when I'm upset. "I got expelled from school."

"What!?" I shriek, my jaw unhinging. "Expelled? For what?"

So she tells me. About Stacia and the exams—my exams!—and the money for Joss. My vision goes red.

"Are you crazy, Abbie?" I'm yelling now, all my rage coming out on her. "What the hell were you thinking?" She's crying, her head dropped and shoulders rounded forward. "You deserve to be expelled. Cheating? Are you serious? I'm glad they did it. You shouldn't get any special treatment just because of your parents."

I pace the small kitchen in front of her, hands on my hips. "Jesus, Abbie." My daughter, *my* daughter—a cheater.

The irony is not lost on me, and I swallow it hard.

"I know," she says. "I fucked up, okay? But at least I'm owning it. I told the truth and am accepting the consequence. That's more than you can say."

"Excuse me?" I hiss. I may have already picked up on the irony, but I don't need her throwing it in my face.

She glares at me. "You heard me."

"Don't you think I've paid enough for what I've done?"

"What? By getting tenure? Sounds like a reward to me."

"He's fucking dead, Abbie. Dead. Gone. If he hadn't been meeting me that night, he wouldn't have been driving from campus at the exact moment your mother sped into the intersection. I'm the reason he's dead. So if you think living with the guilt of someone losing their life isn't equal to you getting expelled from school, then you're not the daughter we raised you to be."

Heat and adrenaline course through me with such power I feel like I could lift a car. I want to slam my fist through the wall. Feel the pain.

We're in a stand-off, both breathing heavy, neither wanting to be the first to concede. I'm the adult here. She has no right to come at me like that.

Or does she?

We stand there for a long minute, arms crossed. It's then the sadness hits: I'm not as good a parent as I thought I was. I should have seen Abbie for who she was, not dismissed her struggles as frivolous and passing. Her desire for acceptance is what sparked all this, and then her love for Joss is what fueled it.

Just as I'm about to speak, Abbie breaks first.

"I'm sorry," she says as quiet as a mouse, and my defenses soften. My hands uncurl. It's been a fuck of a year for all of us. I can no more be angry with her than I can with myself.

"Come here," I say. Abbie walks around the table and falls into my arms. We both cry. Joss is somewhere in the house, doing God knows what. Did she hear us? Even if she did, I don't know whether she'd understand.

Abbie's chin rests on my shoulder. Her skin smells the same as it did when she was young: buttery and sweet. She holds me tight and I squeeze back even tighter.

"Mom," she says into my ear, "where do we go from here?"

February 2003

*T*he *balloon garland would have been enough, but we had to go one step further. Our house looks like a party store threw up—confetti sprinkled on every table surface, streamers strung from corner to corner, and an oversized banner in three shades of pink.*

Abbie only turns one once.

Her eyes go wide as a cupcake is placed on her high chair tray. She goes to reach for the candle.

"No, no," I say. "No touch. Hot."

Someone gives a little me-me-me-me and we all sing. Abbie breaks into a wide, gummy grin. She claps when we clap, and there's a collective "Aww" from the few friends and family who've gathered in our kitchen.

"Go on," I say. "You want to taste it?" I dip my finger into the frosting and wipe it on her tongue. She smacks her lips and grabs a handful. It's her first taste of sugar. We all beam at this miracle child who's become the center of our lives.

There's a hand on my back. Fisher comes to stand beside me.

"I'd say she likes it," he says, eyes adoring his niece. "You two sure know how to throw a first birthday party. Big precedent for future kids."

I shake my head. "No future kids. She's it for us."

"Really? I'm happy to—"

"No, Fish." I wrap my arm around his waist. "You've given us such a gift, we could never ask for more."

Then we look back to Abbie, and her nose scrunches just like his—just like her father's.

FOUR MONTHS LATER

Joss

FOUR MONTHS LATER

"Taking my books and going to my room. Taking my books. Going to my room. There. I'll read them all, and Dad can't stop me. Oh! Better finish before *Paddington* comes on! No, Dad, no. Don't drink that. Stop, stop. Here, Jossy, hug this. Look, a cat! Mrs. Sullivan's cat. Maybe Dad will let me have one. Here, kitty kitty kitty. Nice kitty. Soft fur. What? What'd you say, Dad? I *am* a good girl. Yes, I am! Watch me, twirl. I'm a ballerina! Spin, spin, spin. One, two, plie. Three, four, plie. Haha! Is he in the audience? Where is he? Meow. Oh, kitty, you're here again! Come here, let me pet you. Wait, where are you going? Come back!"

Abbie

I drench the cereal in a waterfall of milk the way Ma likes it, then replace the box behind the towel rack in the bathroom next to the other random items she's hidden away. It's Ma's secret stash, she says, and no one's to touch it. Never. Don't even think about it. Mom and I use what's there and replenish from the store when Ma's supplies run low.

I carry the bowl to the living room and place it on the TV tray. Ma does a lot of sleeping lately. I like to think it's her brain's way of taking a break. I wonder if her dreams are just as confusing as her reality.

"Ma," I say, giving her shoulder a jiggle. "Breakfast is ready." She's been awake since before seven, but has already dozed off again.

She sits up, reaches for the spoon. She doesn't thank me, but I know manners are just another thing Alzheimer's has taken from her.

I sit next to her and flick on the TV. This has become our morning routine. Mom leaves for campus, and I get Ma her breakfast.

"What do we feel like today? *Today Show* or *GMA*?" I ask, though I don't expect a response. I choose the *Today Show*, mostly because the anchors' banter makes me smile. They seem like friends—*real* friends.

Ma and I sit in silence long after her cereal is gone, but it's a silence that has a presence. She naps again, but I can't. I'm on watch. Ma watch.

* * *

Mom bursts through the door a little after two.

"Sorry, sorry," she says, flopping her bag onto the counter. "Whole line of students after class. You wouldn't think there'd be so many questions the first week." She's holding three sunflowers, their thick stems wrapped in cellophane. When she catches my face, she explains without me having to ask: "Thought maybe they'd— The memory of them—" Then, sadder, "I thought she'd like them."

The dark circles under her eyes are visible through her makeup. New lines have formed on her forehead over the past few months. Deep ones, the kind that have stories of their own. I feel bad she's had to cram all her classes together so I can get to work on time. But taking care of Ma is our new normal, especially after hired help proved to be a disaster. After Ma accused three different nurses of stealing her things, Mom and I threw in the towel. Thus, our tag-team arrangement to do it all ourselves.

We don't talk much. We're partners in caring for Ma, but that's about it. Forgiveness, I'm learning, is one thing, but forgetting is another. Ma's mind might be mostly gone, but mine is still very much intact, and the image of Mom and Micah burns as clear as crystal despite my every attempt to let it go.

How can I? It's not every day you walk in on your parent having an affair. I'm here to tell you, it's not easy to come back from.

So, we do our daily dance of working and nursing and half-sleeping. I'm no dummy—this isn't sustainable. We both know it.

But for now, it works. I take the morning shift while Mom teaches, and then Mom takes over when I head to the gallery. The days are long, draining. Even sitting around doing nothing takes effort.

"You won't be late, will you?" Mom says.

"It's fine." I grab the keys from her outstretched hand. They're like a baton in the relay. It's my turn to go.

If you would have asked me four months ago if my expulsion was a good thing, I'd have said you were crazy. But here I am, doing something I enjoy—showing art, watching others fall in love with colors and canvas the same way I do.

It took a while for Mom to get over my expulsion. If I'm being honest, I'm not sure she's really over it completely. It only took a week for her to insist I get a job as a consequence.

"It didn't have to be like this," she'd said with the slightest air of smugness. "You could have been enjoying college like everyone else your age."

What she didn't see was that I was totally in my element at the gallery. College was never for me. It only took getting expelled for everyone to get it, and for me to learn a hard lesson: sometimes the things we think we need most are the same things we should actively avoid. People who are dark in the heart. The Stacia Kings of the world.

What I would tell people is this: Find yourself a Trina. Someone who forgives when forgiveness isn't deserved. I was a bad friend—but a confession and an apology goes a long way. We spent the summer hanging out like old times before she left to go back to Nebraska for sophomore year and I stayed put. Her texts no longer go unanswered. We talk every day, and the authenticity I'd been missing this past year has settled back into my life.

Now, in the relay race of our day, Mom slips off her heels. "How was she today?" Her questions always tip up at the end, infused with hope, like all of a sudden I'll forget what she did. Like our relationship can go back to pre-Micah.

Somedays I think maybe it can. Somedays my head is clear. She fucked up—but so did I. Betrayal is a commodity we've both held.

The keys rattle in my hand. "Tried to argue that we had a cat named Skittles. But turns out she was just talking about the stupid rabbit's foot."

She nods. There's not much to say at this point.

I leave, thankful to put some space between me and the house, between me and my moms. It's a double-edged sword, taking care of Ma, both a duty I accept and a burden I despise—emotions too similar to decipher. Did I ever think this would be my life at nineteen? Not a chance.

* * *

The Price is Right blares through the living room, as though a higher volume will somehow reach Ma's brain better. Another day, another morning of game shows.

"Fifteen hundred," I say to the screen, though I have no idea what a washer/dryer set costs. "Ma, what's your guess?"

She doesn't respond.

By the time the final showcase comes, my eyes are drooping. I didn't sleep well after Ma woke the whole house up, yelping from a nightmare.

I slide down the couch, closer to her, and rest my head on her shoulder to keep it from bobbing. Ma doesn't flinch. She doesn't seem to mind our touch. Not like some Alzheimer patients I've read of who freak out when they don't recognize someone. Mom and I hear those horror stories and worse in our family support group.

I'm not sure how long I've dozed, but I'm startled awake by the feel of fingers combing through my hair. My eyes shoot open, but I stay still, not wanting to frighten Ma by jerking away. She starts to hum, then speaks.

"I sang this song to you when you were in my belly," she says. I blink several times. "I'd run my hands over my stomach, imagining you all curled up in there. It was an easy pregnancy. Never got sick once."

My heart swells to where I think it might burst. I bite my bottom lip, scared that if I move, it will break this lucid moment. Is what she's saying true? Or is this just the dismantling of her mind spinning daydreams?

"I gained almost fifty pounds with you," she continues. "Couldn't stop eating. Never saw a biscuit I didn't like. Your mum was always on me, but then would turn around and come home with frosted donuts because she knew I was craving them. She loved to lay her head on my belly and talk to you. Cup her hands around my belly button, like it was a direct line to your ears. I would have done the same thing if it were her, but I chose the short straw. We both wanted to carry you, but it was me in the end, and your mum was just as excited. I can't even tell you how many baby clothes we had before you came."

She laughs, and I think I might cry. I haven't heard her laugh for so long. There's a stretched pause. My gut seizes, hoping she hasn't fallen back into the land of darkness. Don't leave, I silently plead. I gently tip my head so I can see her face. She's serene, present. Her eyes meet mine.

"I loved being pregnant with you," she says. She touches my cheek, trails the pad of her thumb under my eye to my temple. "You are the best thing I've ever done. The thing I'm most proud of."

I clutch her shirt in my fist, as though it will keep her here with me. But within a few seconds, she's gone again. The light goes out in her eyes, and the corners of her mouth settle back down into a straight line.

"Oh, Ma," I say, and the tears come freely.

I stay like that, curled up against her, until I hear Mom pull in the driveway. When I quietly slip off the couch, I look back down at where Ma sits and picture her pregnant with me. I grew inside this woman. She carried me, brought me into this world. This bright force. This brilliant mind. This person who's now disintegrating before my eyes.

I bend down and kiss her forehead.

"Thank you, Ma."

Christine

The funny thing about tenure is it doesn't feel any different than before. I teach the same classes. I have the same office hours. Only now, the name plaque outside my office is a bit shinier.

CHRISTINE GRAHAM, PH.D.
PROFESSOR OF ANTHROPOLOGY

It's the second week of classes, which still feels very much like the beginning of the year. My desk is yet to be inundated with assignments. I can still breathe.

I'm teaching in the same lecture hall as last year—the classroom where it all began. When I first saw my room assignment, I'd shuddered. How could I possibly teach in that space again? I'd gone so far as to draft an email to the Registrar, requesting a change, but stopped short of sending it.

I can't run from my past, from my mistake. Maybe it was Kerry who intentionally put me in this same classroom. A small dig. Her way of punishing me. I'll never know, and I'm far too chagrined to ask.

I open the tri-fold pamphlet in my hand and study the glossy image. An elderly man sits on a bed made with neat, military corners. Beside him, a nurse—dark hair, kind eyes—leans in with a smile.

"But she's so young," I'd said when Dr. Kaur had handed it to me a week after Joss's wandering in the rain incident. "All these people are old enough to be her parents."

"She won't know the difference," he'd said, his eyes gone soft at the corners. "The disease has progressed extremely rapidly, faster than any patient I've treated, if I'm being honest. There was no way to prepare for it, nothing you—any of you—could have done. But don't kill yourself over it, Christine. Joss needs round-the-clock care. Places like this have the means to provide that for her."

His words were meant to comfort me, but instead felt like my wife's death sentence. Funny, this disease that claims a life, but insists on infantilizing it first.

I flip the pamphlet back to the front. Caring for those you love the most, the headline reads. Even the font is gentle and welcoming.

My fingers trace the photos of residents, old and helpless. I can't picture Joss here. My Joss. It doesn't seem possible. Yet, here, I am, about to call. About to do what I know needs done—for Joss, of course, but even more so for Abbie. It's in these moments, with the ripples of the disease staring me straight in the face, that I feel the loss most acutely.

But moving Joss to permanent care means it will just be Abbie and I at home. Abbie, the daughter who carries my DNA through Fisher alone, yet is the one person I'd gladly step in front of a train for. The daughter who used to be my friend, but now can barely look at me. I don't know where our future goes from here—can it be salvaged?—but I do know one thing: I'll spend every day trying to put the pieces back together.

I leave my office for class, and as I do, the last visible thing before I close the door is the picture of Joss, Abbie and me. I pause and stare at it for another second. Warmth fills my body. Joss, my wife. Abbie, our beloved child. Despite it all, I am so lucky.

***

The class is half full when I walk through the door. I go to the front table and drop my bag, then log into the podium computer to pull up my lecture. I do a quick scan of the room. By now, I know most of their names. I've become good at remembering, having told myself in those early years that it would help me stand apart from the other faculty who never put names and faces together throughout an entire semester.

That's when my eyes land on the chair. Four rows back, dead center. Micah's chair. But he's not here. Instead, a girl named Heaven with bouncy blonde hair fills the seat. She puts her ombre notebook on the fold-out desk top. She couldn't be more opposite from Micah, and her name alone is some sort of cruel irony.

Heaven glances up and spots me staring. She smiles, and I quickly look away. I clench my hands and then release them. Once. Twice. The memories are strong, but my therapist says I need to let them go. Last year was a hiccup, a delusion—one I'm not proud of, but one I have to own. The things I felt were real, at least I thought so. But feelings don't have to be mutual to be real. Turns out, people only see what they want to see.

Three more minutes pass. The class fills. Fifty young, impressionable minds, waiting for me to impart my wisdom. Ready to learn about the human experience, the way in which we work.

What can I tell them? That we're all just wandering this planet trying to do our best? That mistakes are part of life, and that what defines us is not the mistake itself, but how we react to it?

I know these things. Maybe once only superficially, but now on a level no one would envy.

Can I tell them how short life really is? Their brains aren't wired to process mortality—not yet. I don't want to taint it for them. They deserve to be carefree a bit longer.

I'm light on my feet. Tenure's not going to change me like it does many faculty. I want to be here. I want to watch the lightbulbs come on above my students' heads. I inhale, deep into my core. Feel my mouth stretch into a smile, a real one. The freshness of a new academic year is just what I needed. I'm in my element, here in this classroom with these students. This is what I'm good at, and—at fifty-one—I hope I'll have many more years to do it. I'm lucky to turn another year older—something I once feared, but now realize is a privilege not afforded to all.

"Good morning," I say. "Welcome to Anthropology. Let's see who all is here, shall we?"

ACKNOWLEDGEMENTS

There's a particular feeling I get whenever I step onto a college campus—a specialness, for lack of a better word. It's something I can't quite describe. Maybe it's the grand buildings, or the sense of wisdom that wafts from the grounds. Maybe it's the sense of community, the camaraderie of a place where friendships are formed and lifelong ties to institutions begin. Or, perhaps, it's the fact that I worked on a college campus for over a decade.

My time as a college instructor undoubtedly influenced the origins of this novel, and although the characters and situations are not based on anything I encountered firsthand, the setting is an homage to the liberal arts university experience I love so much. Academia will always hold a special place in my heart—and will likely be a reoccurring theme in my writing. So, thank you to my Mercyhurst family—former coworkers, students—for the lasting impact.

The writing process is often a solitary one, and for that, I'm eternally grateful to my writing community for the support and encouragement. Thank you to my beta readers and critique partners for their invaluable feedback: Kerry Chaput, Caitlin Weaver, Debra Pappler, Ruaridh Frize, and Hayley Pisciotti. To those who leant a (constant) ear to the highs and lows of the writing and publishing journey, just know I don't think I would have survived without you.

To my fantastic editor, Carmen Lewis: I'm blown away by your eye for detail, and I'm confident this novel wouldn't be where it is today without your special touch. Thank you!

Friends and family have been my sanity and sounding board—listening even though they didn't understand my rants, reading early drafts even though they were littered with typos, and giving me the grace to pursue this dream, even when it meant a lot of alone time behind a computer screen. My family truly is the greatest—they sing my praises with such genuine excitement it makes me blush. To my parents, brother, grandmas, extended Gildea clan, cousins, in-laws, and tons of friends: Your unending support means the world to me. To DJ, Josephine, Elizabeth and Michael—my four favorite people—I love you.

Finally, to you, the reader. Books wouldn't exist without you. Thank you for being a consumer of stories, and for sharing—either by written review, or by word of mouth—so others can discover new authors and books to love.

If you enjoyed this book, I'd love for you to leave a review on Amazon. Even a couple words are enough to help boost visibility for up-and-coming authors, and especially indie books. Your three minutes mean more than you know—thank you!

ABOUT THE AUTHOR

Jen Craven lives for stories where one decision changes everything. The author of two historical fiction novels, this is her debut work of contemporary women's fiction. She writes from her home in northwestern Pennsylvania.

Follow her on Instagram at @jencravenauthor or visit www.jencraven.com